WEAVERHAM

VILLAGE
OF
MOONBEAMS

by

George Moss

CHESHIRE COUNTRY PUBLISHING

First published in the United Kingdom 1998 by
Cheshire Country Publishing, Chester.

Copyright © 1998 Cheshire Country Publishing
& Roger Moss.

A catalogue record of this book is available from the
British Library.

ISBN 0 949001 13 9

It was George Moss's dream to write a book about
Weaverham... his Village of Moonbeams. Sadly, George died
in 1998, before his work could be completed, and this fascinating account has been painstakingly pieced together by his
old friend and fellow Russet, Bill Elson. A keen and perceptive
local historian, George had a vast store of personal memories
and Bill has ensured that they carry the unmistakable authen-
ticity of a man writing about a village he knew and loved.
George's family are indebted to Bill Elson for, without all his
efforts, this book would simply not have been possible.

PICKER-INGS

Pipe Lines

Weaver Holt

Actoncliff

The Cliff

Acton Hall Farm

Acton Hall Farm

ACTON BRIDGE C

Warrington 8
Tarporley 9½

G.P

Willow G

Valley Farm

Acton Bridge

Acton Bridge

Oakhill Farm

Yew Tree Farm

Poplar Farm

Mount Pleasant

Ash House

Lower Green

Hall Green Farm

Acton Bridge

Merebrow

Hilltop Farm

Mill

P.H.

Sch

Pol Sta

Crowton

Hall

Birch House

GANDY'S MILL

Ivy House

CROWTON CP

Filter Beds

Acton

S.W.

The Wood

F.B.

M.P.

F.P.

MARSH LANE

Bent Lane Farm

Onston

Hilton Farm

Mill

BLUE BELL WOOD

Hefferston Grange

Grange Brook

Cottage

Hollies

Holly Bush Farm

The Cottage

Ruloe

Barncroft Farm

Rydal Farm

Sanatorium

W E A

SANDHOLE FARM

The Riddings

Brook House

Grangelane Farm

SMITH

G.P.

The Home Farm

Works

HANDLEY

SMITH LANE

Beechwood Farm

Bratt's Bank

Cuddington Hall

MILL

M.P.

Delamere Park

Poplar Farm

Bryn Fm

Works (dis)

Hunts Hill Wood

FB

Cuddington

Royalty Covert

FB

Foxey Hill

Ravenhead

Ba

F.P.

CUDDINGTON CP

Cuddington Station

G.P.

1

THE early roots of my family were established in the 1830s, when Josiah Moss and his wife Sarah and family came from Cranage to farm in the Weaverham area. This farm was Handforth Brook Farm, Gorstage.

Times were difficult in the early 19th Century. A Church vestry meeting was held on 7th July, 1831 to discuss unrest in Weaverham Village. It was unanimously resolved "that in consequence of the disorderly state of the Town and Lordship of Weaverham (which we in a great measure attribute to the evil effects of the Beer Bill) that a lock-up house has become necessary for the preservation of the respectable inhabitants of Weaverham". This resolution was seconded by Mr Benjamin Burgess of High Street. It was also resolved that Mr Barry be requested to allow the said building to be erected, on the waste piece of ground, at the entrance to the village from the Warrington Road end. It was also resolved that the building be 13 1/2 ft. square and be built of stone.

The Committee of the following persons be appointed to put the above resolutions into effect: Mr Wild, Mrs Andrews, and Mr William Norman.

Following the Napoleonic Wars, there had been a recession and in the early 1830s poor corn prices and a general state of distress and unrest among farmworkers did not help the situation. However, there was one bright spot in Josiah's life, because he was fascinated by the building of the Grand Junction railway, through his farm. Stories were handed down through the generations about Josiah's interest in the power of steam and how he would rush with his men to the railway side to watch the steam trains chugging through the farm and wave to the passengers in the open-topped carriages. Steam always had a fascination for men and boys alike and 100 years later, I found myself rushing home from school to watch the "Coronation Scot" steaming through the village just a few hundred yards from where my great-great-great-grandfather, Josiah, watched trains with the same enthusiasm.

He would never have visualised such progress in the power of steam and yet now just over 50 years on from my times of watching for the streamlined "Coronation Scot", steam is but a memory, except for an occasional time when enthusiasts organise and fund a train drawn by a steam engine, with the smoke billowing from its funnel and giving off that very special smell. On these rare occasions, small groups of people would gather at vantage points along the line to experience the nostalgia of their childhood. When the building of the Grand Junction Railway was proposed, it was met with strong opposition which was eventually overcome, in both Parliament and in the country. Locally, there was the Hartford Contract, the Preston Contract and the Basford Contract. For the Hartford Contract, agreement was made on 25th June,1834, that Benjamin Seeds and Son of Prescot, Lancashire, would complete the seven miles three furlongs of railway by 1st April, 1837, for the sum of £92,066 and to forfeit £30 per day for each day beyond the contractual date. The Contractors were to be paid a capital sum less 10% every two months and they were to maintain everything in working order for 12 months after the Engineer's Certificate of Completion had been signed. The Grand Junction Railway was to supply the land.

The track was described as 12,000 yards in cuttings and 982 yards in embankments, for which would be required 80,000 cubic yards of ballast, 48,000 stone blocks, 1,960 wooden sleepers, 48,000 pieces of patent felt, 103,836 iron spikes and 96,000 oak pins. A five-arch bridge, of Runcorn stone, was to be built over the Weaver; there would be mileposts, hedges, and the building of three cottages.

"Gates at foot crossings must be Heart of Oak or best memel timber. Mortar must be made of best Welsh lime mixed with clean sharp sand, prop: 1 to 2. For double track, 2 sleepers or 4 blocks for every linear yard, and for every 2,500 yards of embankment track there will be 5,000 sleepers, each 9 ft by 10 inches by 41/2 inches. For 5,814 yards of cutting there will be 23,256 blocks needed and 46,512 oak pins to fit exactly into holes in the blocks; and each chair, to carry the rail, would require two wrought iron bolts with mushroom heads."

The most difficult part of the Hartford Contract would be the construction of the Dutton Viaduct, over the River Weaver, between Acton Bridge and Preston Brook, contracted to David McIntosh, of Bloomsbury Square, London, at a cost of £54,000. A decision in favour of piers had to satisfy the Weaver Navigation and the Weaver Trustees, who, by the summer, were still not satisfied with the safety of the project and suspended it during the summer and autumn of 1834. Agreement was eventually reached and the viaduct, 1,400 feet in length, with 20 arches, each with a span of 63 feet, was duly completed in time.

On Friday, December 2nd, 1836, the last stone of the viaduct was laid by Mr. Heyworth. It was the first structure of its kind in the Kingdom and it had been completed without loss of life or limb. This marvellous achievement was celebrated with a fireworks display as large crowds gathered to enjoy this great occasion. It was a wonderful sight, with the whole viaduct lit by torches and fireworks, and great credit was given to Locke, the designer.

The workmen were treated to a good dinner and excellent cheer, according to the "Chester Courant". Not always had the relationship between the workmen and their employers been so good. Men had been taken on from all over the Kingdom, many from Ireland, and many lived in rough encampments along the way. Poultry, eggs, potatoes and vegetables were continually stolen from farms near to the line and I would imagine the newly built gaol at Weaverham would often be put to good use to hold the wrongdoers until they could be taken to Knutsford Gaol, or some other prison.

On one occasion, the military had to be brought in to restore peace at Sutton Weaver, where a Harvest Supper was being prepared, at a local inn. In fact, the whole village was in danger of being taken over when 200 soldiers, from Chester and Liverpool, were brought in, and 27 of the ringleaders were arrested and sent to Birmingham Gaol. During drunken randies, there were many brawls between the railway construction workers and the local farmworkers. Nevertheless, the railway was completed and the first train passed through Acton Bridge Station, in July 1837. A new age of travel had dawned.

Meanwhile, life on Josiah's farm carried on regardless. Horses had taken over from oxen for ploughing; haymaking, as ever, relied on good weather and if the weather was right a start would be made in early June. The hay was mown by scythes and then the swaths were rowed up into the wind into haycocks using pikels. When the hay was dry it was carted in using horses, and either built into haystacks or carted into the barns. When the corn was ready to cut, usually in early August, once again scythes and hooks were used just as they had been in Biblical times. When the scythes and hooks were not in use, it was customary to hang them in an orchard tree to become covered with a layer of rust. Consequently, when the blades were sharpened with a stone, this coating of rust was removed, leaving the blades thinner and therefore sharper.

Nowadays, the giant combine harvesters cut and thresh the grain allowing the straw to fall out in neat rows onto the stubble. But I remember old men talking of times when they used to go reaping. True reaping was done with a hook, and the hand was used to draw the corn to the hook. This, incidentally, was the origin of the saying "by hook or by crook." Then came mechanical Reapers, which were the first horse-drawn machines to cut the corn, but they left it lying flat on the ground. These machines were gradually improved until they were able to drop the cut corn into bunches ready to be tied into sheaves. Then came the miracle machine, the horse-drawn Binder, powered by a large land wheel. This not only cut the corn but gathered it up into sheaves and an automatic knotter bound and tied each sheaf with string. The sheaves were then kicked out of the side of the machine, falling into neat rows in the stubble ready to be set up into stooks or "attocks" as old Cheshire men called them. Strangely enough, in those early days of Binders, the reaping hook still endured on some farms as if the men were loth to change methods. In itself the reaping hook was an enlarged sickle and probably the oldest of old implements.

In Josiah's day, teams of skilled reapers would travel around the farms cutting the corn. They would start around 4 o'clock in the morning when the dew was keeping the corn moist, allowing the sweep of the blade to cut through it easier. They would start to work side by side, maybe a team of six men, and they would progress forward perhaps 50 yards, and then walk back to the beginning to repeat the operation parallel to the first cut. The "walking back" gave them time to straighten their backs out of the crouched position so giving them some respite from the strain of the job. It was hard work and as soon as the sun rose in the sky, towards noon, the men would rest awhile and have their "bagging", usually Cheshire cheese.

The men mowed the corn and the women worked close behind gathering it into sheaves and tying each one with a band of twisted straw. The sheaves would then be set up into stooks and would be carted in by horses after they had stood out to dry for "three Church bells". This was an old Cheshire farming custom meaning that the corn would stand out while the Church bells rang out over the fields for three Sundays, allowing the grain to harden off in wind and sun before being carted in. When the time came to cart the corn, the men divided themselves into "reachers", "loaders" and "stackers". Usually, the tallest men reached the corn onto the carts, while the loaders placed the sheaves, in an orderly fashion. Round the load they would go with the butt ends of the sheaves outwards, keeping the corners well squared off, and then filling in the middle. In this way, layer after layer, the load was built up. A full load, one which a horse could comfortably pull, was roped onto the cart by the wagoner before it left the field, as a carelessly loaded cart, if it was not secured, could shed its load on the way to the stackyard. An experienced loader would use the wheel tracks in the stubble behind the cart to help him build a square and safe load. Usually, a young lad would lead the horse and cart with its precious load up to the stackyard. An endless procession of horses and carts would wend its way from field to farmyard. It was always a fascination and a treat for farm children to ride back to the fields on an empty cart or wagon. On the floor of the cart would be a host of insects and beetles of all shapes and sizes which had fallen out of the sheaves as they were unloaded. Thousands more would end up in the barns or stacks.

The barns were filled by the same methodical pattern of stacking, so that as much corn as possible could be stored inside. Every spare moment was used to walk around the barns treading down the sheaves to make room for more. Stack-building was an art in itself and usually the stack was laid out lengthways roughly North to South, as it was said to "weather" better in this position. The barns and stacks became the home for the winter of hundreds of mice and rats, which in turn became food for the predators such as barn owls and an army of farm cats. The damage done by these mice and rats as they fed and bred in the corn depended on the length of time before threshing. Soon after the corn was safely gathered in, a new sound would be heard in the village. The sound of the flail pounding the grain out of the kernel would issue forth from every barn, large and small, in the neighbourhood, and it would carry on throughout the long dark hungry months of winter. At the end of the harvest, women gleaned the fields for wheat from the stubble and this would also be threshed by flail. Most cottagers had flails of their own, but it did take a lot of practice to become skilled in its use and many a lad suffered a few knocks on the head until he got used to the rhythm of the job.

It was not until later in the 19th Century that steam-powered threshing machines started to appear in the village. These new machines were greeted with anger and fear amongst the farm labouring community. There was widespread unrest, leading to riots and rick and machine burning. The previous method of separating the corn from the chaff, flailing, had provided winter-long work for thousands and there was fear of widespread unemployment. Eventually, the military were used to subdue this and some hangings and deportations took place. However, in the Weaverham area, there was adequate alternative employment in the building of the new railway, and the introduction of this new machinery was achieved without trouble.

The first machines were horse-drawn and, very often, the farmer, whose corn had just been threshed, would provide horses to remove the machine to the next farm. Then, as the self-propelled traction engines became available, the fascination for steam grew. The names of the engine makers were often proudly displayed in polished brass under the front of the tall smoke stack and in addition, very often the engines themselves were given names of their own. Many a young boy would slip away from school to watch the engine nudging its box into position in the stackyard to be "set up" ready for an early start the next day.

The box was fitted with spirit levels and had to be absolutely level all round for it to work properly. With the old steam engines this was a very difficult and highly skilled job. When the ground was uneven the wheels had to be driven up onto planks of wood of various thicknesses and considering the steering wheel had to be spun dozens of times to turn the front wheels a fraction, it can be understood what a lengthy job it was to set up the machinery. The steam engines needed a continual supply of water, and the fire had to be kept burning well to keep up a good supply of steam.

When the box and press had been set up, then the engine itself had to be set up to the box so that the driving belt would run smoothly and drive the machinery. The second man would arrive very early at the farm, to fill the boiler with water, get a good fire going under the boiler and build up steam. Milking on threshing days had to be finished early as once the machine started, there was no stopping until noon.

As speed picked up to the required revs, the threshing box would hum loudly and the whole village would know which farm was threshing. At least a dozen people were needed to run the thresher and while it was in motion, they became its slaves. Two or three with pikels on the stack would pass the sheaves out and on to the box where sometimes another man would pass the sheaves on to the "feeder" who would cut the bant (string band) and spread the sheaf on to the moving canvas which bore it down into the threshing box. It required a competent man to do this properly, sometimes the farmer himself, and I know that Frank Moreton, at Lake House, always did this himself.

Early machines were not fitted with the canvas conveyor and then it was a much more dangerous job. As the corn was threshed out of the straw by the fast moving drum, the grain still in its sheath of chaff dropped into shakers and riddles which separated the chaff which was blown out by a fan into a box with two alternate settings, so that as one bag filled with chaff, a lever was thrown which diverted the chaff through another opening into a new bag and this would go on non-stop. The chaff was carried away to a spot well away from the farm and set on fire, apart from one or two bags of good clean chaff which were mixed with horse or cattle feed. The separated grain then fell onto a selective screener consisting of circular revolving screens of different mesh sizes, through which the grain was graded into firsts, seconds, and thirds, and weeds, each grade falling into its respective waiting sack. With a good thresh, the corn handler changing the sacks and weighing each full one before tying it, had a heavy job. Sometimes these sacks often containing 2 cwts of wheat or oats, would have to be carried up a rickety set of granary steps.

Early machines had a trusser instead of a baler. This machine trussed the threshed straw and knotted two bands of string around each bundle, in the same way that the binder put its single band around each sheaf. This trussed straw was in great demand, for thatching and for bedding down cattle and horses. The threshing was often done at the "back-end" of the year and, if the weather took a turn for the worse, the machine would sometimes stand days, sheeted-up in farmyards. Then as the days brightened up, the job was renewed.

It was dusty work, with the dust particles and chaff swirling around and settling most uncomfortably down your neck or in your eyes, and the more you perspired, the more it would stick to you. But later, when the baler came into being, the bales were tightly packed and bound with wire, the man responsible for threading the wire into the needles of the press became known as "the needler." As the stack was reduced in size and the bottom of the stack or bay came nearer, so the runaway rats and mice diverted the attention of the workers who would run after them flailing with sticks and pikels. Dogs and cats would be in attendance. I remember Jack, the small fox terrier at Hefferston, would catch 60 or 70 during a thresh, sometimes two in his mouth at once. When all was over, he would sleep by the barn for 24 hours or so, completely exhausted, and usually scarred by a few rats. The farm cats had an equally busy time killing mice by the hundreds and occasionally getting bitten themselves by the dog in all the excitement. Rats used to live and breed in abundance under corn stacks and in the barns and I remember at one threshing a rat running up George Ward's trouser leg causing great amusement as he held his trousers tight at the top until it ran down again.

The threshing machines became a familiar sight on the roads, travelling between farms, each with its following of assorted workers hoping to be taken on at the next farm. Sometimes they were lucky, but very often some were turned away if the farmer had enough workers of his own. Many of the "machine followers" would sleep rough in the barns or shippon bings and were said to be as "lousy as jays" and because of the danger of fire, Grandfather George would make them give up any matches they were carrying.

It was no easy task driving one of these machines complete with its box and press. Because of the gearing, the steering wheel had to be spun furiously to obtain a slight movement of the front wheels. However, many farmers loved to chance their arm at it. Charlie Gleave at Church Farm liked nothing better than driving the machine from Church Farm to Nook Farm. But many hair-raising accidents occurred whilst moving the machines, very often through brakes failing on steep hills, or lack of steam, or ice on the road making it impossible to haul the heavy weights.

Tom Gleave went through the hedge into his garden at Grange Lane Farm and on another occasion got Alf Stringer's engine stuck in his pit. Mr. Dickenson of Little Budworth, a quiet man, once had one of his machines over in a ditch in West Road, by Nook Farm. Another steam engine, driven by "Puddin" Ashbrook, came to pull it out. The tow chain was connected and "Puddin" went full speed ahead to pull out the ditched engine. His own engine reared up, its front wheels leaving the ground and then crashing down again to smash the front axle, blocking the main road for the rest of that day, and most of the next, before repairs were finally made and the ditched engine pulled out.

The Stringer Bros., Alf and Henry, had a few machines, but Henry Massey was the king of the fraternity and had the best machines and the most reliable, although he once shunted his machine into the ditch at Walker's Gorstage Green Farm, blocking the drive, and the milk had to be taken through the orchard to Horners Creamery. Ralph Oultram worked for him and when Henry died, Ralph bought one of the machines and started his own threshing business, from Gorstage Green where John Smith worked for him. Later, he moved to Yew Tree Farm, Crowton, where, succeeded by his son Ted, the business carried on and flourished.

When all the corn was threshed, the stacks gone, and the bays empty, it was a time of satisfaction and relief, because the danger of losing the lot was enormous, as the following reports show:

"On the 30th day of May 1886 at 2 o'clock in the afternoon, a fire was discovered at a farm occupied by Mr. Peter Darlington, Weaverham. Engine Weaver prepared, horses procured. Two firemen, Arrowsmith and Earlam, at once set out. Fireman Hollinshead followed on foot. An abundant supply of water was obtained from a pit nearby. At length the fire, which was in a stack of old hay, was subdued. Engine and brigade arrived back at station at 6.30. Stack was insured with The Liverpool, London & Globe. Agent Mr. James Pimblott of Weaverham. 35 assistants helped the firemen. Cause of fire unknown. Horses and driver from Mr. Chambers, distance 3 miles. Time taken 5 hours. Estimated Loss £35. William Chadwick. Supt.

On the 10th July 1890, Stacks and Farm buildings were destroyed at Mr. William Horton's Mere House Farm at Weaverham.

A messenger arrived at the station at 11.30. Horses were harnessed to the Engine Weaver and arrived at the farm with several firemen at 12 o'clock. Several stacks of hay and straw and a block of farm buildings containing carts, implements, hay, straw and other produce were well ablaze. Water from several pits was used and considerable damage to a field of oats. It was only possible to stop the spread of the fire and it took nearly 12 hours to do this. Cause unknown. Loss considerable, amounting to about £800. William Chadwick. Supt."

And in 1897, the worse blaze in living memory took place at Wallerscote in the tenancy of Mr. George Dean. Damage was estimated at £1,500. The fire was spotted at 1 o'clock in the morning by two railway men walking home, and they woke Mr. Dean. A man was dispatched on horseback to Northwich to summon the fire brigade. Led by Superintendent George Chadwick, from "The Bleeding Wolf" pub, five firemen, aboard the engine Niagara, journeyed "at a gallop" to the scene, arriving at around 3 o'clock. Some time later, the Marbury Estate Brigade was on hand. With the help of some 50 local people who had left their beds, the firemen ferried water from a pit 20 yards from the blaze and fought through the night to control it. When they left for home at 11 o'clock the following night, 15 stacks of corn and 200 tons of hay had been destroyed. It was suspected that the fire had been deliberately started, by someone with a grudge against the owner, Mr Smith Barry of Marbury Hall.

Old Josiah would have been in his element if only these steam powered threshing machines had happened during his years of farming, but by 1851 George Ellis had taken over Handforth Brook Farm and he and his family were to remain there for the next 70 years.

Old Josiah Moss farmed through difficult times; we know of his great enthusiasm for the railway and of how he and his men would leave whatever job they were doing and rush to the railway side to watch the trains chugging through their land.

One local farmer said: "Ah canna understand thee, Siah, wasting so much time watching these "foos" going past in these new-fangled trains, an' ah wouldn'a let my men stop for it neether."

Old Josh replied in no uncertain terms: "Me mon, if my men weren't as interested as me in this wonderful railway, they would be no use to me."

We know of the recession following the Napoleonic Wars, poor corn prices, falling land values and a general state of unrest amongst farmworkers, which led to the building of Weaverham prison. Many farmers went bankrupt, but old Josiah still battled on. The Repeal of the Corn Laws, in 1846, caused further lowering of corn prices. Old Josiah's son, John, married, in 1846, for the second time, after losing his first wife, having taken on a job, as a labourer. In 1847, he and his new wife, Mary, presented Josiah with a grandson, also named John.

Neither of old Josiah's sons had worked for him on the farm. John spent much of his life in forest clearance and was also skilled at making homemade bricks, while Thomas had served his time to saddlery and also spent some time as a tanner. In fact, in later years, the nickname "Owd Tanner Moss" stuck with him.

As the enclosures progressed with the successive Enclosure Acts, land clearance was being undertaken locally. Much of the Gorstage area had been covered with gorse, hence the name, and John did much to clear these areas. By the time his young son had reached 12-years-old, father and son were striding out at 5.30 each morning from their cottage in Gorstage to a site in Delamere Forest which was being cleared to extend a farm belonging to a Mr Snelson.

This was Crown land which was to be divided up, in later years, into small holdings, for soldiers returning from the Great War.

Old John carried a felling axe, while young John had a small axe with which he trimmed the brushwood off the felled trees and helped to heap this up for burning. It was hard work and, sometimes, it would be 7 or 8 at night before they returned home. During those hard years of forest clearance, the burning desire to become a farmer never left young John and when he reached 14 years of age, in 1861, he decided to put himself up for hire at Over Hiring Fair.

He often recalled his anguish on that day, when he stood among a group of carters, wagoners, cowmen, shepherds, general farmworkers and apprentice lads. They were a strange and varied crowd; some were hardened annual attenders at the Hiring Fair, some were seeking new employment because of disputes with their masters, and then there were the new attenders seeking work as apprentice lads, not knowing what the future held in store for them. The men all carried some item of their particular trade for recognition by the farmers. The horsemen usually showed a tuft of horsehair, either in their coat lapel or attached to their hats; a piece of plough cord for the ploughman; and the cowmen likewise a tuft of cowhair. The shepherds carried a crook, and the thatchers wore a braid of plaited straw, and so on.

John was nervous and wondered what kind of master he would have. It was quite an ordeal for the young lads, as the farmers requiring serving lads made their choice and it was quite a shock when Farmer Newall, who farmed at Lake House Farm, Weaverham, chose young John Moss and took him on at £1.00 per year plus his keep.

John and Mary were pleased that their young son was to work locally, and so at weekends, after a week living in at Lake House, the young lad would return home to Gorstage, to relate stories of his work. His mother was greatly concerned about the state of his velvet jacket, each time he came home. The pockets were so full of grease and with the soil sticking to it, that young John needed cleaning up every time he arrived. It was a while before the truth came out. It seemed that the Newall household fed their servant lads on a diet of cheese and fat bacon and bread baked on the farm and John (not being fond of too much fat), used to stuff the bacon in his pocket rather than leave it on his plate and be chastised, and then he would quietly feed it to the cats and dogs in the farmyard hoping no-one would notice. Thus he was never short of animal friends in the farm-yard.

Comforts were few and it was very much a case of work, eat and sleep. The day started at 5.30 a.m. and usually lasted until 6 in the evening, or longer, at Harvest times. One of the main jobs was pumping and carrying water from a large well in the yard. There seemed no end to the demand for water, both to the house and to the farm buildings, particularly in win-ter time when the cattle were inside. Other jobs included sawing logs for the fires on which all cooking was done, and feeding the poultry, pigs, and small calves.

He was also required to run errands and it was on one of these journeys that he met young Mary Gleave, at "Back o' Church", the popular name for Church Farm. It was at Lake House Farm that young John completed his apprenticeship in farming. He learned to handle horses and to plough and cultivate with them. He also learned about animal husbandry and how to look after a stock of cows and to milk them by hand. But as he matured, he worked on other local farms and for some time lived in at Gorstage House Farm, next door to his old family home. He continued his courtship of Mary Gleave, daughter of George Gleave, who farmed Church Farm, and on 26th September, 1872, they were married at St. Mary's Church, Weaverham. John was 25 years of age and Mary 23. But Mary was determined to become a shopkeeper and the couple took a shop in Copyhold selling provisions, becoming very popular with their customers.

However, when a bigger shop became available in Church Street, Mary's father, being a highly respected farmer in the village, secured for them the tenancy and they moved in, allowing Thomas Gleave and his wife to take over the Copyhold business.

John, however, could not settle in the shop and, after allowing treacle to run all over the cellar floor when he forgot to replace the barrel bung after running a jugful to sell in the shop, Mary decided he would never make a shopkeeper and realised where his heart was. Then John came by a lucky chance.

After a series of bad harvests due to bad weather, Walter Bradford retired from Beach Farm and John and Mary secured the tenancy from Lord Barrymore. John's dream had come true. I am sure that George Gleave was influential in securing the tenancy for Mary and his son-in-law, and I am equally sure that he, being a shrewd and well-established farmer, would have assisted the young people in their efforts to become successful farmers. The rich soil and good pastures, many of which were on the banks of the Weaver, made it very acceptable to the new tenant.

He had saved enough money to buy a few cows and a horse and taking one step at a time he gradually built up a small herd of shorthorn cattle. This breed was popular in Cheshire up to the middle of the 20th Century.

When the family moved to Beach Farm in February 1888, Harry was just a babe in arms, but George, Arthur, Edwin, Annie, Ada and Ethel, were growing up, and soon Tom and Percy would be born. Two more boys died in infancy and Ethel too sadly died at an early age. Mary was a good cook and taught the girls how to bake and to cook good wholesome food. John was a good farmer and although he lived through troubled times, he saw many changes.

He saw the coming of the threshing machines, firstly as a horse-drawn steam engine and box and then as a self-propelled steam engine which hauled the machine from farm to farm and provided the power to drive it. In John's early days, corn was threshed by a flail, an instrument consisting of a staff with a piece of hard wood hinged to it, the hinge usually being a stout piece of leather. With this, the corn was beaten on a hard barn floor and winnowed by the wind blowing through the open barn doors. Flailing was a practice which was both arduous and lengthy and could be a dangerous job to someone not skilled at it. It did, however, provide employment for men all winter and, consequently, the new idea of the threshing machine meant loss of work for many, and met with disapproval in the farmworking community. Nevertheless, although the new machines were treated with suspicion, in Weaverham farmworkers did not stoop to burning the farmers' barns and machines as they had in other parts of the country.

From the mid-1870s to 1880s, bad weather and the consequent poor harvests that went with it, coupled with the imports of American grain, and American, Canadian and Irish cattle, brought more worries to local farmers.

The boys were to be a great help to John on the land and soon he was taking advantage of the large amounts of manure brought up the river from Liverpool where it had been obtained from the American and Canadian cattle boats. The "muck boats" as they were called, were berthed at "Wilbraham's Quay", a popular landing quay on that part of the river known as "Forster's Bank", a hundred yards on the right beyond

Marshall's Hill, where, until recently, Billy Martin had his yard. These boats were unloaded by means of a simple derrick pole powered by a horse. The muck contained a lot of straw and after being carted back to the farm and put in a heap, it would get very hot and decompose, leaving behind a wonderful compost to fertilise and add fibre to the land. It was very cheap, its main costs arising from carriage and labour.

Jimmy Fairclough, who farmed an arable farm at Mere House, and old John carted load after load to use on their fields. However, after a few years, an Anthrax scare among the imported cattle, brought an end to the use of this manure on Cheshire farms and John went on to experiment with chemical fertilisers using bone meal.

In the meantime, his herd of shorthorn cattle had continued to grow and soon John had taken on a milk round supplying the canteen at Brunner Mond and quite a few customers in Winnington. His sons George, Edward, and Tom, usually took their turns at delivering the milk each morning. It was quite a profitable milk round and any milk left over was usually made into cheese or butter.

So it was at Beach Farm that John and Mary reared their family. George and Edwin married and moved away, George to Nook Farm, and Edwin, after a period of time keeping a shop in West Road, moved to Milton Farm, which was one of the original farms of the Heath Estate. Tom went to farm at Ruloe, on another Barrymore farm, and later moved to Whitegate, while Arthur had the Market Garden further along Wallerscote Road, on the right hand side where Mr Kuypers later had his pig farm.

Only the coming of the Great War interrupted their peaceful lives; Harry and Percy joined the Army and fortunately survived the conflict. After coming home from the war, Percy took a farm at Wilmslow, while Harry settled at Beach Farm where he took over, after his father's death, in 1921, and farmed there the rest of his days. He was the last member of the family to farm there. Albert Garner followed him.

Beach Farm, like Beach Hill, Beach Wood, and Beach Road, has been spelt in this way since time immemorial. It is not that we "Russets" cannot spell, but it derives from the old Saxon word "Bache", meaning stream.

Going down the hill, past the farm in the large meadow, on the left hand side, which stretches to the river, can still be seen a number of small raised mounds. These are the "butts" or firing positions for the rifle range which existed here for many years, and are at distances of 50,100,150, and 200 yards from the targets which were in Owley Wood at the bottom end by the river and with the high bank of the Wood behind them. This rifle range was used by the Militia, volunteer regiments forming a National Defence Force from the time of the Napoleonic Wars to the First World War when it was abandoned. In the wood and in the meadow there is much evidence of its long use. For years children have found hundred weights of lead in the shape of musket balls from the first half of the 19th Century, to large calibre bullets from the smooth-bored rifles of the 1850s, and slightly smaller bullets of the Zulu Wars to the .303 bullets of the Lee-Enfields of the Boer War and 1914-18 War which they found in the wood, and which can still be found there. In the meadow can still be found waxed paper cartridges from the time of the Indian Mutinies and brass cases from the spent bullets of the Martini-Henry rifles of the Zulu Wars and the later Lee-Enfields.

The men who operated the targets were protected by a thick metal palisade behind a raised earth bank and Tom Gleave remembers a wooden building being there to house the equipment when not in use. It was approached by a well constructed roadway which entered the wood opposite Keepers Cottage. Unfortunately, in recent years, a large land drain burst at the top of the bank cascading tons of water into the wood washing away trees and the roadway and much more of the evidence in the consequent mud slide, but many older people will remember it.

Great-grandfather John had two sisters, Emma was one, and the other was always known as "the Duchess" who always wanted to be waited on when she visited Beach Farm and considered herself something out of the ordinary. Emma married Tom North, who was a Sea Captain and known as the Old Skipper, but after marrying he ceased travelling abroad and went to work on the Manchester Ship Canal boats. They had two children, Elsie and Hilda. Hilda went to London to work and Elsie went to live in Wales in a bungalow built for her by Ernie Moss, Amy's brother. The Duchess married a man named Kent, and also had two daughters.

2

COMING TO NOOK FARM

DURING the First World War, my grandfather, George, the eldest of John's sons, was farming at Nook Farm. George and Ned, his younger brother, had married Edith and Clara Forster, daughters of the blacksmith from Weaverham Smithy, opposite the Gate Inn.

For many years, Ned and Clara had kept a small grocery shop, in West Road, before they moved to Milton Farm, just over the railway bridge, at Acton. George and Edith had often walked past the lovely old Nook Farm in their courting days after Chapel on Sunday evenings and George would proudly say: "One day, Edith, that farm will be ours."

He was not to know what fate had in store for its present tenant, nor what tragedy was going to befall the lovely old farmstead in later years. Nook Farm was one of the four farms belonging to Squire Robert Heath's Hefferston Estate. One of its earlier tenants, by the name of Samuel "Champion" Hornby, had been quite a legend in his time, because of his phenomenal strength, and stories, passed down through the years, told of how he would carry two large bags of wheat, one under each arm, to the middle of the field with no effort. Then he would sow the grain by hand from a bowl, as was common practice in those days. Later, William "Wiggin" Gerrard became tenant, before taking up the tenancy of Weaverham Wood Farm which, at that time, belonged to Lord Barrymore. (Nicknames were very common in those days and most people were known by them.)

"Wiggin" had two sons, George and John, but sadly lost his wife at the birth of the younger one. He then went to France to marry his wife's sister because it was not legal in this country for a man to do so.

It was in 1890 that "Wiggin" went to farm at Weaverham Wood and was to remain there for the rest of his days. It was then that William Rigby, son of John Rigby of Heath Farm, Little Leigh, applied to Squire Heath for the tenancy of Nook Farm, and it was granted to him. William was a deacon of the Baptist Church, at Milton. He loved the Nook and got on well with his landlord the Squire, but sadly, around Christmas, 1902, he contracted rheumatic fever and became very ill. However, by the end of the first few weeks, going into 1903, he had made a reasonable recovery, and after a period of convalescence when he had been walking out a little, one of the villagers claimed she had seen him riding down Grange Lane in his horse and shandry with his coat-tails flying in the breeze. Sadly, on this journey he must have caught fresh cold which turned into pneumonia, which at that time was highly dangerous, and he died at the early age of 38, leaving behind a widow and two little children, a girl, May, and a boy, Joseph.

Mrs Rigby's father, Joseph Longshaw, who farmed at Milton Bank Farm, which was situated part way along the old cow lane (also the road to the old Onston Mill), leading off the Weaverham to Frodsham road, came to their assistance. However, it was decided some time after William's death, that his widow and the two children would go to live at the Milton farm and that William's brother Tom would apply for the tenancy. This was duly granted, but, unfortunately, Tom ploughed up the whole farm, greatly angering Squire Heath who had always demanded that his farms be farmed on a strict crop rotation system. Tom was given notice to quit.

My grandfather, who was living at Salisbury Terrace, Weaverham, at the time, saw the chance of his dream coming true and went to see the Squire, who gave him the tenancy of the farm, to start on February 1st, 1906. And so, with £100 in the bank, a few cows from his father John's Beach Farm, a little black horse and lots of ambition, he settled into the lovely old farm, with his wife Edith and their family.

Tom McCann and his brother Joe were still living in the shant in a corner of the little cobbled yard which lay at the back of the house. The shant was a small one-up, one-down building, with the bedroom reached by a vertical ladder. My grandmother kept Tom, and his brother, supplied with clean bedding and good food. They drank at the "Wheatsheaf", in the village, and, sometimes, if they had over-indulged, they would sleep downstairs by the fire, rather than risk the vertical ladder. They also slept by the fire if the weather was severe because it was quite cold in the little bedroom which had only a slate roof and no insulation. When grandfather George took over the farm, they had pleaded with him to be allowed to keep their jobs.

Tom McCann was an experienced horse man and good ploughman; he was very quiet with horses, and they trusted him and worked well with him, and he continued as teamsman until his legs began to be troubled with rheumatism. He also knew the farm like the back of his hand, having laid new drains in many of the fields for Billy Rigby, and his knowledge of the positions of these drains was to prove invaluable as the years went by. Soon after the Great War broke out, Joe McCann returned to Ireland, but Tom was to remain at the Nook until the mid-twenties, and became a popular figure in the village.

An interesting story was told about Tom, soon after the end of the First World War. His only holiday was a trip to Chester Races and he usually went each day of the three-day event, held in May. The year was 1919 when a horse called "Air Raid" had taken Tom's fancy in the Chester Cup. During the war, Tom had always had a fear about the possibility of air raids. In fact, when a bomb was dropped by a Zeppelin, at Bold, near Widnes, Tom got up the next morning and told my grandfather he had heard bombs dropping in the night and, as news travelled slowly, it was some time before it was verified that the bomb, or bombs, had fallen on Widnes, exactly at the time Tom was supposed to have heard them. On another occasion, when a Navy Blimp had been travelling towards Liverpool, flying along the railway line, Tom had fled the potato field, to seek cover, thinking he was being attacked.

So he just had to place his bet on "Air Raid". The Chester Cup was run, but Air Raid was beaten by a horse named Tom Pepper. But all was not lost as a new colt had arrived at Nook Farm that week and on arrival back from the races Tom christened the new horse "Tom Pepper" a name that was to stay with it for life, although, gradually, the name was reduced to "Pepper" and, as time went by, to become affectionately "Owd Pep." He was the fastest horse in the district and had a very distinctive racehorse look about him. He took the milk each morning to Acton Station and there were always a few children waiting for a lift to school when Pepper made the return trip to Weaverham.

My grandfather used to recall the night when the local "Bobby" knocked him up in the early hours and asked if he would take two prisoners to Northwich Police Station. He had caught the two men robbing a hen cote at Milton Farm and handcuffed them together. Pepper was harnessed up and the two prisoners with their captor were soon at Northwich where the men were put into the cells to await trial. Burglary was not very common in those days but hen thieving was. The policeman was brought back to Weaverham when my grandfather returned home.

During the War Years, many farm horses had been taken from local farms for service at the front and Pepper would certainly have been called up if he had been born a few years earlier. Tens of thousands of horses died in the Great War, very many of these were commandeered from the farms in this country. Many horses taken to France only lasted about a month, and a horse which did return from the War must have had a charmed life like the little milk horse, "Dolly", belonging to Edwin Walker, at Gorstage Green Farm. She had been shot in the neck and the bullet remained lodged there for the rest of her life. She lived on for many years and the wound did not seem to trouble her as she travelled twice a day to Horner's Creamery with Edwin's milk - a true heroine of the Great War.

A fine specimen of a horse was taken from William Moreton's Lake House Farm and sent to a remount depot, near the frontline. Frank Moreton, William's son, had become a Lieutenant in the Army and by an amazing coincidence was sent to the same remount depot as the horse from the family farm. The story is told of how the horse started whinnying when he heard Frank's voice. Frank was allowed to have the horse for his own use, but unhappily the horse fell victim to a sniper's bullet and like so many conscript horses, never returned. The horses in France were mainly used to move gun positions - a very dangerous job because of heavy shelling and snipers. Mules were mainly used as pack mules, to transport food, ammunition and equipment.

The carnage of the Great War of 1914-18, for both men and horses, was beyond all expectations and as one old Russet told me: "The cream of the village youth was lost during that terrible war".

The Army sent officers around farms to buy much-needed hay for horse-feed and there was a remount depot at Cuddington which also used a large amount of hay. This remount depot was George Thompson's stable. It was on the left, after turning left near the White Barn. Dad and Tom McCann used to take hay and straw there.

Fred "Radish" Johnson from the little thatched cottage at the end of Forest Street worked at the remount depot and became head groom. He had a way with animals, particularly horses, but he could handle and control mules, which were very stubborn creatures. They had many mules at the depot in transit from America to France, and just as he could ride Frankenburg's donkey at Hefferston Grange, when other lads could hardly stick on its back, he would ride the big American mules at Cuddington, to the surprise of his workmates. He was regularly seen exercising the mules along the country lanes around Cuddington until he became of an age to join the Army.

On the morning of his departure from the village, he called upon his old friends at Nook Farm, where he had spent many a happy hour playing as a lad. He was on his way to catch a train to Chester. It was early morning milking time at the farm and they all put their cans and milking stools down and walked to the farm gate with Fred.

He shook hands with them all and bid them farewell, with the solemn words: "I had to come and see you all. It will be the last time. I dunna think I shall ever come back."

And with that strange prediction he wandered off, turning round once more on the top of Grange Bridge, where he paused to have a last look at the old cottage - his family home - and with one last sad wave he was gone. Fred made his way to Cuddington Station where he was to catch a train to Chester where he would receive his short military training, before being set to France, and the frontline. Sadly, Fred was killed by a sniper's bullet soon after moving into the trenches. His prophecy had come true; his family and friends were distraught; a man so gifted in his handling of horses would be missed so much by all who knew him.

The carnage went on and every week more and more local lads were lost on the battlefields. Percy and Harry Moss, two of the sons of John

Moss of Beach Farm, my great-grandfather, went to serve in the war; Harry in the Royal Field Artillery and Percy in the Cheshire Regiment, while Arnie Forster, the old Blacksmith's son and brother to my grandmother, joined the Army Service Corps as a driver, and because of his driving ability he was given the job of driving officers about around the front lines. He always had some hair-raising stories to tell of his exploits at Hell Fire Corner and such other places. Little Arnie survived the war and came back to continue his taxi and garage service, which had developed into a thriving concern, as the motor car was becoming a more familiar sight on the roads and the demands on the blacksmith's shop declined.

While Arnie continued his taxi-service, mainly for women shopping in Northwich, the ironmongery business became a booming business and the shop on the corner of West Road and Station Road began to supply all manner of goods. Farm tools and farm machinery parts could be purchased there and David Forster, after dropping his role as blacksmith, ran the shop with great success. As the years went by, almost anything could be purchased at the old shop. Bicycles, motor cycles, and their accessories were sold there and in later years, household goods, crockery, purse nets, Hornby trains and Dinky toys, and rabbit snares.

The mid and late 1920s saw lean times in the village, and the humble rabbit provided food for many who would otherwise have gone hungry. But it was also in the mid-twenties that Tom McCann was recalled to his home in Ireland, to look after his ageing mother. I assume his brother Joe, who had returned to Ireland several years earlier, must have died. No-one knew Tom's true age, but assuming he was around 70 then, his mother must have been in her nineties. Tom was heart-broken to have to leave the village, and particularly the lovely old Nook Farm, which had now been his home for so many years. He had become one of the family and it was my father who took him to Acton Bridge Station where he was to take a train to Liverpool and from there a boat to Ireland. To make matters worse, it was Old Pepper who took him on this sad journey. The day was a very blustery one and after unloading at the station, he threw his cases back into the shandry and pleaded with my father to take him back to the old farm. After some debate, he accepted that he must go on his way and tearfully he said good-bye.

Every year for some time, a note would arrive on St.Patrick's Day with a sprig of shamrock. Tom could neither read nor write but someone always sent his best wishes to my father and the rest of the family. News of the old farm and his friends was sent to Tom until some years later the greetings and the shamrock ceased to come and it was presumed old Tom had passed away. Although Tom had left the farm, and gone home before I was born, I heard so much about him in later years I always feel I knew him well.

The old farm house at the Nook, where I spent most of my early life living with my grandparents, was a quaint old building with three chimneys and ivy-covered walls. Built of brick and with a slate roof it presented a beautiful picture, nestling among the apple and pear orchards, on the corner of Grange Lane, as it turned into West Road.

The orchards in May became a mass of pear and apple blossom providing their own special fragrance, and such was their beauty that the pear orchards were featured in May 1936 in a National daily newspaper along with a lovely photograph. A little wooden gate in the roadside hedge opened onto a winding pathway which led to the front door by the side of which a lovely old tea rose "Gloire de Dijon" climbed the wall. The pathway was bounded on either side by lupins, forget-me-nots, and many other lovely flowers. Rose bushes and orange blossom, and an archway covered in wild dog roses, added charm to this wonderful country garden, which seemed to have a continual buzz of honey bees during the long hot days of those summers long ago.

The house itself was quite spacious with a large kitchen, containing an equally large kitchen table made of oak. I always remember two chairs which had once graced Dr Smith's surgery, and which still survive, were placed nearest to the fireside, and at the other side of the table was a long wooden bench stretching the full length of the table. This bench was always used by the Headman and his mate when they came with the threshing machine. These two were always invited into the house to have dinner with my grandfather. Afterwards, they would yarn for a while with grandfather about past harvests and then they would suddenly stand as one man, and putting the bench back in its proper place close to the table, they would duly thank grandmother for the meal and return to the farmyard, ready for the afternoon session.

The kitchen grate, where the kettle was always on the boil, was a massive affair on which all the cooking was done, and at its side was a large oven. Two hand-hewn oak beams, of immense strength, ran the whole length of the house, and the perimeter walls were between 14 and 18 inches thick, a feature that was to be of immense importance in time to come. A large cellar underneath the end of the house was entered by a flight of stone steps, and in the corner of the cellar was a well which never ran dry. Halfway down the stone steps was a doorway which led into what I would imagine had been a cheese room in older times, or perhaps a food store as it was always known as the "far pantry." But at this time it had become a most fascinating store-room and was full of the most intriguing objects. A collection of old 'fiddles', an ancient clarinet, every type of cartridge and shotgun ammunition imaginable, together with all manner of tools, sets of scales, and farming relics of bygone days. A seed sowing "fiddle" hung on the wall. I found this room a most enchanting place in which to spend an hour or two delving into its mysteries. There was all manner of cheese-making equipment, a butter churn which I remember being used in the 1930s, and all the necessary tools for making butter stood in the corner. My grandfather was very fond of buttermilk, a commodity hardly heard of today, and he continued to make a little butter from time to time even after the Milk Marketing Board had been formed and a more ready and consistent market for milk had been made available. Previously most people made butter and cheese to use up the spare milk.

The back door of the house opened out onto a small cobbled yard, with an old-fashioned water pump in the middle. Across the cobbled yard stood the coal shed, a goose cote, and an outside toilet which had a long wooden seat arranged with three sittings; one large, one slightly smaller, and a small one for children. In the far corner of this cobbled yard there was a pigsty just beyond Tom McCann's shant, although by this time he had long since gone back to Ireland. Hens lived above the pigs so that any heat generated by the pigs below made the hens warmer and hopefully induce them to lay more eggs. Nearer to the house there was the milk house containing a water-run cooler for the milk which was poured from the milking cans into a large vat which emptied down either side of a metal cooler. This metal cooler was about 2-feet square with a corrugated front and back through which cold water passed from bottom to top where it ran out into a large sandstone trough. It was a wasteful way of cooling because after the trough became full the rest of the water just ran away and in the course of a year thousands of gallons of water would be lost. The milk in those early days was filtered through a muslin cloth to take out the sediment, except for a time when George Horner decided he wanted milk straight from the cow, without sieving, as this made better cream.

In the cobbled perimeter of the yard, a few geese and hens roamed freely. The main farm buildings consisted of a stable with five stalls to hold two teams of Shire horses and a milk horse, with a hayloft above, which always held the best quality hay - horses being more fussy than cattle about the quality of the hay they would eat. Nearest to the house was the cart house where the milk float was kept, and above this was the granary reached by a wide set of steps which were strong enough to bear the weight of a man carrying a 2-cwt sack of wheat.

Next to the stable, towards the lower side of the yard, was a large shippon to hold 32 cows, in four rows of eight, with a "byng" or passageway between the cows. The shippon was a wonderful building, with a large sliding door leading off the yard to a broad central passageway, opening out, through another large sliding door, to the duck pond in one direction, and to the fields in another. Each cow had a stone trough with a wooden chute in front down which the food was passed. Hay was also fed to them from the byng, having been thrown down from the hay loft at the end of the shippons. Underneath this loft was a bull cote and a loosebox, and also a mixing house where food was mixed. Altogether the arrangement was very well thought out. Behind the cows was a group to hold the muck, and between the group and the wall was a walkway. All the cattle were tied by the neck with a chain and each cow knew its own stall and on coming in from the fields they would walk straight to their own stalls. The cows were "mucked out" to a midden yard, situated just at the back of the shippon. The muck was carried out in a wheelbarrow, and as the pile of manure got higher in the winter, planks were used to wheel it higher; hard work, but warm work, and very treacherous on slippery wet planks. Many a youth would end up with his face in the barrow on a wet slippery day. In winter time, the shippon became very warm when all the cattle were kept in at night. Milking was done by hand and, at night, the only lights were shippon lamps. I recall that the old farmhands used to say that on Christmas Eve, at midnight, all the cattle would kneel down and bow their heads, and so convincing was their story that we children believed it to be true.

There was no more warm and comfortable a place than a shippon well-bedded down with straw, on a winter's night, with just the grunting of the cows as they lay chewing their cud. One of the greatest hazards of these warm shippons was the attraction to wandering tramps who could find the perfect bed with a bag of straw in the byng. There was great danger if they smoked, as many of them did, because amongst all that straw, one spark could spell disaster, and my grandfather was always on the alert.

On the other side of the farmyard at right angles to the shippon section was a very ancient barn, with hand-hewn oak beams, and the upstairs loft which had at one point a willow floor. Beyond these buildings was the stackyard where large haystacks and corn ricks would stand, being built from North to South, as was the custom, to have the best drying from the sun. There would also be a couple of huge mangold and turnip hogs or clamps as they were sometimes called, covered with straw and then soil to keep out the winter frosts. Potatoes were also stored here in this way. The farmyard itself was a lovely flat square with cobbles, leading from the shippon to the dairy and milkhouse, along which the men carried the pails as they milked the cows.

In the corner, near to the road, there was a small pond which filled with frog spawn during the Spring. When the steam threshing machines visited the yard they used the pond to fill up with water and it was surprising how much was needed during a few days threshing. And I remember as a small boy seeing a travelling circus stopping and using some of the water to give the animals a drink before moving off in their brightly-covered wagons.

On another occasion, a herd of goats came into the yard and the goatherd asked permission to water his animals and, if possible, to have shelter for the night. It was a lovely summer evening and as the cattle were out grazing in the Barn field which adjoined the farm, and the shippons were empty, grandfather gave the man permission to use the shippons and take his thirty or so goats inside for the night. Then, the man borrowed a milk can and proceeded to milk the goats. When he had milked them he took some bread and cheese from his knapsack and ate a good meal, washing it down with goats milk. Then, with his little herd safe and sound, he settled down in the byng, on a bed of hay, and went to sleep. In the morning he had breakfast sent down from the house and by the time the men arrived for early morning milking, he had moved the goats out of the shippons ready for the journey, having brushed everywhere clean. With only his trusty sheepdog to help he left the yard with his unusual little herd, pausing to give a wave as he travelled over the railway bridge in a southerly direction towards Ludlow.

Nook Farm seemed to attract travelling folk; gypsy folk, Romanies, tramps and roadsters of all manner would call to beg a crust of bread, a cup of water, or milk. Grandfather never came to terms with these folk and detested their visits, but my grandmother had a heart of gold and, on many occasions, I would see her pass her own dinner over to the beggars.

She would say: "I know that I will be eating again before long but these poor beggars don't know where their next meal is coming from."

As a result, this little old lady became loved the length of the land by these travellers. One odd couple were a brother and sister who were on their way to London from Scotland. They were terribly foot sore. They hoped to find work in the big city and I often wondered what happened to them. One of my uncles brought an old bicycle out of the cart shed and offered it to them, to ease their blistered feet, hoping they might take their turns riding it. They were overjoyed and, after bathing their feet and having a hot meal and a rest, the boy took the bike by the handlebars and, tying a folded sack on to the crossbar, he seated his sister on it and rode unsteadily away, heading south.

Some of the roadsters called at regular intervals over many years as they drifted with the seasons from North to South, or South to North. Then, of course, there was the little old lady who resembled a Spanish gypsy woman and always wore a black cape which exaggerated her already mysterious appearance. Grandfather detested her visits and she would try to time them so as to miss him. He always looked upon her as an omen of bad luck, and, on one of these occasions, her visit coincided with his visit to the old "privy", on the opposite side of the little cobbled yard. I can see him now coming out into the morning sunlight to order her away from the farm, only to be met by a string of abuse from this little wretched woman as she put many curses upon him, even to hoping it would rain if he ventured out that night. We never saw her again.

She had travelled the roads for many years and on one occasion on a very dark night Tom Gleave had been going to Weaverham to call the doctor to come and visit his sick father when he met this figure bent double against the wind. It seemed supernatural and a shiver went through Tom as he urged his horse on towards Weaverham where Dr Smith lived, at Ivy House. Of course, in the early Twenties and Thirties, much of the local traffic on the roads was horse-drawn and motor vehicles were few and far between, being either commercial or the odd privately-owned motor car.

In 1925, in about July of that year, a Romany carpet salesman and his family had visited Nook Farm, and there are photographs showing the old-fashioned motor wagon and its caravan trailer. Many people came up from the village just to look at these quaint old vehicles and I would imagine that Mr Harris, the owner, was very pleased to let them have a look round.

As more motor cars came on to the roads, horse users became more accustomed to them. At first, the noise of the engines, combined with the occasional back-fire, caused a great deal of upset to the horses which frequently shied and sometimes bolted, causing accidents and many frayed tempers.

3

PEOPLE, PLACES AND PASTIMES

THERE is still one old villager, now in his eighties, who recalls taking the back shippon door and using it as a raft on Nook Farm's duck pond. This pond, with its island of willow trees in the middle, was a great attraction to young lads throughout generations of families. In winter time, when the pond froze over, it became an ice-rink, as did the flood which usually came up to Lawyer Burton's garden. Winters were much more severe and large sheets of ice would form on many flooded areas. The local blacksmith, Rafe Broad, made dozens of pairs of skates, many of which were just a blade which screwed onto the bottom of a boot or clog, and, in Forster's Ironmongers, a simple pair of skates could be bought quite cheaply. Each skate consisted of a piece of carved wood with a blade attached to the bottom and slots to insert straps for attachment to boots or shoes. Jack Gleave, from Church Farm, had the idea of blocking a drain down on the meadows, near the river, just before a cold spell. Consequently, when the frost came there was a wonderful stretch of water to skate and slide on. Storm lamps would be set up at night if there was new moon and the revelry would go on until a late hour. Homemade sledges, usually with the flat bedsprings used as runners, were taken to various steeply banked fields in the village when winter snows began. There would often be six weeks of this very wintry weather. Gerrard's Bank, on the old park, near to the Church, was a popular place, as was our own steeply sloping field, near to the railway line. Once again, shippon lamps would be taken out on dark nights and a great time would be had by all.

Another great enjoyment in winter, when the weather was more normal, was football. For the Russets, of Back o' Town, Weaverham, our field, known as the Outlet was the venue, and, because of my grandfather's ban on Sunday football, that was the day we were sure to be playing. Of course, it was always necessary to keep a look out for old Grandfather George, because, on such occasions, he always carried an ash plant and would think nothing of laying it across the backside of any youth he could catch, if they had been misbehaving in any way, especially footballing on a Sunday.

It was here that Reg "Blimmer" Jones started his footballing days and my father, despite being in peril of being caught by the old man, also played, acquiring the name "Dimock" after a footballer of the day. Kite - flying became another great pastime. The kites were made out of brown paper and thin cane, or strips of other suitable wood, with a tail of pieces of newspapers.

As Spring turned into Summer, trundles or hoops would be run along the dusty roads, and games of marbles would take place. In the Autumn of each year, at acorn time, flop guns would be made out of a hollowed out piece of elderberry wood, with a straight piece of wood for the stale or plunger. Working similarly to a bicycle pump the acorns were forced out of the end of the barrel with a loud pop. These were happy days and there was always something to do and a lot of enjoyment to be had, at little or no cost.

The village "Bobby" kept his eye on everything that went on and, generally speaking, lads and girls of the village behaved well. There was, of course, a keen rivalry between the boys from the village school, in Forest Street, and those from the old Grammar School, higher up the road, and it was customary, as Tom Gatley, recalled for the "Cocks o' the School" from Forest Street, to challenge the pick of the Grammar School bunch and then proceed to either Lake House Field, or Tower Field, at the back of the Grammar School, where a large crowd would gather to watch the fray. These events were held in good spirit and the worse that came out of them would be a bloody nose, or a black eye, and then all would be back to normal.

The Council School was extended in 1907, but the original schoolhouse was next to the Institute. The first headmaster of this school was Mr Harper. He had retired before the First World War, but came out of retirement so that the new young headmaster could serve in the army, and, after coming home from the war, Frank Nixon duly took up his appointment. When this new part of the school was built, each of the local farmers lent a man and a horse and cart to carry the bricks from Thompsons' brickworks, in Northwich, and to bring other materials which had been brought by train to Acton Station. Early this century, not many children went to school after the age of 10 and many of the older children could neither read nor write.

Anna Hignett, Arthur Davies's wife, was the first teacher in the Infants' School. A teacher at the Senior School in the early years of the century, was Nettie Ashbrook, daughter of Joseph Ashbrook who farmed Valley Farm, Little Leigh, for 50 years until a few years before his death, at the age of 87. She was a fiery person who did not believe in sparing the rod. However, she took to the whisky bottle and, caught with a bottle in her desk, was dismissed. She had courted and then married, probably in her forties, Jim Roberts (the milkman), son of William Roberts, of Northwich Road. He kept his horse at the back of his house in a field which would come up to where Russet Road is now. Later, they went to live in Tower Lane where Joseph Ashbrook, her father, went to live with them in his retirement, about seven years before he died, in about 1915.

Some of his near neighbours were Ted Buckley's father, who lived in the first cottage past Rose Cottage, going towards the Gate Inn, where Ted Ellis's father lived, and Joey Ormson, who lived where Mrs. Metcalf lives, Tudor Cottage, which were then two thatched cottages. Jim got his milk from Moreton's and had possibly also traded with Valley Farm and sold in the Northwich area. He used to collect bets, which had been left with Joe Johnson, and take them to the Northwich Betting Shop.

A Mrs Penny followed Nettie at the school and she was followed by Violet Fisher. Mr Trickett was headmaster of the Old Grammar School which was founded in 1638.

The school was described in an early directory, by Samuel Bagshaw, in 1850, as:

"... a stone building, of considerable antiquity, now undergoing a complete reparation. It is endowed with the Pickmere Estate, situate in the Parish of Great Budworth, and let from year to year at a rent of £30. The estate was bequeathed by Mr Barker in the reign of Charles II for the instructions of children residing in the parish of Weaverham. In 1835 a house and farm buildings were erected upon the estate at a cost of £310. Of this sum, £250 was raised from a fall of timber, and with the addition of a year's rent, and the price of the old materials was found sufficient to cover expenses. The entire rent is paid to the schoolmaster and this income is increased by a portion of the rent of the Gorstage Estate and the interest on certain moneys in the Northwich Savings Bank. All the boys are taught English, reading and Latin without any expense, and for writing and accounts there is a quarterly charge of 7s.6d for each boy from the town, and 2s.6d for each boy from the lordship. There is also a charge of 1s. entrance fee and an annual payment of 1s. for firing and 1s. for cockpence. A portion of the latter is appropriated to the purchase of cocks, for which the boys raffle on Shrove Tuesday.

The master had usually been appointed by the Trustees of the Weaverham estate, but the question as to the patronage of the school was raised some years ago by the vicar. We may observe that the school was in existence at the time that the Pickmere estate was bestowed upon it by Mr Barker; his trustees, therefore, could have no right to appoint the master, but such right must, of course, remain with the persons who lawfully exercised it before the accession of this endowment. It was contended that the fact of the school having been popularly called the Vicar's School, raised a presumption in favour of the vicar's claim to be the patron.

However, in the absence of confirmatory evidence, this is certainly very shallow ground upon which to support such a claim. There is no doubt that the school was originally erected at the expense of the parish and the repairs are paid out of the church rate to the present day. On this account, it would probably appear that the vicar and churchwardens, or perhaps the vestry generally, are the parties in whom the right of appointment is vested."

Children of many of the village farming families were educated at the Old Grammar School. My grandfather and grandmother attended and there was a study of agriculture which helped some of the pupils to spend a period at the Reaseheath College of Agriculture. The Grammar School is said to have been plundered and damaged by the Royalists during the Civil War.

A large number of the pupils were the sons of local farming families and this led to the school's closure in 1916. As the young farmers reached the age at which they could serve in the army and joined up, and went to the Front, their places on the farms were taken by the younger sons who would normally have been at school. Consequently, the school had to close for lack of pupils, but one of my friends had a work colleague who was actually a pupil at the school in its final year. George Hough, from a family of butchers in Barnton, used to walk every day across the Locks, at Saltersford, across the bridge over the old river, and up Wood Lane to the school, with a shilling in his pocket for his tuition.

The double line siding at the Coal Wharf went in off points, near the bridge, with the buffers near the Barnfield end. The London, Midland and Scottish Railway Company had been forced to put in the siding when they were negotiating to purchase more land from Squire Heath, in order to widen the track to four lanes. The Squire also insisted on the company planting trees on a stretch of land in front of the hall, to screen it from the railway.

Bill Hignett, a tall man who walked with a swaying gait, ran his coal business from the wharf and lived at No 40 Nook Cottage for many years; these were formerly known as Wharf Cottages. He had stables, an office and a weighbridge by the road near our house, and two or three horse-drawn lorries. One day, the front end of one of his lorries had broken and over the weekend, while he was waiting for Rafe Broad the Blacksmith to come to repair it on the following Monday, some youths came and took the two front wheels down the Barnfield under the bridge and into the swampy part of the outlet near the brook. It was ages before old Bill and Ralph found them.

A shunting engine came about midday every day to bring full wagons of coal and take empties away. Tenants of Mr. Heath could use the wharf to receive or send goods and according to Tom McCann, who had worked at Nook Farm for many years, many tons of timber were loaded there in early days. Tom Newton used to work for Bill Hignett as a driver of one of his coal lorries. He had a club foot, was as hard as nails and could carry coal with the best. No matter how cold the weather, he would sit on the front of the lorry without heavy clothing. He was often teased by young lads and if he caught any of them, he would lock them up in the weighbridge building, frightening them to death. There was a high signal near the bridge and this was really high to enable it to be seen over the bridge from a distance in either direction. One of the jobs Bill Hignett detested doing, although he was paid by the Railway Company to do it, was to go up to the ladder to trim and fill the old oil-lamp. He said it swayed violently in high winds.

Rough coal in those days was 4d cwt and best coal 6d cwt. My grandfather had 5 cwts of coal each week, and Bill would have 2 quarts of milk a day, at 4d a quart. Bill used to have the hay from the railway batters between the wharf and the underbridge to feed his horses, but when the wharf ceased to be a coal wharf when work began on widening the track and when Bill moved his business to Acton Station, he still came for the hay and this led to a dispute with the Ganger in charge of the length of the batters past Nook Farm.

In those days, the grass on the railway batters was scythed by the railway gangs, particularly before the Royal Train was due along the line, on its way to Scotland. The two footbridges further along the line towards Acton were erected in 1925 when the work on widening the track was finally finished. Previously, there had been a footpath over the line and where the footbridge nearest to the station now stands, there was a level crossing for horses and carts going to Joe Effersham's farm which was farmed by the Clark family who had a lovely orchard and a barn and small shippon.

The first remembered tenant at 38 The Wharf was Ned Gerrard who worked for the railway, and, at a later time, Ella Davies and her sister were occupants. Ella was the dairy maid at Hefferston Grange (Grange Hall). The dairy was later converted into a bungalow by Warrington Corporation and its first occupants were Hughie Nield and his wife, Bertha.

Hughie Nield was farm bailiff for my grandfather at Home Farm until his untimely death in 1936. Ella Davies became the second wife of old man Greatbanks, father of Fred and grandfather of Norman. Fred ("Pecker") Greatbanks won the bowling cup at a match held at the Grange on the day of the Pageant, September 14th, 1909, beating amongst others his own father. He would be about 10-years-old. Old Greatbanks moved later to Forest Street where Hiram Curwell later lived. They had a sideboard just through the door, covered with pottery and ornaments which over the years the old man and Pecker coming into the house at night in a state of drunkenness gradually swept on to the floor. Ella's daughter Ida, after leaving school worked for my grandfather George at Nook Farm and Dad used to take her home to the house in Forest Street.

After the Greatbanks's moved out of number 38, to go to Forest Street, Mr and Mrs William Woods moved in. They were the parents of Arthur ("Parrot") Shaw's mother. Arthur will be remembered by many as being the teamster for Frank Moreton, at Lake House Farm, up to the outbreak of the Second World War. Mr and Mrs Woods moved to the cottage after retiring as licensees of the "Star" public house, opposite the Wheatsheaf. They were the last licensees before it closed. Then a Mr and Mrs Doyle lived at 38. Mr Doyle was a groom for Mr Pillings, but sadly his wife died in childbirth and when he left the wharf he was followed by "Rookie" Woodward and his family. Rookie was handyman to the Frankenburgs between 1910-1919, doing repairs and looking after the chickens, and after him came Mrs Waterman, Jim Waterman's second wife.

Mr and Mrs Sarson also lived at the cottages. He was coachman to Squire Heath and followed Joe Johnson in that capacity after Joe had been sacked by Mrs Heath for an indiscretion which we will learn about later. Bill Hignett had to move out of the cottage, as Mr Heath required it for the Sarsons and he went to live in West Road, in Mrs Cryer's house. Mr Sarson was a good looking fresh-faced man who used to ride to Weaverham on horseback each morning for the daily newspaper for Mr Heath. It is said that Mr Sarson committed suicide by hanging himself in the Tack Room at the Grange. This room was later to become the laundry for the Sanatorium. Ned Gerrard's brother Jim, who had been a sergeant in the London Metropolitan Police, took to drink and lived much of the time in the stable of old Hignett and was much tormented by Tom Gatley

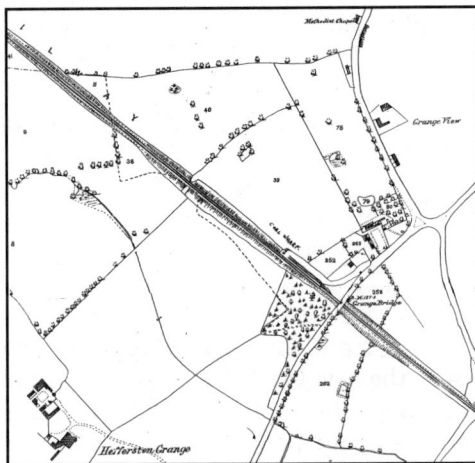

A map showing the former railway sidings near to Grange Bridge.

and his friends with hails of stones onto its tin roof. These are still lying in abundance at the bottom of Coal Wharf.

After the Sarsons, came Bill Hornby with his family and they lived at No. 40 for a while. Rosie was born there, before he bought the shop in High Street near to where Barber Joe Foster had his barber's shop. Then Arthur Jones, who worked at the Sawmill at Cuddington, moved in with his family; there was George, Sam, Ethel, Emmie, Jack and Arthur; and later Reg ("Blimmer"), son of Ethel, and another Arthur, son of Emmie.

Either just before, or just after Bill Hornby, a Mr and Mrs Smith lived at No. 40. Mr Smith had married a widow, Mrs Chetwynd, whose husband had been killed in a mining disaster at the same time as "Tish" Ashley's father, and he brought up Arthur and Cyril ("Squib") Chetwynd, who was a good footballer and could have played professionally. Cyril married Jessie Scott.

The old road, going down past Nook Cottages and to the wharf, was the original road which, before the coming of the railway, carried on through the wood and the park, passing within 100 yards or so of the hall and eventually coming back to its present alignment. Later, when negotiations were in progress to build the railway, it was decided to carry the road over the railway, skirting the big park at Hefferston. When this road, Grange Lane, was cut in 1830, it was put in the care of the Landowner, but when the responsibility eventually fell to Robert Heath, his only repair was to continually level it with sand, which became completely useless in wet weather. The stretch of road between The Nook and the Gate Inn became known as West Road because of its position in relation to the village, previously it was "Back o' Town". Tom McCann recalled that when he first knew this road, it was little more than a sandy track heavily rutted in wet wintry conditions.

Perhaps the most important man in the village and certainly one of the greatest characters, was Dr Smith, who when he called on his rounds never refused a cup of tea. He always called at "Nan" Allman's shop in Forest Street. He was very annoyed about old man Allman taking to drink and leaving home. My grandmother said he was such a nice man when he got married, and very clean, always wore a bowler hat and went to Chapel regularly, but he later became a drunkard, lived rough on farms and followed the thresher.

Bill Whitley put his father's Army greatcoat on and went to Dr Smith.

"Well, William, how long have you been enlisted?".

"Just a fortnight, Doctor," replied Bill.

"What can I do for you?" asked the old Doctor.

"I was wondering if you could lend me a shilling, sir," said Bill. "You see the Army doesn't pay very well and I haven't got the money for a drink."

"Oh, I'll mix you a drink better than any the pub can sell you," said Dr Smith, and he mixed him a concoction of his own.

Bill drank it and as he was leaving, the Doctor gave him a shilling, but he had only been in the Wheatsheaf a few minutes, when a strange feeling came over him. He fled from the pub and lay down under a large hedge in Lake House Field, behind the school, and remained there sick all night. When daylight came he staggered home. Needless to say, he kept well away from Dr Smith for a long time.

Another malingerer named Jones, from Church Street, went to complain of backache and feeling too ill to go to work. Dr Smith examined him and said: "I am afraid there is nothing I can do for you, there is no cure for your complaint."

The startled man said: "Surely I am not that ill, am I, Doctor?"

"Yes, very ill," said the Doctor, "You are suffering from that awful disease called Lazyitis, for which there is no medical remedy. Now go from this surgery and never come here again until you are genuinely ill."

During the annual rook shoot at the end of May, the Doctor would always join Mr Heath's rook party. Everybody used small bore rifles; the rooks were to be made into Rook Pie. The old Doctor would never leave a rook which had been caught up in a forked branch; he would keep on shooting with his rifle until the branch was cut through. He was reputed to have silenced an argument by throwing bottles in the air and shooting them down with either hand.

When Mr Heath sold some trees to Littlers' Timber Yard, the timber wagon had to be loaded in Dr Smith's field, next to Heath's croft. The men were having their dinners in the shippons at Nook Farm and the horses had been brought across for a drink before the journey to Northwich, (the trees were cut down with cross-cuts and trimmed with axes), when Dr Smith passed on his return to the surgery in his pony and trap. He came into the Nook Yard in a terrible rage and ordered that no timber was to be drawn off on his field; also, he threatened to bring a gang of men from the village to throw it off the wagons.

However, when he had gone, the wagoner in charge calmly said: "Yoke up the horses and we'll put it on to the King's Highway."

This they did, but in so doing they sank deep ruts into Dr Smith's field, which he rented from Lord Barrymore and this caused a terrible row between Mr Heath and the Doctor.

Dr Smith died in 1917 and he was followed by Dr Moore who had a large Airedale which was terrified of Fred Allman's fox terrier and dared not come out of Doctor's Lane, even though the fox terrier, which Fred had got from the Hunt kennels and was a descendant of Dark Admiral, was much smaller. Another well known professional man in the same mould as the Doctor, but, unlike the Doctor, not so prominent in public life, was the local Veterinary Surgeon, "Farrier" Bates.

John Willy Bates was a much sought after man in the early years of this century. During the First World War, he was appointed Veterinary Inspector for all horses commandeered by the Government for service with the Army at the Front and stabled at the Remount Depot at

Cuddington. Also, he was appointed vet to the railway horses, on the recommendation of William Marshall, of Mere House. He was college-trained and one of the best vets of his day. A great character, he would be seen dashing about the district on his large red Indian motorcycle, complete with bowler hat and coat-tails blowing in the breeze. Before each journey, he would fasten a stout piece of brown paper under his jacket to keep off the cold wind. When he arrived at a farm to attend to an animal or calve a cow, his bowler hat, his three-quarter length jacket, brown paper and shirt would be rapidly removed and dumped in the corner of the shippon and he would go to work on the job in hand. If it was a difficult calving, he would call for Tom Platt, his great friend, who would ride pillion on the large bike which had no kick-start and had to be started by running alongside and letting the clutch out and jumping on at the right moment. It rarely let him down and was a regular sight on the local roads and farm tracks.

John Willy, having split from his wife, lived for a long time in Manning's yard in a caravan which John Heffen had previously occupied, but, later, he bought a bungalow in West Road, where he startled neighbours by having his coffin made while he was still alive and keeping it behind the door in his front room. He was said to have slept in it many times, but in the winter time, he kept a few potato sets in it to induce them to sprit. He liked a drop of whisky and was often heard to order a "dog's nose" at the bar of the Wheatsheaf. This was a whisky concoction, but what was added, I do not know. He never wore a top coat and in the coldest of winters he would look round at the men rugged up in thick coats and scarves and say: "What the devil is wrong with you all, it's not cold. Get a drop of whisky down you, it'll warm yer marrow".

There was a story told in the Knowledge Room at the Wheatsheaf for many years. It appears that John Willy would pay out £1 to anyone who would sleep in his coffin for a night. After a lot of discussion, Sgt. Allen, always on the look out for a bit of spare money, took up the challenge. So off they all trooped at closing time to see the Sergeant get into his "bed", but none had realised that John Willy was so short of stature that none of them would fit in the coffin and it would be impossible for any of them to sleep in it.

Farrier Bates's close friend, Tommy Platt, farmed Well Bank Farm with his mother, Sarah Platt, and his sister, Maggie. Tom and Maggie were as alike as twins, and although Tom called Sarah his Aunt, it was a fact that both children were her own. Sarah never married, but one of her close friends from the past was Sam Keay, from one of the black and white thatched cottages in Church Lane, near the Church Hall, but on the opposite side of the road. Sgt. Allen said that the children had a very strong likeness to Sam.

The following is an extract from the Census of 1891:

Church Street   Born

100 (Well Bank Farm)
Sarah Platt. Farmer 42.   Weaverham
Maggie Platt. Daughter Scholar 8   Weaverham
Thomas Platt. Boarder 12   Weaverham

Well Bank Farm was a little farm up the bank, on the left of Well Lane, and the land stretched down to Weaverham Well, where a footpath entered the field and, passing close by the farm, carried on to High Street, by way of Smiths Lane. When eventually old Sarah died, Tom carried on farming with some help from John Gerrard from Weaverham Wood. There was a shippon with stalls for nine or ten cows and Tom grew a small field of potatoes and some turnips and he would often be called upon by his friend Johnny Bates when the vet was in need of some help. Johnny would sometimes use Tom's leggings to hold a colt for castration. Sgt. Allen once took a cat for such an operation and it would give the old vet great pleasure if the cat would squirt all over the unfortunate holder. Sgt. Allen was only just able to dodge this, and refused to pay the full half crown, saying that a shilling would suffice.

Eventually, when the Barrymore Estate was sold, the farm came up for sale and it was offered to Tom for £2,000, but he had not the money to buy it. His old friend Johnny Bates offered to lend him the money without any obligation, but he was afraid to take the risk and while he dithered, Arthur Davies came along and bought it over his head.

Tom's sister married a man named Collins, Ken Collins' father, and John Gerrard gave Tom a job and a house in Moss Street, where Jack and Margaret Sayle lived with him for many years.

Aunt Annie Moss and Aunt Ada used to tease Tom about his marriage chances with a girl named Winnie Carney, but Tom, like John Gerrard, remained a bachelor all his life. He was a good worker and a very honest reliable man. Arthur Davies's mother, when her husband died, married Robert "Bobby" Howarth from the Gate Inn, who during his time as Landlord kept a small herd of cattle in the shippon there. These were walked daily to and from the pasture by his stepson, Arthur Davies, who looked after the cattle. When he died, he left enough money for Arthur to buy Well Bank where he was followed by Jack, who developed a milk round and farmed there until the Leigh Way housing development.

Well Bank had sufficient pasture of its own, but others, like Jim "Huckster" Woodward, when he moved to The Limes in West Road, Bobby Howarth, and also Tom and Mary Gleave from the little shop cum farm in Church Street, had to rely on renting land from Lord Barrymore, or the Vicar.

Although not so big as Well Bank, Adam Forster's Village Farm, later to become Ellison's, so keeping it in the family, had a few fields of its own and when Fred Ellison went there after Adam, he kept seven or eight cows. The milk was churned, and he made a good trade in buttermilk. Fred was my grandmother's uncle and he and his son, Rowley, had a coal round, although not so big as Bill Hignett's. Their coal came via Greenbank Station.

Adam used to sell cheese and once when he had a theft, the local policeman was put on guard, but the cheese still went missing. When the constable was told of the second theft, he asked Adam if he thought he had taken it. Adam replied, "Well I don't know, but when thar went, the cheese went."

At the end of the 19th century, Adam used to go to Blackpool on bicycle to preach and said there were only a few houses on the front. Such a long journey you would think too daunting to contemplate, especially when you consider that in 1867 a coachman on the London to St Albans run was fined for whipping a cyclist who was overtaking him. The guard on the same coach was also fined for hurling an iron ball on the end of a rope into the cyclist's spokes, felling the rider.

It was Adam who claimed that the "Grange Lady" jumped on the back of his horse while he was riding down Grange Lane, and jumped off at The Nook. He wasn't the only person to have seen the apparition. Alfred Catley saw the ghostly figure of a hooded person, whom he took to be a monk, in the old wood, near to the railway, and young Reg "Blimmer" Jones insisted he saw a hooded figure which he described as a woman carrying a jug. She actually spoke to him saying, "Take this water to that old man, he needs it." This was in the Back o' Town area of Weaverham, and young Reg never stopped to look round, but fled towards his home at Nook Cottages, his little clogs striking sparks off the road. On meeting his brother Arthur and gasping out his story, he carried on home. Arthur went immediately to investigate, but could see nothing and the incident remains a mystery.

Over the years, so many people have reported seeing the ghostly figure of a woman always carrying a jug in this area of the village and when old Tom Parker, from Acton, was coming home late, from Cuddington, with his horse and float, he noticed with alarm the ghostly figure standing in the entrance to Grange Wood along the lane. He tried to urge the horse on to get past quickly, but the horse stopped and refused to go on any further. The old man had to turn round and go home by way of Bag Lane and Onston. No-one seemed to know who the lady was or how the haunting originated, but it is known that when the Hall was taken over to house nurses and domestic staff for the Sanatorium, one room remained locked and barred from the occupants and it was thought to have some connections with the supernatural happenings there.

There were, of course, many pranks played and some people were frightened out of their wits by others dressing up in white sheets. There is the story of the staff at Hefferston dressing up two dummy figures, a man and a woman, sitting with arms around each other in the potting shed to give Mr Holden, the head gardener, quite a fright when he opened up one morning to start work. However, real or imaginary, very few would venture into the wood or the Park, and certainly not after dark, except if you were out rabbiting and had company. Like Arthur Short one night, when he took Stewart Brown. When confronted with Lowe's dapple-faced horse, Stuart thought it was a ghost and his heart nearly stopped. Arthur, however, did see the Grange Lady one night after walking out with a girl from the Grange. Returning through the wood to the entrance onto the road, he saw the ghostly figure of the veiled and hooded woman, close to the spot where Clarence Holt saw her some years later.

Speaking of ghosts, reminds me of other supernatural happenings told to me by members of my own family. Ernie Williamson, my great-uncle and husband of great-aunt Ada Moss, used to tell the story of how one night, as he was leaving Beach Farm to walk home, a vivid bright light passed him and as he turned, it appeared to enter the house. My great-grandfather John, standing by the corner cupboard in his kitchen, saw the bright light come in through the wall and shortly afterwards, he found great-grandmother had passed away in her chair.

Aunt Ethyl Moss, she was the wife of Tom Moss, one of great-grandfather John Moss's sons, who had gone to farm at Bawsgate Farm, at Whitegate, recalled hearing a girl's voice singing a hymn upstairs at the farm. Thinking it was her daughter, Mary, she was not unduly surprised until she went upstairs and found that Mary was not there, nor was anybody else. Then she found Billy, one of the farm workers, dead in his caravan down the yard.

Another great character was Martha Andrews, Jack Sayle's Granny, who lived in one of the two thatched cottages further down "Narrow Lane" opposite the Ring-o'-Bells yard. The cottages had long gardens stretching back as far as Church Lane. Her one-up and one-down cottage was kept spotlessly clean and like most village cottages, it had a pigsty, which she also kept wonderfully clean. This sty at the bottom of the garden, was arranged well, with a small yard with a feeding trough just outside the cote. She liked pigs that would keep their sleeping quarters clean, so that if she kept the yard mucked out, woe betide them if they messed up the interior. They would get Martha's brush behind them.

Either my great-grandfather, or Grandfather George, would bring her four pigs at a time from Beeston Market, and after fattening them up she would sell three and keep the fourth for herself, which she would kill and hang up in the house. She was a giant of a woman, at least 6 ft. 6 ins. tall, very broad and of immense strength. She smoked a clay pipe, liked a pint of beer and frequented the Star where William Wood was Landlord. Martha went out to work on local farms, picking potatoes, or thinning turnips, and she could turn her hand to anything. In fact, when work was short she would take in darning and mending socks. Because of her great strength, she was often called upon to go with my great-grandfather,

John, from Beach Farm, to help him kill pigs. She travelled around the district with my great-grandfather in his horse and float as they went out to kill pigs for local farmers and also for George Horner, for whom they would kill over 200 pigs each year. She could hold a pig better than any man and once she had straddled it, the pig was held like a vice; there was no escape.

There was one pig they killed for old man Groves, from down by the river. It was a very large pig and the old man wanted it hung from a beam in the kitchen. The hooks were in place, but when they lifted the pig it was too big to hang so my grandfather suggested "cutting his yed off." "Nay, thee shanna, I'll not have his yed cut off, it'll spoil him," said old man Groves. After struggling for some time, they gave up and the pig was left on the table. But the next morning, when old John and Martha were driving past to another job, the old man rushed out and told them to come and look at his pig. There was the pig hanging from the hook in the kitchen complete with head, but with a large hole dug out in the kitchen floor to accommodate it.

Martha's husband, "Nibby" Andrews, was a quiet little man, rarely allowed in the house, who had little to say. Wearing a little pork pie hat, he walked with one hand behind his back giving the impression that he had some deformity or lack of use in it. He was fond of watching cricket and rarely missed a match, and, in fact, helped to look after the ground. Lads used to shout to him: "Bowl straight for the wicket, Nibby," as he headed for the cricket ground, when a match was to be played. Many an unsuspecting, tormenting lad received a nasty shock if he came too close to little Nibby's "weak" hand. Nibby would catch hold of the lad with it and clout him with his other hand.

Other old cottages stood in Narrow Lane, now Wallerscote Road, near its junction with Northwich Road. There were five of them, a terrace of three, and a group of two. Old Jack Vaughan lived in one of them and in another, Bill Crook, who claimed Lord Crook in Parliament was his uncle. There were also two other thatched cottages a little further along Narrow Lane, on the left hand side. Martha Andrews lived in one and old Alan Gregory in the other. There were also a couple of thatched cottages in Station Road opposite the driveway to Mere House, and another where the Scout Hall now stands, and another in Sandy Lane where Frank Mainwaring was born; his father was brother to Dick Mainwaring's grandfather. Abraham Youd lived in the thatched cottage in the poplar-lined High Street; he was gardener to Dick Burton's father who lived in the "Limes"; his son Ernie Youd went to live in West Road where Arthur Davies had lived, and Bill Groves then had the cottage and lived there until it was demolished, to make way for road-widening. Richard Walker of the local land drainage firm "Walker Bros.", tragically lost his life recently in an accident with a trailer at Bryn Farm on Cuddington Hill. He was a hard working man, well-liked and respected by all who knew him and it was a sad loss to the local farming community.

Strangely enough, his father, Forester Walker, worked for many years on this same Bryn Farm which they had recently bought, as cowman for Arthur Youd when he had the farm. It is recalled how he threatened a motorist who had been abusive to him about not being able to control his cows on the way to the farm from the fields, in Millington Lane. The motorist told him not to wave his cow stick at him, while Forester told him what he would do if he didn't shut up.

Much to the dismay of his family, after finishing at Youd's when the farm was sold, Forester turned a bit wayward, but before he passed on, he had quietened down somewhat. His wife, old Granny Walker, used to kill pigs at the little farm in Bent Lane which Alice (nee Walton) Dutton and her husband Johnny kept. Alice worked, in the early 1920s, with my mother at Hefferston Grange. Granny Walker went on to keep the Cabbage Hall and for an annual "do" for the jockeys and stable lads at Sandy Brow racing stables, she always made a rabbit pie, using five rabbits which she paid Hiram Curwell and old "Nasser" Aspell to catch. However, on the night they went netting they caught only four, so they caught the old woman's cat, took its head off and skinned it with the rest and no-one knew the difference. It seemed to be enjoyed by all, but the two didn't accept an invitation to a piece of pie that night.

Forester's brother, Tom, married one of the Johnson sisters who were working at Grange Lane Farm, which at that time belonged to the Cunninghams. There were three of these sisters. Arthur Jones married one of them and the third was responsible for rearing all the calves born there. The Cunninghams, who had come to Forest Hill, which had been Littledale's place, had bought Grange Lane Farm and Gorstage Lane Farm and had been the next highest bidder to Warrington Corporation when Frankenbergs sold up.

A Mr Johnson was farm bailiff at Grange Lane Farm and a Mr and Mrs Scott, who kept turkeys, went to live at Gorstage Lane. Cunninghams bred horses, but their money came from their cotton business, and in the slump about 1926, they lost everything and were made bankrupt overnight. The Bank took over the farms, but the Johnsons stayed on until the farms were sold. Gorstage Lane Farm was bought for a Mr Hook, who was a vagrant, by his uncle for £1,800 and eventually Grange Lane Farm was bought as an investment by a gentleman and rented to Tommy Gleave. The price paid for the 143 acres was £5,400.

Miss Hall, who was a friend of Miss Hatton, head gardener at the Grange, and who Tom Gleave was courting, wanted Tom to buy Handforth Brook Farm for £2,500, but Bradburys did a private deal with the Barrymore Estate and bought it over his head. Some of the Barrymore farms were sold at giveaway prices; Edwin Walker's Gorstage Green Farm was sold to him for £2,400; ICI bought Weaverham Wood, Wallerscote and Beach Farms and some years later Handforth

Brook as well. "Shoot" Groves, from down by the river, bought his little house and bit of land from Lord Barrymore for £600 and then held up the ICI pipeline until they met his demands.

Mr Fairclough, who farmed Mere House Farm, was a short-tempered man. He sacked one of his workmen, "Skelly" Dutton, at a minute's notice for stealing a button hole rose from the glasshouse on Sunday when he went to feed, water, and muck out the horses. Skelly used to cart off the potatoes, kneeing them up onto the cart three sacks high with the knees of his trousers worn out. He would keep three Irishmen going picking the potatoes with forks. Skelly lived in High Street and was a friend of Tom Gatley at Weaverham School. Tom Gatley passed on in September 1985 and George Tickle also that month, as did Bernard Wilkinson who worked with George at Joe Rigby's.

One of Fairclough's sons was an officer in the Army and was a friendly chap who always stopped for a chat if he met you across the fields. The other son, Max, became friendly with Charlie Bebbington's daughter, Nancy. Charlie's son Jack had emigrated to Australia and had acquired a large acreage of land there which had to be cleared of bush and scrub. When old Fairclough objected to his friendship with Nancy, Max eventually left home and went to live with the Bebbingtons, later going out to Australia to Jack's farm, where Nancy later joined him and they were married. When she arrived at the farm, she was dismayed to find the nearest milk was six miles away and they had to go on horseback to get some before she could have a cup of tea. Also, drinking-water had to be brought in tubs, from some distance away.

Eventually, the land was cleared and they prospered. Max and Jack have now passed on, but Nancy did return some time ago, maybe 1983, and Tommy Gleave met her in the churchyard.

Farmer Fairclough insisted that his ploughmen ploughed so that the furrows came up to the roadside in very straight lines as if by a ruler, because he knew that the old men of the village would walk out and cast a very critical eye on them on their Sunday walks. Corn sown by hand would fall into the cocked up furrows. He was reputed to be a hard man, but in later life when he was in a wheelchair and the farm came up for sale, he asked his daughter to take him out to where his fine horses were in the sale ring and he cried like a child as they walked past him for the last time before going with their new masters to their new homes. Such was the love of a man for his animals which had been his pride and joy.

Arthur Dean, who was farming at Wallerscote as a tenant of Lord Barrymore, until ICI bought the farm to cover with the limebeds, then came to Mere House Farm which he rented from the Fairclough. He was offered Mere House for £9,000, but instead he moved to Handforth Brook, after the Bradburys moved out. While he was at Mere House, our cattle got out into his corn. He was angry about this and said he would forgive just this once, but if it should happen again he would seek compensation.

Within two months of the corn being cut, he put over 100 sheep to graze on the stubble. They got through the hedge on to Nook Farm and a very red-faced Arthur Dean came to take them back, with neither explanation nor apology.

Fred Allman worked at one time for Captain Townshend, at Gorstage Hall. Captain Townshend was a joker and loved to play practical jokes on his friends and his workers. When the local Bobby, Sgt. Ellwood, went to supervise the dipping of the sheep, which by law he had to do at each local farm, he left his tunic and helmet at the hall and went off with the men to the dipping trough. During the course of the dipping, there was suddenly a commotion with loud whistle blowing and they looked up to see running across the field in the distance, the figure of an irate police-man blowing his whistle furiously much to the consternation of the sergeant who thought something serious was afoot. But it was one of Captain Townshend's jokes; he had donned the sergeant's tunic and hel-met, unearthed his whistle and come running across the field blowing for all he was worth.

One morning, he called Fred to tell him to get the boilerman, old Bill Heath, to get as much steam up as he possibly could as the house was cold. Old Bill stoked up until a great pressure built up and the safety valve started blowing off, but when he came to leave the boiler house, he found himself locked in and in his panic he burst through a window cov-ered in soot, much to the amusement of the Captainwho had locked him in.

Mrs Townshend had a herd of pedigree Friesians, some of the earliest ever imported into the country. My grandfather went to buy two bull calves from her, one for Nook Farm and one for his father at Beach Farm. She said she could only supply one, which went to Beach Farm, but that her friend Mrs Dewhurst had one which we could have. The Beach Farm bull turned out very nasty, but the one at Nook Farm became a very good bull and was reasonably quiet. One of the best cows in Mrs Townshend's herd was "Gorstage Gouder", which was reputed to give over nine gallons a day, but Mr Horner was not impressed; he said the butterfat was too low.

Captain Townshend was a prominent member of the Cheshire Hunt, but had another great love, greyhound racing. He had a greyhound called "Tied Time" which was trained by the Wrights, at Whitley. It won the Waterloo Cup and Captain Townshend was very proud of it; he said it was worth more than all of Mrs Townshend's pedigree herd. He was an engi-neer and in his garden, he had a large model railway he had built himself which would carry several adults. He had been playing with his family on this railway all one day and caught a chill, but despite being warned by Dr Smith to stay in bed for a few days, he continued to go to London on business. As a result, his chill turned to pneumonia and he died. Group Captain Peter Townshend was connected with this family.

Thomas Gleave and his wife, when they first married, had a shop in

Copyhold. It was here they spent their honeymoon and stayed up all night to bake bread. Thomas said: "It was the finest batch of bread we ever turned out." Later, he bought the little shop in Church Street which he paid for with sovereigns, to the surprise of everyone. In those days, a cash purchase like that was the talk of the town. At this new shop, he had a small shippon and the use of several fields scattered about the village. One such field stood at the spot where the Ring o' Bells now stands. This was a round field, while the triangular piece at the junction of Northwich Road and Wallerscote was a lovely garden entered by an archway which stood about the entrance to Ring o' Bells yard. He also had the football field and the field where the cobbler's and the new housing development now stands. The cattle had to be walked through the village to their pasture and back to the shippon for milking, but there was nothing unusual about that in those days, as cattle were several times a day herded through the village. Johnny Ormson was Tom's cowman and Tom used to say to customers in his shop when Johnny went missing: "Anybody seen my man Pokey?"

Johnny also had another nickname, "Whistling Johnny", because of his habit of whistling hymns as he walked the little herd of cattle to and from their pastures. He lived with his sister, Nancy, who used to take in sewing in the thatched cottage next to the Grammar School. They had milk from Nook Farm and one day as she walked past the other cottages opposite, she was struck on the wrist with Bill Johnson's spinning top, the blow breaking her wrist. Children played with top and whips in those days

My great-grandmother was Mary Gleave, daughter of old George Gleave, from Church Farm, and sister of Charlie, Thomas, John, and another sister who married Mackam Ellis. Thomas and Mary used to run about Church Farm barefoot. Great-great-grandfather George Gleave came to Church Farm as a young man. He was a very particular man, and all the jobs done for him by his men had to be done well. He had Hessian sacks attached to the thrippers and bottoms of his carts to catch any corn that was accidentally shaken out of the sheaves.

Grandfather George on one occasion went to Charlie Gleave's place to borrow his horse and shandry. There were two large round stones at either side of the gateway, to protect the gate stumps, and, unfortunately, Grandfather hit one of these and upturned the cart. Old Pinder from the pie shop happened to be walking past.

"By the times, George, whatever 'an you bin doing?" (All his sentences were punctuated by "by the times".)

Mrs Pinder, always called "Cissy", used to make lovely pies and black puddings, also savoury ducks, and these were on display in the little shop window in Church Street. Fred Allman recalled as a lad, how they used to loop a piece of wire and by careful manipulation pull an odd pie to within arm's reach of the door which was always slightly ajar.

Mackam Ellis, who as I have previously mentioned married one of

Tom's sisters, farmed Handforth Brook Farm where his housekeeper, after the early death of his wife, was a Mrs Turner. Jack Burrows, who was a good worker, excelling in hedge-cutting and laying, helped him work the farm. Old Mackam was a staunch Churchgoer and never missed a service, but he was known to be a bad-tempered, irritable man with all who worked for him. In fact, one of his critics painted on his white farm gate: "God on Sunday, Devil on Monday."

One fine harvest day, he was driving the reaper on the field on the left side of Gorstage Lane near the "Firs", when the horses were a bit sluggish and his language became very choice. Suddenly, he saw the Vicar watching him from the roadside and his mood changed immediately.

"Good morning, Vicar, what a beautiful day."

The Vicar nodded and looking rather bemused went on his way.

Mackam was a small, thin-featured man with the countenance of a badger. He would travel miles at night in a spring cart with Tom Gleave to such places as Frodsham and Mrs Turner would never know what time old Ellis would return and so she would lock the doors and answer to no-one but Jack Burrows who would come back frequently to see to cows calving.

There was an occasion when Mackam went with Tom and Charlie Gleave and Tom Platt to the "Tunnel Top" inn at Barnton, when an argument broke out with some of the "Boaties" who were notorious for fighting. The Weaverham men on their way home were followed by the boatmen, who were intent on throwing them into the canal. Mackam fought a rearguard action with a walking stick, while the others made good their escape. Eventually, only the handle of the stick remained, but it stopped the wild boatmen who were taken aback by the ferocity of the little man who fought like a tiger. If anyone came to the farm with a horse to borrow a light roller he had and allowed the horse to nibble at the hedge by the gate spoiling the look of the hedge, then Mackam would get very bad-tempered and refuse to lend the roller.

A regular path was trodden between Handforth Brook Farm and Grange Lane Farm, from where Tom Gleave would walk each day, to see Mackam and every Saturday morning, old Tom would take a gun around our farm at Hefferston, as far as the willow beds, returning via Nook Farm and Handforth and then back to his own.

Mackam had two horses on Tom's bottom field. Uncle John, who was married to Mackam's daughter, took one while my grandfather took the other. Neither had been broken in and Uncle's never did much good, but my father managed to break the other, a dark little mare by the name of Madam, but she would accept no other driver. After Mackam's death, Tom Gleave, cousin to Jack's father Charlie, came to farm Handforth Brook and Fred Thomason, as a lad, went to work for him. Fred remembers being sent regularly to Northwich cattle market with Tom's calves, calling at Nook Farm, to pick up any of my grandfather's, and also to Charlie

Gleave's Church Farm.

Each calf was put into a hessian sack with its head out and the neck of the sack then tied or stitched with string. So long as the calf stayed in a comfortable lying position, the journey would cause no discomfort and half a dozen calves or so could be carried in this way to market, where they would be freed out of their sacks into pens where they could stretch their legs ready for the auction. Any requirements from Burgess Bros., Agricultural Engineers, would be picked up and brought home on the way back. Fred went on to work for Edwin Walker, at Gorstage Green Farm, and he was there during the war years. Fred was well educated and left the Grammar School with a good School Certificate, but he had suffered at one time with tuberculosis and it was considered an open-air job would be better for his health. His mother and sister, for many years, ran the bakery in Wallerscote Road.

Another well known family, who for many years were at the heart of the village, were the Woodwards and on one Acton Club day, many years ago, Tommy Gleave, who was then at Handforth Brook Farm following Mackam Ellis, was coming out of Acton Station, having unloaded a cart-load of potatoes, when he came upon a group of people standing around a man lying on his back on the grass verge. It was Danny Woodward completely drunk. The crowd persuaded Tom to take him home to his cottage, down Gorstage, in his cart. They threw him in the cart where he lay until Tom got to his own farm gateway.

Now Tom couldn't bring himself to throw out old Danny so near to his home, so he took him to his own gate, whereupon Mrs Woodward rushed out in a rage and demanded of Tom: "Draw the kecker bar and tip him out." However, Tom refused to do this and manhandled Danny out and stood him on his feet. Without more ado, Mrs Woodward drew back her fist and with a monstrous punch felled Danny and left him in a heap and there he stayed until he sobered up.

Danny and Harry Hornby were out on a brickying job in Liverpool. They went into a pub at noon and when a fight broke out, Little Danny hid under a table, but Harry, a big rough lad, said: "Come out, Danny, I can look after both of us."

Chairs were broken and a real brawl ensued, but thanks to Harry they made good their escape. Danny's brother Fred, who was married to Matty, who kept the little shop in Forest Street, next to the school, claimed to have built a house with its bricks on end rather than flat as he didn't have enough bricks.

"Brownie" Woodward, who lived at "Tea Pots" house, was known as "Points man" Woodward. This was his second job on the railway. His first job was as a cleaner, but one day when he was cleaning an engine in the sheds, he accidentally started it up. It smashed through the shed doors and then through buffers; it was a miracle they employed him again. His first wife died and he then married a widow, a Mrs Wild, who had two children, Joe and Rose, both of whom became teachers. He used to come to the Nook to get away from their "learned" talk. He used to call them a Secret Society.

Jim Woodward, always known as "Huckster" Woodward, from Woodward Street, the same gentleman who traded with the poachers for hares and rabbits, used to travel to Holland's at Nantwich every Tuesday to collect his cheese which he would sell on Warrington Market. He occasionally took my father with him to Warrington where some cheese was sold at a pub, possibly the "Norton Arms" next to the cattlemarket.

Old Jim had a shandry which was set low on its iron-rimmed wooden wheels and my father recalled the days of the "Cinder Road." This was a section of Narrow Lane, now Wallerscote Road. The first length of this road, from its junction with Northwich Road, was very stony and it was always a pleasure to get off the hard road onto the softer cinder length, nearer to Beach Farm, for a smoother ride. When Jim moved to "The Laurels" in West Road, he kept a small herd of cows in the shippon there. Joe Atherton was his cowman and twice a day herded the cattle through the village from shippon to pasture and then back for milking. Joe lived in one of the white cottages, just past Sextons, at Greenbank.

Sammy Woodward, known as "Happy Days" Woodward, because of his happy disposition, and was Ivy's grandfather, carried on a market garden business and lived in a house, set back off West Road, that was sometimes known as "Woodwards in the Field." He had two horses, but when he hadn't enough keep for them, he would lend one out to Nook Farm in return for its stabling and food. It was a lovely little mare named "Kit" and Jack Sayle, father to Jack and Norman, used to drive it; this led to the expression "working for his keep".

Uncle Fred Woodward was a happy little man and he would pick out a tall man at the Gate Inn and offer him £1 if he could wheel a wheelbarrow, which he kept at the pub, twice round the big tree and to the Wheatsheaf, without lifting the wheel from the ground. One victim was Levi Vernon, from Church Street, who was over 6ft tall. Bets were taken and witnessed and Uncle Woodward then produced the barrow, which was a child's wooden toy barrow and to the amusement of his friends, old Levi could only manage to wheel the barrow a few yards before straightening his back and lifting the barrow from the ground at the same time.

On another occasion, he shouted to Sgt. Allen who was walking down Brickley footpath: "Would you like some duck eggs, George?"

"Yes, I would," said the Sgt. "The wife will be very pleased, I'll go and bring a basket."

He then went home and came back with a basket and cloth to cover the eggs to keep them from prying eyes, as old Uncle had suggested.

Uncle said: "I'll put them ready for you when you go home."

On returning, he called for the eggs, but was flabbergasted when he arrived home and his wife Nellie uncovered a basket full of round coal "duck eggs" and to make things worse, he had paid half a crown for them. Uncle carted night soil by night with a horse and cart, first onto a field behind the Grange and then onto a field down by the river at the bottom of Marshalls Hill, upstream of the garage. He also carted ashes to the tip beneath the underbridge and to fill in any number of old pits on Grange Farm and other farms round about. Fred was Les Peake's grandfather and his wife was Martha, always called Mattie. She was old Dick Mainwaring's sister and their father was Tom Mainwaring, great-grand-father to Dick, who became gardener at Hefferston Grange Hospital, and grandfather to Bert, who was Dick's father and who died at a young age.

Old Tom Mainwaring had a donkey cart and lived for a while down near Woodbine Cottage, along the Warrington Road. One night, Ralph Whitley was returning along the Warrington Road and, on reaching Marshalls Hill, he heard a very strange jangling sound. He took fright and thought he was about to see the ghost which was supposed to haunt Marshalls Hill and Forsters Bank. He was too far from Acton Hill to retrace his steps and make a detour, so he had to face whatever was approaching. Much to his relief, he saw Tom Mainwaring's donkey head-ing for home dragging his tethering chain behind him.

Dick Mainwaring carried on with a horse and cart and lived in the fur-thest cottage of the three, which were later to become Inglenook Cafe, near the Hanging Gate. He had a shed at the far end where he kept his horse and cart, but at one time, he kept them at the Laurels where Jim Woodward lived. Dick was a quiet man, similar to Mattie, very wizened looking, and his old horse was very quiet and well behaved and they seemed never to be off the roads.

Fred Woodward was brother to Danny from the Brook and the one who Danny claimed had built a house with the bricks laid on end, instead of flat. Fred and Mattie kept a little sweet shop in Forest Street, near the footpath, which ran between the cottage and the school, across the top of Lake House field, and into Withens Lane. Mattie kept a few pigs at the back and would travel miles gathering sticks for the fire. Herbert Percival, Maynard's father, carted the night soil before Fred Woodward took on the job and he was reputed to rub his tobacco with not very clean hands and then enjoy his pipe. He, also, tipped ashes in a pit on Grange Field and on the outlet under the underbridge and had a shandry with which he taxied passengers to Acton Station. Pulled by his big black horse, it was said he could do the journey in two minutes from the Star, and he did so, several times a day.

Many of the old characters with a horse and cart, like Herbert and Tom and Dick Mainwaring, could earn money by carting bones to the Bone Works. The rail wagons with the bones, horns and hooves were backed into a siding at Acton Station and the contents carted with high-sided horse wagons to the factory. The Bone Works, or to give it its proper title, "The Weaver Refining Company", had a football team for which Harry

Hough and Fred Allman played. Their biggest rivals were Barnton Vics who beat them on the Barnton ground, but were heavily beaten 9-0 on the return match on Hough's field, at the bottom end of Acton, opposite the Company buildings. Opposite Woodwards in West Road lived Sammy Newall with his wife and daughter Lily. Lily later went to live at the end of Grange View. Sammy Newall had a market cart and took women shopping with their large baskets. He sat up in front with a row of seats behind him and two rows of seats, one down each side of the cart, with a step at the back for getting on and off. When old Sam Newall died, his widow took up with Joe Johnson who had lost his job as coachman with the Heaths through his indiscretion and Joe carried on with the market service and also took to buying and selling fruit and vegetables.

Two girls, the Knowles sisters, one named Anna, lived in and worked for Joseph Burton, at Tilstone Heyes. A brother of the Knowles girls worked for Tom Gleave for a while, and then emigrated to Canada. Mrs Laidman, before she married Lance, worked for the Burtons after the Knowles girls had left.

The Laidmans had lived in the far end of Grange View in the house which Bill Hignett had moved into after leaving Wharf Cottages and this is how Lance met his wife. Hughie Nield had worked for Squire Heath as a lad on leaving school and after the old Squire died and the Grange Hall was sold, Hughie went to work for Arthur Youd, at Bryn Bank, and then for Jack Marrow when he took the farm. Bertha, who later became Hughie's wife, was a servant girl living in at Arthur Youd's and had previously worked at Nook Farm. Her sister married a man named Jack Turner who used to drive a wagon for Warrington Corporation; the family had originated from Warrington.

Other helpers at Nook Farm included Ethel Sale, Jack's mother, who was strict with the children and didn't hesitate to keep the peace, and Ethel Jones, who was a good worker who could always make a good meal and could turn her hand to anything. Hughie Nield had a sister and a half-sister; his sister married a Billy Lightfoot who had a small farm near Crabtree Green, while his half-sister married Joe Yoxall. Fred Groves's first wife also helped at the Nook.

At one time, Joe could not get a dentist to pull a large tooth out. Tom Gatley took him to Mr King, Peter Knowles's father-in-law. Tom was told to hold Joe down by his ears from behind and the tooth was duly removed. Hughie Nield's family lived in one of the cottages down Gorstage, Danny from the Brook Woodward in the one nearest the brook, Nields in the middle one and Orams in the end one. Granny Oram used to sell nettle pop and ginger beer for a penny a bottle and on Sunday walks, no-one would go by without buying a delicious drink. Jim Griffen was another character who helped at the Nook. He would eat his sandwiches and drink a can of tea, then every dinner time without fail, he could climb up onto the horse feed box in the warm stable and sleep as fast as a rock for the rest of his dinner hour.

Also living in West Road was Ted Buckley's father, Chris. Now corncrakes at the turn of the century were common throughout the district and their calls in spring could be heard rasping all down the Weaver Valley, but as the century progressed they began to disappear and became quite scarce, but in Footroad Field, Chris would sit in the hay or edge of a corn field and with a piece of leather stitched to his trousers and a ratchet wheel, he could produce a perfect corncrake call and he would start them calling to him for hours on end. Footroad Field was the only field on which they would appear in the whole of the district. There were waterhens and coots in abundance in the pits and marshy places by the brook and the willow beds and lads of the village, such as "Blimmer" Jones, used to love to eat their eggs raw or fried, and they were so numerous their numbers never declined.

Peter Darlington, who farmed Weaverham Bank Farm, was a shabby little man always wearing a bowler and old frock coat which had seen better days. He had four daughters and one son, George, who never married, but took over the farm when Peter died. Another well known family were the Whitleys. John Whitley, nicknamed "Smirt", was Sexton and also school caretaker and lamplighter. He was possibly Billy Whitley's uncle, or even his grandfather, and had two daughters, Dot, who married Cyril Stockton, and Rene.

The Whitley family, Billy, Jesse, Ralph and Tom, all worked on the land. Bill began his working life as a servant boy to Billy Marshall, of Mere House Farm, who had taken the farm after Horton who had cleared it of gorse and scrub.

One of Billy's jobs was to see that Mr Marshall's mother, who lived at the next house, Mere Brow, was alright. She would insist on Billy having a good dinner and would watch over him while he ate it. Unfortunately, he would already have had his dinner at the farm and being over faced, he would have to resort to surreptitiously putting some in the pockets of his velvet livery suit provided by his master. Very often, Mr Marshall would catch him coming up the cellar steps with a mug of ale, but he always overlooked this misdemeanour. Billy Marshall and his wife did not get on very well, however, and, one day, she summoned young Billy to tell him to get up early the next morning and put the horse in the shandry to take her to the station.

"I'm leaving," she said, "but don't say a word about it, just say I am going to town."

Next morning her packed cases were loaded in the shandry and she was gone, but Billy Marshall, who had been having an affair with his maid, now to become his housekeeper, carried on to have several children with her and eventually they were married.

Mr Marshall was such an important man in the LMS Railway Company, he could arrange to have any London train stopped at Acton

Station for his convenience. It was on one of these business trips to London that he caught pneumonia from which he died. Billy Whitley as a lad was caught by a policeman, named Turner, stealing apples from the Maypole orchard and was taken to Acton Station to be put on a train to Northwich. He said to the policeman: "What time does the train come in?" "Very soon," was the reply "and tha'll be on it, and tha'll not be seen around here for a while."

"Not if I can help it," thought Billy, and as soon as the Bobby put his head in the Ticket Office, he was gone, off down the path, by the side of the smithy, which leads down to Acton Cliff and Dutton Locks, and over the river on his way to Runcorn with the policeman hard on his heels, blowing his whistle to no avail. Billy stayed away for over six months, by which time all was forgotten.

Billy worked for many years for my grandfather and would "sub" his money at the rate of 2/- a day to buy beer. He must have developed a taste for it, helping himself in Billy Marshall's cellar, but on Sundays Grandfather would not "sub" him and he would then turn to my father or Uncle Cliff. Billy left Grandfather when the call of the threshing machine got into him and one day when he was "following" the machine, the engine came to a stop to draw water from the little pit at Nook Farm as it was passing. He shouted to my father: "Come and have a look at my dog." Opening his shirt he drew out a large rat, one of six he had running round his stomach, prevented from escaping by a large leather belt round his cord trousers. When threshing a stack or bay he would catch these rats and sell them to Mr Pilling who used them for training his fox terrier.

On Saturday nights, Billy would go to the "Sheaf" with his brother-in-law and on his way home he would invite Dad in for a "bite of supper", and then he would start singing all the old Cheshire folk songs, mainly about farm work, ending with a hearty rendering of "Johnny the Carter's Boy."

"I sit upon my wagon, I'm as happy as a king, the horses they are willing... etc.".

On Sundays, old men like Hiram Curwell and Bill, would go on a farm walk begging a pint of rough harvest ale where they called. Harvest ale was a shilling a gallon and was brewed by Chester Northgate Brewery, who would offer it free delivery in 41/2, 9, 18 and 36 gallon casks. Billy's brother, Jesse, was a rather nasty character and would cause fights wherever he went. He used to catch rats, but always with a pair of gloves on. He would always have a ready market for them, and Bill had to keep his hands off them when Jesse was about. Jesse used to provoke people into fighting him until, one night, at the Gate Inn, a little man took him outside and struck him a mighty blow over the heart. He had to be carried home and put to bed and never recovered, eventually dying of what Dr Smith diagnosed as pneumonia.

Ralph Whitley worked for most of his life for Tommy Gleave. He was a good worker, but he would suddenly bring his horses out of the fields, stable them, and go on a drinking binge, until he had no money left, sometimes being away for a month.

Tom was the quietest of the family and lived in Forest Street. At one time, he worked for Bailey Bebbington, Charlie's father, at Poplar Cottage. One day, Tom had gone to sleep, after his dinner, on one of the benches in the yard, on his back and snoring away with his mouth open, when "Ned" Burrows cracked an egg, dropping the contents into his open mouth. Tom woke with a start, choking and coughing, then took off to chase Ned all round the village. Ned was quite a character himself; when young lads called him "Ned", he would say, "My name's Edward in your mouth".

And then there were the Johnsons. Old Myoh Johnson (he was father to Alf, and his son Bill was Clara's Dad) lived in the thatched cottages at the top of Forest Street, the one nearest the Grammar School. Alf Johnson lived in the middle one and Stanways in the one nearest Nook Farm. Alf Johnson was Albert's grandad and there were also three girls, Beattie, who married a man named Hunt, was one, and Florrie, who married Ernie Bradley, was another. Florrie already had two daughters, Lily and Hilda. The other daughter married a Stanway from next door and went to live in the old farm house at Beach Hill Farm. Her husband worked as a gardener for Johnsons at Weaverham Grange in Beach Road, later the Max Woosnams, and now the Water Board, while she delivered groceries for Price's store in Hartford with a cart pulled by a white horse which she stabled at Beach Hill. She was a familiar sight around Hartford and the district. George Henry Dean had moved out of the old farmhouse into a new house he had built at the roadside.

Old Alf used to sit under the oak tree, opposite the houses, on warm summer evenings, enjoying a last pipe of tobacco after supper and he would take a pint of beer in moderation. Fred Johnson, one of his sons, was the skilled horseman who worked at the remount depot at Cuddington and who lost his life in the Great War, and another son was "Trot" Johnson's father and another was Arthur Johnson's father. As well as his three daughters old Alf had five sons, George ("Skimper"), Arthur (Albert's dad), Jack ("Tabsy"), Fred and Harry, who worked at Horners Creamery. Bill Johnson's eldest daughter was Dora who courted and married a Shallcross who worked as a cowman for Mackam Ellis at Handforth Brook Farm. One day, confronted with a bull in the field at the back of the cottages when he went to take the cows across the level crossing to the farm for milking, he came back to cut a stick from the holly bush and armed with this, he forced the bull to retreat and took the herd for milking, much to the amazement of the Johnson family who were watching from the garden.

Arthur Johnson married Ethel Jones, Arthur Jones' daughter, who was living then at Nook Cottages. Lily Johnson, now Mrs Lily Hall, widowed and turned 70, remembers her old grandmother saying that a Mrs

Pickering, from the East Lodge at Hefferston, used to walk to the old cottage in Forest Street, to sit with her during thunderstorms, because she was terrified of them. On the night Nook Farm was bombed, Lily remembers being terribly worried about fire. She was in service at the time, but was having a night off and her mind kept thinking of the thatched roof of the old cottage which was vulnerable to fire at the best of times. In fact, fire was what destroyed the adjoining cottages some time later, but with this new danger from the sky, she was forever opening the door to see if all was well. Suddenly, she heard a whistling noise which became increasingly louder. Little did she know it was the land mine coming down on its parachute with the wind whistling through its shrouds. Luckily, she had gone back indoors before it reached the ground.

In the 19th and early 20th Centuries, poaching was rife in the countryside around Weaverham, as it was all over the country, and very often men who could barely read or write became experts at making purse nets or "poss" nets as they were known locally. They would use a 2-inch piece of wood to form the loop made on a brass ring and used bone needles. Seventeen or eighteen loops would make a net of about a square yard. Long nets were also popular, but needed two or three people to use them. The net would be pegged out along a hedge used by rabbits returning to their burrows after being driven from their night feeding grounds by the "runners in". Lengths of hazel were used to hold the nets up and on a good night dozens of rabbits would be caught on one netting. Many of the local farm workers would set snares on the rabbit runs they had noticed during their working hours. These snares could be purchased at David Forster's hardware shop, along with the nets. These snares would be "looked up" early in the morning and the rabbits caught would provide much-needed food for the families.

Most men were capable of catching a rabbit for the pot. The old Russet poachers could count amongst their numbers such men as "Ned" Burrows, "Rafe" Whitley, Billy Whitley and Lenny Groves to name but a few. There were many too numerous to mention who became experts in this nightly profession. Then there were also lone poachers like Jack "Tabsy"Johnson who had an amazingly powerful and accurate throwing arm who could kill hares and rabbits with a stone. He would throw out a challenge that he could kill more rabbits with a stone than anyone with a shotgun in the same length of time, and to demonstrate the strength of his arm would throw a stone clean over Lake House Farm stackyard and all, from Lake House Field. He spent most of his time poaching, but Dr. Smith caught him setting snares on his land and took him to Court. Dr. Smith was also a Magistrate and sat on the bench that day and sentenced him to three-months in Knutsford Gaol.

The old Doctor visited him in jail and said:

"Well, Jack,how do you like this place?".

Tabsy said: "Ee, mon, 'ave never felt so hungry in my life."

The Doctor replied, "Aye, its the rappit broth th'art short on, but this should teach thee a lesson."

Tabsy married a girl named Stringfellow and he was always in trouble with his wife because of his behaviour and he would sleep most of the time in the pig cote, at the bottom of the garden. He was brother to Albert's grandad and lived in the row of cottages, nicknamed Rabbit Row, opposite the cobblers in Northwich Road, at the junction with Wallerscote Road. He was a difficult man to get on with when the mood was on him, but perhaps part of the reason for his odd behaviour was so that he could wander off into the wilds, rabbiting at any hour of the night without disturbing anyone.

Tom "Stosher" Allen was another who poached alone with snares and nets, but he always had a whippet or lurcher dog with him. But in the early days when gamekeepers looked after the local estates, the most dangerous type of poaching was carried out by organised gangs who worked by night. They were often referred to as "night men" and were greatly feared. More often than not these poachers used long nets. The local policemen, like the game keepers, were hard men and feared no-one but they had some rough experiences with the gangs who would stop at nothing to avoid being caught as the penalties for poaching were severe, men were even deported to Australia for it in the early 19th Century. The poachers were quite jovial and friendly people by day, but once they had turned out on a poaching expedition they became ruthless and animal like and people greatly feared them. Most of them had worked over a large area of the land and knew every inch of it, and many of them never went home for months on end sleeping rough wherever they could. When the rabbits were caught there was a ready market for them. "Huckster" Jim Woodward, living in Woodward Street, had a shed at the bottom of his garden which came within a few yards of a public footpath. The market dealer would arrive at his shed early in the morning and a deal would be struck for the catch which was often quite considerable;always there would have to be a careful lookout for the village policeman. Soon the rabbits would be on their way, in old Huckster's horse and shandry, to Warrington Market.

The Star Inn, in High Street, was the poachers' pub and they would retire to it as soon as it opened. There was always a good fire going and soon damp clothes would be steaming as they dried. They would enjoy their ale and feast on bread, cheese and pickle as they yarned of the night's escapades and adventures of previous years. Martha Andrews would be usually the only woman customer amongst these rough outcasts and loved to yarn and laugh with them.

On one occasion in the Star, a group of Northwich poachers met up with some of the Weaverham "night men" and they decided to join forces in a spree of poaching at Delamere House, the home of the Wilbraham family. It was a pitch-black night as they set off on their journey and as they arrived at the park, in front of the old house, they ran out their nets.

When they gathered in the first "catch" of rabbits they moved much nearer to the old house, running out more nets, when suddenly one of the poachers caught his foot in a trip wire and triggered of an alarm system, causing a collection of bells to start ringing, loudly echoing across the night air. They brought out the gamekeeper, grooms, and gardeners, together with a pack of yapping dogs.

Several shots blasted out as the gamekeeper fired his shotgun in the direction of the poachers who fled, leaving behind their nets and rabbits. The distances covered by these men at night was unbelievable, and before daybreak they had recovered at least half of the rabbits and some of the nets, the rest having been found and confiscated by the gamekeeper and his men. Talk about the incident had to be very guarded in the Star, in case the village Bobby got to know.

Many village farms belonged to Lord Barrymore's estate and had an abundance of rabbits on them, but Owley Wood, known in those days as "The Owley", was a strictly forbidden area where pheasants were reared by the Barrymore gamekeeper.

For many years Dr. Smith had the sole shooting rights. The gamekeeper's house, still there, was in Beach Lane (Wallerscote Road), opposite to the Wood, which was entered by a wicket gate. Any young boys, or youths, entering the wood risked a good hiding from the gamekeeper who always carried a good ash plant. The keeper also looked after Beach Wood which had many magnificent trees which were felled for timber when ICI took over the Barrymore Estate in the early 1930s. The gamekeeper at one time in Keepers Cottage was a Mr Carson who had a daughter named Annie. She courted a boy from Weaverham who, when she became pregnant, left hurriedly for Canada. However, he eventually returned to build the two houses in Northwich Road, on the opposite side of the road to the Ring o'Bells, by the side of the entrance to the old football field, and opposite the triangle. They married and lived there many years.

Another keeper was David Hindley, upon whose death, Mrs Hindley and her family of seven were given a lovely house at Claycroft, Marbury, by Lord Barrymore, and a pension for life.

The new and last keeper was Mr Tomkinson whose daughter May worked in Mrs. Collier's paper shop which was next door to the Star, and later became Mrs Burns' shop.

May courted Frank Collier but he died early and May never married. She then went to work for David Forster in his Sandiway ironmongery shop; she was a very quiet, somewhat shy, girl and could often be seen riding her bicycle between Weaverham and Sandiway, usually wearing a long leather coat. She cut hair in her spare time.

There was a period of time when for one reason or another, perhaps between Mr Hindley's death and the appointment of Mr Tomkinson, Thomas Gleave from the shop in Church Street was asked to look after the wood for Dr. Smith, and one night it was visited by "night men".

It was a dark night and old Thomas was patrolling the wood, carrying a storm lantern. When the poachers saw the light approaching they lay in wait and ambushed him, brutally attacking him and leaving him on the ground unconscious and bleeding heavily. When he didn't return home the alarm was raised and my grandfather and his brothers went to search for their uncle. When they found him they were deeply shocked and carried him to the surgery, at Ivy House, where Dr. Smith dressed his wounds and patched him up. His opinion was that Tom must have had an exceptionally thick skull, or he would not have survived. It took him a long time to get over it and he never risked going into the wood alone at night again, and the poachers, realising what would happen if Dr. Smith found out who was responsible, gave the area a wide berth for some time to come.

Tom was never happier than when with his brother Charles, from Church Farm, and his nephews, from Beach Farm. He would set out on a night's rabbiting, travelling the Weaver Valley as far as "Throstlenest Field", the field at the bottom of Marshalls Hill, opposite the garage. This field comes up to Mere Bank and carried the old packhorse road along the top, connecting by way of Strawberry Lane to Acton Cliff and beyond. From these forays they would come back with a grand haul of rabbits, most of which had ready customers in his Church Street shop. The rest would be consumed in rabbit pies on the two farms. Also many a poor family were beneficiaries. Occasionally they met up with other poachers, even the notorious "night men", but they had enough stout-hearted young men in their party to take care of themselves and each man carried a stout stick or ash plant with him.

As the large estates broke up after the First World War, and the battles between gamekeepers and poachers gradually died down, a new form of rabbiting began to emerge. The rabbit was still a wonderful help for the working man and his family and, as I have mentioned earlier, most men and boys alike were capable of catching a rabbit for the pot. Some used ferrets, and others nets.

Charlie Gleave and his son, Jack, started to organise ferreting parties to local farms during the rabbit season. There would be my grandfather, George Moss, from Nook Farm; Tom Gleave, from Gorstage Lane Farm, and, later, from Grange Lane Farm; Harry and Arthur Moss, from Beach Farm; and usually the local Bobby would join the party.

For many years they had a rotation of the village farms. They would each have a gun, and Jack Gleave took charge of the ferrets. Jack was an excellent shot and equally accurate from the hip as from the shoulder. Armed with shotguns, ferrets and spades they would know every likely burrow to be found over hundreds of acres of land. A couple of rabbits were sent back to the house early so that a large rabbit pie could be made for when the hungry men returned after their day's rabbiting. My father, who was Jack Gleave's friend from schooldays, often joined the party.

When they had eaten and drunk their fill, they would play "Nap", a popular card game of the day.

My own memories of these early ferreting parties were enhanced by their tales of olden times. Uncle Harry, from the Beach, would talk of his adventures in the Royal Field Artillery, in the Great War, and their yarns of old Weaverham were always fascinating to listen to. Their visit to Nook Farm was particularly rewarding to me because they invariably lost a couple of half crowns either under or down the side of their chairs and by the end of their card game they were too weary to notice. It would be well after midnight when they departed for their respective farms and, generally, they would be on foot or bicycle. Their catch would be carried home between them. Jack Gleave kept down the rabbit population to a manageable amount during his lifetime. Besides providing a day's sport, the problem of keeping rabbits under control was an endless one on each and every farm.

Inevitably it was Jack Gleave who was responsible for keeping the village's fox population down. His knowledge of wildlife and nature in general was far above that of the average countryman. He never stopped observing animals and birds and their habits. I remember, on one occasion, he went with my father to observe a large fox earth one moonlight night. They were sitting at the foot of an old oak tree, and the moon had just risen, when, suddenly, an old vixen appeared, followed by cubs. She walked along the pathway at the side of the field, and as she came nearer it was possible to count the cubs. The two silent watchers stared in amazement as the full contingent went on their way. Twelve cubs trotted behind the one vixen. Jack observed that no man would see that more than once in a lifetime. The only explanation was that a vixen had died, either by shot or accident on the road, or a similar fate, and her cubs had been adopted by another already with cubs and she was about to introduce them into the big world and show them the dangers lurking there once outside the safety of the fox earth and its proximity.

"If we'd had a gun, we'd never have witnessed that," said Jack. Because like crows and rooks, foxes seem to have an uncanny sense in detecting the presence of a gun.

In his younger days, long before the Owley Wood housing estate was built, and when the wood itself was much more extensive, and long fields of meadow grass and corn rolled down to the river, Jack used to relate the story of how on a quiet summer evening, he was sitting on a gate leading off Wood Lane, which led down to the river, when suddenly a small army of stoats came into view led by one large stoat. As if by some strange ritual they approached the gate walking on their hind legs following the "King" stoat who walked tall as if on tiptoe. Jack remained perfectly still and the stoats passed under the gate and hurried on their way in the direction of the river. Along the banks of the Weaver was an abundance of wildlife and in the Spring time the hedgerows were full of birds' nests

Page 52

of every kind. A favourite pastime in those days was bird nesting, but no more than one egg would be taken from a nest, carefully blown, then labelled and put away in either sawdust or cotton wool.

Kingfishers darted about or sat poised on a branch over the water ready to dive in; the streams running into the river were clean and fresh, even up to the late 1930s, just before the Second World War. The stream running through Beach Wood ran over a clean sandy bottom and was pure enough to drink, and held fish, as did the river.

My father recalls being taken by his father from Nook Farm to Milton Farm which was at that time farmed by John Lewis. The purpose of the visit was the purchase by my grandfather of a horse called "Snowball." Snowball turned out to be a very good horse which we kept for many years at Nook Farm. It was always said that in icy conditions he would slide down Station Hill with a load of milk in the morning before turning right to the milk loading platform.

Sometimes as many as twenty horses and shandries would converge on Acton Station going over the bridge and turning right to the platform. This was a hazardous manoeuvre in frosty weather and sometimes studs were screwed into the horses' shoes to give better grip, but these would not last long if the horse did a lot of road work. The spring carts used for the milk runs were quite a bit higher than the platform and this made it much easier work. It was much heavier lifting the churns up to the platform from a low shandry than lowering them down, and in snowy weather snow used to drift down at the loading area and would very often reach as high as the platform. The drivers used to tie their horses to the rails and wait for the train. About three goods vans were reserved for the milk and the Porter and Guard would be urging every one to hurry up with the loading so the train could leave on time, but if one of their friends had not yet arrived the farm men would work slowly to allow him time to get there, much to the annoyance of the railway men. Old "Pep" used to hear the train whistle and fly down Station Road. Sometimes the swing bridge would hold up milk floats coming from the North side of the road, and one horse, Dan Massey's crashed through the bridge gate, but luckily the bridge had not begun to swing.

One farmer taking his milk to Acton Station every morning would be Mr. Walker, from Ash House Farm. Each morning he would call on his sister, who was John Lewis's wife, at Milton Farm, and ask her to get down one of the hams hanging from a beam in the kitchen. He would then have ham and eggs for breakfast before returning home. His daughter married a Nield, a short, stocky, fellow, who he always said was not big enough to be a "mon". Nevertheless, they went on to have fourteen children, losing two of them. At one time they kept the Tigers Head, at Norley, but later developed a business selling fertilisers and straw.

One of their children was Daisy, a favourite with the boys and always full of devilment, and another daughter was Lily, who was in my father's class at Weaverham school, and used to walk daily from Acton Cliff to school and back. John Lewis was brother to Sam Lewis, who nearly became tenant of the Home Farm, at the Grange, and he had another brother who worked for the Warrington Corporation.

When Old Pepper was taking milk, very often the train would be approaching Grange Bridge blowing its whistle as "Pep" was just leaving the farm, and he would get to the loading platform before the train. Arthur Jones was very often driving the horse and was once stopped by the local policeman and warned to drive with more care, after seeing him drive around the corner by Forster's shop on one wheel. There was keen competition for milk prices and farmers had to watch the market. One man, a Jim Manning, was the buyer from St. Helen's Co-op. He was a happy little man, but slow to pay. Snowball was accidentally backed into the brook with a load of muck on the cart, the weight coming down heavily on him. My grandfather was driving him at the time and was sure the horse must have broken his back. The only way to free him was to pull the cart away from him with another horse after dismantling Snowball's harness. The problem was that a horse will not pull if it thinks it is going to hurt another horse, and it took ages to coax this one to pull. As soon as the cart's weight came off him, Old Snowball scrambled to his feet and walked along the brook eating grass from the banks as he went, much to the amazement of the onlookers. He had to be led out at a place where the banks of the stream were not too steep, and after a few days rest he was back at work, none the worse.

George Tickle recalled that Old Pepper came as a colt from Hignetts at Onston Hall where he had been broken in, and he remembers borrowing him with a shandry for Tom Gleave, when he was at Handforth Brook, to take crates of fowl and some calves to the Northwich Auction, and the occasion when Uncle Cliff was driving him to Greenbank and he bolted. As a small boy, Cocky Waterman, from Nook Cottages, was in the float, but, eventually, Pepper was brought under control and there was no harm done. Another time George was coming across the old Park, at Hefferston, after walking a nurse home to the Hall, and in the pitch black of the night he fell head over heals over Pepper who was lying across the footpath. The horse never moved - he probably knew it was George.

A horse similar to Pepper was one owned by Enoch Jones, grandfather of the cattle truck Jones's. He was a very smart man and kept his horse beautifully groomed. He used to plough at Whitegate, using this single horse, and when not ploughing he would saddle him up and jump the field gate with him. When Enoch was in the "standby cavalry" a form of "Territorials", he used to win, with the same horse, first prize at "tent-pegging", a form of target practice with a lance.

The way of life depended upon the horse and a farmer was judged by the quality of the animals he kept and the manner in which he turned them out, either behind a plough or pulling a cart. Great pride was taken in their appearance by their owners and the men working with them, and the horses would look magnificent sights, heads nodding, crotal bells jangling, polished brass decorations on the shining harness gleaming in the sun, as they made their stately progress. The name of each horse was as familiar as the name of your best friend and his strength and prowess compared with another's favourite.

So it was with the Gentleman; his social standing, his worth, and the respect accorded to him, were measured by the quality and appearance of his horses, as well as the luxury of his transport, be it coach, trap or float. One such Gentleman was Henry Pilling, who lived at Mere Brow, after Billy Marshall's mother. He worked on the Stock Exchange, in Manchester, and every morning, at 8.30, he would travel to Cuddington Station, in a horse and trap with his coachman, Pat Doyle. He would return home at 5.30 pm. The coachman had to be smartly dressed, complete with bowler hat, but would only drive the empty coach. If Mr. Pilling was on board he would drive himself, whilst the coachman sat behind. His horses were well bred and always kept in top condition.

Harry Woolley used to be in charge of the stableyard and got very cranky if any hay or straw was left on the cart after a load had been delivered, and he always expected a tip from the vendor to keep the order. Old Pilling paid over the odds for good hay and straw and also oats for his horses. He used to ride with the Cheshire Hunt and was badly scarred due to a riding accident. It was no doubt due to his connections with the Cheshire Hunt that he managed to get his groom, Mr. Doyle, into one of Mr.Heath's cottages at The Nook. As a parting gift when the Pillings finally left the village, he gave to Harry Woolley and old Bill Elson an oil painting each. When these turned out to be worthless oleographs, Mrs Woolley threw Harry's in the fire and burned it, but Bill Elson still has the one given to his grandfather.

Another Gentleman to be seen on his way to Cuddington Station each day was Buckley Taylor, from "The Oaklands", in his tub, with the door at the back. His driver used to pull so hard on the reins with his feet placed firmly to the front of the tub that it was said the horse was pulling the cart by the reins, rather than the traces.

Mrs Buckley Taylor was the daughter of Sir Edward Houlton, proprietor of the Daily Dispatch and other newspapers, and it was said that Mr Buckley Taylor had been only a "shoe-black" before his marriage.

Another man who travelled everywhere in a pony and trap was George Henry Dean, from Beach Hill Farm. He was not very tall, but a very fat man and when he stepped up into the coach from the rear he almost lifted the little grey pony off its feet. He was a jovial character. Another character was Tom Pope, his handyman, who was a friend of Tom Allen, and, when they had the chance, the pair used to drink George Henry's beer, in the cellar. Joe Johnson, one-time coachmen at the Grange, for the Heaths, before he was sacked by Mrs. Heath for an indiscretion, said that Mrs

Heath preferred to drive her own trap herself and rarely rode with the Squire, who usually travelled with a coachman in his own trap which was much larger and had large wheels with yellow spokes and rims.

Mrs Heath was a keen horsewoman and rode with the Cheshire Hunt. She kept several good hunters which were stabled in loose boxes set around the stableyard. On leaving school, Joe had started work as a footman for Robert Heath and had then become coachman, in succession to his "father". Joe's natural father was reputed to be "Wiggin" Gerrard who supplied Mrs Johnson with potatoes and other vegetables for her shop in Church Street and was paid "in kind", hence Joe, who had a strong resemblance to the Gerrards.

Joe's "father" continued to work as an odd job man for Mr Heath after ceasing to be coachman. One of his jobs was to collect fallen leaves at the "back end" of the year, compost them, and mix them with crushed bone from the Bone Works to use as a fertiliser on the land. Robert Heath had a very wild horse for sowing this home-made organic fertiliser, a horse which no-one would approach in the stable, except Robert himself. He used to take it some carrots and go to its head, and it would then never turn a hair while being harnessed.

Joe's "father" was a very keen fisherman and used to buy cows' intestines from the butcher, and Joe recalled going with his father to hang the bag of innards in the old river to catch eels, down by the bridge across to the island. This is not the present bridge but an older bridge, only the plinth of which now remains some 50 or 60 yards downstream. Others using fine horses were the milkmen, such as Albert Hinde who used to travel the district. He used to call at the Wheatsheaf on his way home in the early afternoon. The horse, which would be facing towards the Hanging Gate, would be waiting patiently for Albert to have his refreshment and would know in a minute or two if Albert was over the mark. As soon as he put his foot on the step, to climb into the float, the horse would know if he was in his cups and would turn round at the bottom of Forest Street, turn left down Church Street, into Well Lane, and proceed towards Acton. If Albert was sober, he would take the high road, High Street, Sandy Lane, and Marshalls Hill, to the cottage where he lived, just past the Bone Works, now the site of the Rheingold, and his horse would be turned out to graze in the little croft by the river at the back of the cottage. One old-timer used to say:

"Albert's a mystery to me. He's th'only mon I know as can set out from womm in the morning with th'empty churn in his cart, and come womm at a neet wi'it empty, and still make a living; it beats me."

Albert, although not a big chap, and getting on in years, was not to be put off challenges, such as the time when Arthur Davies, who used to work with his horse and cart for the council, met Albert in Northwich Road, as Albert was returning one day from his round. The story had gone around that Albert had been making comments about Arthur's drinking habits, and when they chanced to meet on this occasion Arthur began to rant and rave at Albert, who straightaway hopped off the back of his milk float.

"Now", he said, "tack tha' coat off and I'll thresh thee".

Arthur was glad to withdraw from the conflict even though he was a much bigger man.

Other milkmen who were going the rounds with horses and floats, measures and churns, at this time were Milkman Roberts, from Copyhold, Tommy Forster, from Gorstage, and "Nippy" Jackson, who lived at the old thatched cottage near the Grammar School.

There was a lovely old mill at Milton. It stood in a valley, sometimes referred to as "Happy Valley", or "The Little Heaven", by Joe Rigby. At one time there was a beautiful mill pond created by damming the stream just beyond where the two streams, Cuddington Brook and Handforth Brook, meet. The water was held back by a wide stone wall with an iron sluice gate in the middle operated by a pulley and chain. It was approached down a little road which turned off to the right down Sandfield Lane just past Joe Rigby's Milton Bank Farm, and wound down into the valley. It must have been a heavy pull for pack horses, or horses and carts, when bringing back the ground grain.

After passing by the mill, the stream crossed the road at Milton Rough, on its way to the next mill, Gandy's, but in the 1920s at this point there would not have been a bridge, and travellers between Acton and Crowton negotiated the stream via a ford.

At one time, old Tom Tanner Moss lived there, but by that time it would have ceased to function as a mill. Tom Moss was Amy's father and worked in the early days for old "Bailey Bebbington", who was Charlie Bebbington's father, and who lived at and ran the family cabinet making business at Poplar Cottage, the old black and white thatched cottage, with workshops to match.

After leaving the mill, Tom went to Dane Bank Farm, at Davenham, with his sons, Ernie and Bert. Ernie later went into business, making a fortune out of cakes, "Scribona" and making special packages of the same. Old Tom sold my grandfather a very wild horse which was brought back tied to the back of a shandry.

After it had been well fed it became almost impossible because it had been only half-broken in. Old Stringer, the threshing machine owner, told grandfather that it had already broken most of old Tom's implements. Tom's wife was a little woman, very careful with money, and had been a schoolteacher before marrying. Later when Dane Bank Farm was sold, old Tom and his family, after he had decided he wanted a bigger place, went to live in a large house at Alsager while he looked for a suitable farm. This house had a big garden with large lawns and a swimming pool. There were two daughters, Mabel, taking after her mother, a careful girl, e.g. when the cat ran off with a slice of bacon, Mabel ran after it, and taking the bacon off the cat washed it and returned it to the frying pan. The other girl, Edie, used to wait for the old folks to retire to bed, then leave the house, staying out till the early morning, leaving and returning via the drainpipe.

Joe Rigby told me of a time when Dave Holland's grandfather, Jim Holland, was farming at Acton Bridge, with his son Jim, who later farmed at Dane Bank Farm, Leftwich. Jim came to ask Joe if he would like to go to a dance at Frodsham. Transport was to be a small gig belonging to old Jim and the best horse in the stable, a little mare who could fly. This caused Joe some concern because he knew what the consequences would be if the old farmer found out what was going on. But young Jim assured Joe that if they waited until the old man had gone to bed and then quietly yoked up the horse and gig no one would be any the wiser. It was a lovely moonlit night as they sped off to Frodsham, and they stabled the horse at a farm close to the dance hall. The dance was a wonderful affair and the lads enjoyed every minute of it. They returned in double quick time in the early hours, along the moonlit country lanes, but by the time they arrived home the little mare was white with lather. Unfortunately, young Jim had not wiped the old man's favourite mare down, and the first place the old man went to, when he got up to start the day's work, was the stable. He went wild when he saw the condition of the little mare, and that was the end of their horse and gig transport.

One of Joe Rigby's stories of his cattle dealing days was the buying and selling of a cow off Miss Ravenscroft. She had always milked the cow while it ate its corn out of a bowl. When she sold the cow to Joe, she warned him not to attempt to put a chain on it, and when he got to Beeston he repeated the warning to the drovers, but they ignored him, much to their regret, because it went berserk, stampeding through the market, scattering all and sundry.

This was certainly not a good day for Joe who, accompanied by Philip Bebbington, bought a cow and calf at the market. They put the calf into the back of the float and the cow dutifully followed them home. Joe milked the cow and turned it out to the calf. Immediately it took off and escaping the farmyard it carried on all the way back, with the calf running behind, to Beeston and they had to make another trip to bring it back.

Another of his tales involved Jack ("Jake") Tully who, after one of his annual days out at Chester Races, was proudly walking over Acton Bridge Station in a new slop and boots which he rarely, if ever, laced up. Suddenly a spark, from the funnel of a railway engine, floated up over the side of the bridge and alighted on him, setting him on fire. He quickly threw off the slop and stamped on it to put out the fire, but it was ruined, much to his disgust and verbal condemnation of the railways and all who worked on them.

And then there was the time when old "Clem" Hignett was sitting in the Railway Hotel when a load of hay went past, on its way to Jim

Page 58

Holland's farm. The landlord, a Mr Dallow, looked across at Clem and said:

"Clement, I hope that hay isn't mine."

"You'd better ask Mr. Holland about that," said old Clem.

Sure enough, he had sold the hay to Mr Dallow, but before it had been collected he had sold it a second time to Jim Holland.

And his recollection of Johnny Rylance, in his knee breeches and leggings, taking a party of villagers to Tarporley races, in his market cart. As he prepared to return, he accepted a challenge from a couple of gentlemen in a fine gig. First home to "Wareham Gate" (Gate Inn) would take £1 from the loser. They all set out and the two gentlemen called at each pub for a drink and Johnny and his party would trot past. Eventually, as Johnny passed the White Barn, he had a clear run until almost the top of Grange Hill when, approaching the bridge, the others sailed past him, with much shouting and waving. But all was not lost, because the two were so inebriated that when John and the party rounded West Road, there, upturned in the ditch, was the lovely gig and its two dishevelled occupants. The old market cart sped past to the Gate Inn and awaited the £1 note.

At the turn of the century, the village was full of interesting shops. Benjamin Burgess had built up a drapery business, along High Street. This shop was a very large impressive building which is still standing, but no longer in use as a shop, but since Burgess's time it has been an egg packing station and a furniture store. The business was high class and employed travellers, salesmen, and delivery men, to cover a large area almost as far as Warrington and Chester. He also ran a successful agricultural machinery store, the forerunner of Burgess Bros. Farm implements were actually made in Weaverham for a time, in a shed adjoining the shop.

All along High Street, from Charlie Bebbington's house, "Poplar Cottage", to the Gate Inn, where Lord Barrymore's Agent came to collect his rents from the estate tenants, almost every type of shop and business was represented.

Charlie Bebbington had followed in his father Bailey's footsteps as the local undertaker, cabinet maker and joiner. Cyril Stockton was apprenticed to Charlie and the first job he went on with Charlie, so he told Bill Elson, was to restore the pulpit and repair some pews in the church at Whitchurch. Cyril's first job, before he became apprenticed, was as a footman, complete with velvet and lace livery, at Arderne Hall, Tarporley.

There was Billy Walsh's bike shop; "Putty" Phipps' plumbers and decorators, in the black and white half timbered house, next to the Wheatsheaf, which was thatched until recent years. Bill Hornby had his shop on the north side of High Street, near to Joe Foster's barber's shop, but later on moved across the road. Mrs Postles' cake shop, she also sold lovely ham, was in High Street, on one side of the entrance to Chapel

Wynt, and Mrs Percival, at the Post Office, was on the other side. Next to the Post Office was Hough's butchers, with the slaughter house at the top, of the Wynt, behind a high wall. Cattle were bought on the hoof at local farms and driven by boys along the roads to the slaughter house. On one occasion, Frank Buckley witnessed such a deal between my grandfather and Butcher Hough. They were walking a fine young heifer round to the farmyard at the "Old Nook" and the conversation went like this:

Butcher Hough: "I'll no' gi' thee a penny more than fourpun, mister."

My grandfather: "Nay, a'll tek no less than four pun ten."

This went on for some twenty minutes or so with the butcher smacking his shiny leather leggings with a twitching stick all the while.

Finally, Butcher said: "A'll gi' thee four pun five and that's me last offer."

"All right, then, tek her off," was the reply, and the old butcher summoned the waiting lads to run the heifer back to his slaughterhouse.

George Buckley, whose mother kept the Maypole, where George sometimes played the piano, lived and worked at the butcher's. The son, Eddie Hough, and Harold Booth used to think of themselves as self-styled gangsters and hard men, even to the extent of carrying a gun which Eddie Hough had acquired to protect himself while visiting the wilder parts of Manchester. He even bought a mackintosh with a special pocket, to carry the gun. Eventually, his father had enough of this nonsense and sent him off to Canada to work on a farm.

Bill Elson was born in the Wynt and remembers, vividly, a terrifying experience he had when he was three or four-years-old. On his way to Mrs Postles, with a penny for a bar of chocolate, he was about halfway down the cobbled street when he heard the rumble of a tail-gate being lowered on a cattle truck. For a moment he froze with horror then ran to the nearest door, which happened to be Mrs Peddicord's. There was no-one in, but the door was not locked and he went inside closing it behind him. Standing on tip-toe at the window he looked out to see the frightened cattle filling the Wynt from side to side as they were stampeded up to the pens at the slaughter house.

Arthur Curbishley was slaughter man at the time and the cows and bulls were chained up and pole axed, while the pigs and sheep were strung up head down and had their throats cut. There was always a heap of heads behind this high wall waiting to be carted away.

In the shop, which later became Cyril Catley's, there was a grocer by the name of Isaac Nicholas. He was possibly Arthur Nicholas's brother, he had a son Bert and a daughter Marjorie and another daughter who kept Sandiway Post Office. He was followed by Harry Alcock, a tall man, over 6 feet, who walked with a long loping stride and had very large feet which pointed outwards as he walked, causing small boys to scurry out of his way for fear of being trodden on as they went to school, in Forest Street.

As well as a grocer, he was also a corn chandler and sold pigeon corn, hen food, meal, and cattle feed as well as molasses and sugar. Roy Okell remembers the steam engined motor lorry, which used to bring his supplies, being unloaded. During the First World War, Harry seemed to have an endless supply of sugar which he kept reserved for his regular customers as Tom McCann found out when, on the recommendation of his fellow Irishman, Ned Larvin, he called to ask for some.

"Go and get thee sugar where tha gets thee other groceries," growled Harry.

He would stand for hours outside his shop, in a large white apron, with his thumbs tucked in at the shoulders. His frequent encounters with Maggie, from the shop at the corner of Church Street, which was also a grocery store, led to their marriage and she moved in with him. Her shop was taken over by Fred Pitcher (Calico Jack) and his wife, who was a Collier.

Old Mrs. Collier kept the Newsagents, next to Harry Alcock's. Mrs Burns was the last person to have this shop. Old Mrs. Collier was a very large woman and when sitting behind the counter, she left very little room for anyone else. "Clogger" Wilbraham Buckley rented a room at the back of the shop, where he made his clogs and boots. He lived at Moulton, but when the "Star" ceased to trade as a pub, he moved there to continue his business and lived on the premises. Another shoemaker was Ernie Bradley who lived in a cottage down Shady Brook Lane. His brother went to work in Buckingham Palace.

In Harry Alcock's shop, there was always a flitch of bacon, at the end of the counter, and a large roll of twist tobacco, at the other, and when serving either he would use the same very sharp knife. Villagers used to say that he always wiped the knife clean before cutting the tobacco; he never bothered before cutting the bacon. Maybe he thought it gave the bacon a smoky flavour.

Church Street had quite a number of family shops where groceries and sweets could be bought, like Thomas and Mary Gleave's who also baked bread. And Fred Allman's shop which sold groceries and did a roaring trade. This was a happy friendly place where all kinds of topics were discussed, as they were in David Forster's shop at the other end of the village.

My great grandfather David Forster had built a large house, on the corner of West Road and Station Road, next to the smithy, and overlooking the village tree. He moved out of the smithy, which was later occupied by his daughter and son-in-law, Louis and Jesse Gerrard, and, in his new premises, started his ironmongery business and general store.

Sadly, David Forster died in 1904, before the advent of the motor car. His son, also David, took over the business and later on, after the First World War, his brother, Arnie, began a taxi business. As the years went by the corner shop sold all manner of goods; household utensils, pots, pans and crockery. A fascination for all young lads was an array of pocket watches, "turnip watches", they were jokingly called, which were displayed in a glass-fronted cabinet. The prices for these ranged from 5 shillings to 7/6d, and were guaranteed time-keepers. There were all kinds of garden tools, seeds, lawnmowers, farm implements, and tools such as pikels, forks, spades, plough points; even snares to catch rabbits.

For washing day, the women could get dolly tubs, dolly pegs, and punners. There was nothing you could not buy. There was paraffin oil, carbide, for bicycle lamps, bicycles, motor bicycles, and accessories. Batteries could be charged, and the shop became well known for miles around.

It also became well known as a stage for political argument. David Forster was a staunch Liberal and groups of farmers would arrive at the shop and start a debate which could go on for hours. The shop was quite spacious and heated with a paraffin stove and had its own special smell. There seemed to be no catalogue of where each item was stored within the shop and sometimes you would be waiting for a while before your required purchase was unearthed. The shop was an Aladdin's Cave with storerooms above the shop and another in an outbuilding. David became a Councillor and a County Councillor. Forster Avenue was named after him. His brother Arnie would help in the shop. He was a cheerful little man who went about his business whistling hymns, being a bass singer in the Chapel Choir, and was well liked all over the village throughout his long life.

David Forster also built Mrs. Sinnot's house. Harry Rogers, who worked as a clerk at Horner's Creamery, lived there at one time. Tom McCann recalled giving him a lift in Billy Rigby's shandry in a very violent thunder storm which had caused him to turn back. He was a very quiet man and was so terrified that he prayed on the floor of the cart all the way home.

There was a big shed in the field opposite Mrs. Sinnot's; this was a wheelwright's premises. First it was Sandy Ellison's, who had moved from Acton, then Jack Platt's, who was followed by a man named Clarke. They all worked in conjunction with Forster's Blacksmiths.

Duttons had the wheelwrights, at Bryn Smithy, working with Newalls, at Bryn, and Sam Cawley had the wheelwrights at Acton Bridge. Rafe Broad's and Tom Rowe's smithies were taken over by Nagles.

There was a very special apple tree in my Great-grandfather Forster's garden behind the smithy. It was a Russet, but the apples it produced were far sweeter and the skin of a deeper hue than the usual Russet tree, consequently the old man was plagued by gangs of lads from "Back o'Town", Weaverham, coming to scrump apples from his favourite tree. Old Abraham Youd, who was living in the thatched cottage, halfway along High Street, was a master at budding and grafting fruit trees, and Sammy "Happy Days" Woodward decided he could produce and grow, in his market garden, a fair number of freshly grown Russet trees from the original in the old smithy garden. This new variety of apple tree was advertised in Sammy's seed catalogue under the name "Wareham Russet" and became a great success and as the years went by hardly a local garden was without one of them. So between the three men, the "Wareham Russet" had come into being and, along with the trees, the lads who had been so fond of the apples came to be known as "Wareham Russets" themselves.

The name has become a popular title for villagers, long after the demise of the three men who conjured it up, all those years ago. Naturally in those days, it was necessary to be born Back o' Town, Wareham, to be a true Russet.

Jimmy Hoole, the son of Sam "Saddler" Hoole, also had the gift of being able to graft roses or fruit trees onto any stock. He grafted pears onto the hawthorn hedge, alongside Brickley path, and years later, pear trees were growing in the hedge and bearing fruit.

Just outside the village, but used by many of the village farmers, Bryn Smithy was one of the oldest smithies in the district and is said to have been used by the Monks of Vale Royal. The Newall family kept the smithy for many years, and of course near every smithy was a wheelwright's shop and in this case it was the Dutton's homestead in Smithy Lane.

The smithy was always a busy place and whenever you went by there would be a horse inside being shod and perhaps another couple waiting patiently outside. There was the sound of the bellows, the reddening glow of the coals, and the hammering of the red hot metal as the shoe was hammered into shape, and then there was the smell of burnt hoof, as the hot shoes were pressed to mould to the horses' feet.

It was a place where the tempers of both horse and man could become frayed, especially when the nails to hold on the shoe were being driven in. These nails had to be driven in so that the pointed end came out through the hoof to be neatly riveted up to hold the shoe fast. Horses were not always content to stand patiently, while the shoeing operation was carried out, and could become restive and sometimes difficult to handle, and the job could then become dangerous. Smithies were natural meeting places where farm men and other horse owners would gossip and spin yarns whilst waiting for their horses to be shod, and many an old man would drop by to get a warm near the fire at the forge and join in the gossip.

However, Bryn Smithy had something extra to offer. It was the meeting place of local boxers who came to show off their prowess in a makeshift ring. Here by the light of oil lanterns or shippon lights, they would challenge any man in the audience to fight. There would always be a few who would fancy their chances against the experienced fighters.

Of course many a young man who had come to watch at the ringside was urged on by the crowd to step forward and put on a pair of gloves, although some preferred to fight barefisted, in the old style. Excitement in the old hovel would get to fever pitch as the men hammered each other. I talked to Philip Hind many years later, when he was Landlord of the

Gate Inn, and he said how much he had enjoyed those nights at the smithy. He was of only slight build and his face still bore the evidence of the hard fights he had there. But he assured me that everyone involved in this venture really enjoyed it and continually came back for more.

The smoke from the men's clay pipes hung heavily in the air of the low building and the friendly banter and heckling was all taken good humouredly and in a sporting manner.

After the night's entertainment, the men would saunter off home in small groups some nursing bruised faces and knuckles. Edward Lloyd Clarke's boys were amongst the boxers, also Hiram Curwell. Fred Allman, who at one time worked for Clarke, was also often present. Clarke was quite a fighting man himself and would pull on a pair of gloves any time to take up a challenge.

Always among the audience was retired Policeman Tom Roberts who, on retirement, bought his childhood home in Copyhold where he kept a few hens and a couple of pigs. He would be seen walking past Nook Farm late at night, on his way back home.

Tom Roberts had a rather strange hobby. He kept a gamecock which was always kept in the peak of condition, and nothing pleased Tom better than challenging his neighbours to put their cockerels in to fight his bird. Sometimes, if he got the chance, he would slip the gamecock into a hen pen to watch the scrap. One time, he caught a large crow in his own pen, and fastening him in he threw in his gamecock. To his mortification, he had to rescue his bird before the crow caused it serious injury, and it took the gamecock quite some time to recover his pride.

One of the village's most well known, and respected figures, was Sergeant Allen. Although his name was George, he was always referred to as the "Sergeant", the reason being that he attained that rank during the course of over 19 years' service with the Territorials.

"I was with the Fifth Cheshires under the command of Major Brunner and Lieutenant Freeth and I was the first man in Northwich to have the Territorial Medal pinned on my chest," he said.

He also added that he served throughout the whole of the First World War. When he was boasting that he marched the local T.A. Contingent to the Railway Station en route to France, Henry Gatley, who was also born in Newton Heath, like the Sergeant, told the Knowledge Room crowd in the Wheatsheaf that he used to nurse George as a baby on his knee. Much to the amusement of all, Bill Robinson, an old soldier of the Cheshire Yeomanry, said:

"Th'e owt a dropped him on his yed."

Although born in Newton Heath, his mother came from Anderton and his father from Little Leigh. One of Mr. Allen's two sons, Frank, chose the Army as a career and attained the rank of Battery Sergeant Major in the Royal Artillery, but on returning to this country, from Egypt he lost a leg in a motor accident, while on manoeuvres, and joined the staff of the Air

Ministry. The local Cheshires went to France under Roger Brunner, while the Yeomanry T.A. went under Captain De Knoop, a gentleman and M.P. from the Tarporley area. Other men who had taken horses and undergone training were John Gleave, Charlie's brother, and Enoch Jones from Kingsley, the cattle dealers and movers, but they were both too old to go to war.

Another of the village's characters, who was also a practical joker, was Bob Nash, who became one of the village's early car owners. One day, during a high-spirited discussion in the Wheatsheaf, Sgt. Allen boasted that he would be made welcome in the Sergeants' Mess in Chester at any time, having served with the Regiment during the Great War. As the pub closed its midday session, Bob was waiting with his car outside. "Anyone for home?" he asked. Several climbed aboard, including "Snibby" Crossland who had already overstayed his usual time, and of course, Sgt. Allen. It was soon evident as they turned into Forest Street and made their way out of the village that they were off on an unexpected journey.

"What about my Jinny and the potatoes ?" said "Snibby", as he thought of an irate wife waiting with his cooked dinner.

But all was in vain as the little car sped off on its way towards Chester. Arriving at the Barracks, it was not long before Sgt. Allen was presenting his assortment of friends to the Sergeants' Mess. A most hilarious afternoon followed and it was much later that the little group returned to Weaverham, much wiser and even more inebriated.

The Sergeant served for over ten years on the Parish Council and was a man of strong political convictions.

"I am a radical," he said, "and an old supporter of Sir John Brunner and young Jack when they were campaigning in the Northwich Division."

He was a great admirer of William Ewart Gladstone, whose portrait always hung on the wall of George's house, the old Grammar School, in Forest Street, where he lived with his wife, Nellie, and stepdaughter Bertha, of whom, he would say, he would pay three silver half crowns to any man taking her off his hands. There were no takers.

The large blue stone on Forest Street, opposite the Old Grammar School, was said to be where a man by the name of Nathaniel Morgan was buried. Sgt. Allen was the instigator of this story and called his house Nathaniel Morgan's home.

At election times, Sgt. Allen would have many a political argument with the Reverend Patterson Morgan, the local Tory councillor, politician and J.P.. Patterson Morgan had married Miss Dronsfield and this had made him a wealthy man and he became the owner of Sandiway Lodge, now a nursing home, and its land. Betsy Gleave, who was Charlie's wife, was sister to Jack Fryer, farm bailiff to the Dronsfields. Jack Eaton, Phyllis's father, was estate bailiff to Captain Higson, at Oakmere Hall, while a Mr. Woods was farm bailiff for Robert Heath and lived in the West Lodge, which was surrounded by very thick high hedges. His son persuaded Dad and Harold to walk home with him and then frightened them half to death by shutting the gate and telling them they would have to stay all night.

There are still a number of thatched cottages which have recently been renovated in style in the village and there are a few which in their day were thatched. However, many are but memories from when the village of Weaverham was a very picturesque and tranquil place, in the days of Queen Victoria, and remained so until after the First World War when life began to change with the advent of the motor car.

The population of Weaverham, in the year 1871, was 1,685 and at this time it was a thriving rural community. In High Street, Benjamin Burgess, as I have already mentioned, had built a large house and business premises to sell agricultural implements, seeds and fertilisers. He also dealt as a linen and woollen draper, tea merchant, ironmonger and insurance agent. Some agricultural implements were even made at his workshop in High Street.

Charles Dobell was a corn and seed merchant and John Cossins ran livery stables (hunting horses) near the Sandiway Head Inn, now the Blue Cap, and was also a horse dealer. With horses providing all the motive power for both local farmers and businessmen, there was a steady demand for them.

There was also a heavy demand on footware and, amongst the local shoemakers, were Thomas Ford, John Wood, and Gerard Williams, who also made boots. Arthur Arrowsmith was the Registrar of Births, Marriages and Deaths, and Samuel Johnson was the Parish Clerk as well as being a local tailor. The Postmaster was Peter Harrison, and Joseph William Smith and Samuel Smith were the local surgeons, while John Janion Manifold, of Station Road, was the pharmacist, chemist and grocer, and also sold cattle and horse medicines.

Another tailor was Edward Jones, and Francis Moore was a draper and milliner. Jane Youd was a milliner and dressmaker and a man, by the name of Samuel Hoole, was the local saddler. Anne Percival had a butcher's shop in the village at this time and there were several pubs: The Wheatsheaf, The Gate Inn, The Ring o'Bells, near to the Church, and more often than not, called the "Church Style", The Rifleman, which was in Forest Street (possibly where the Chapel now stands), The Star, which was on the site of Buckley's shop, and The Volunteer, at the corner of Smith's Lane and High Street. There is also mention of another pub in Forest Street, called The Lord Nelson, but there is no reliable information about it, and it could have been a previous pub, renamed. The date of the Star is unknown, but in 1850, and in 1857, it was kept by a Mary Pollock. The last Landlord was William Wood, who retired with his wife to Nook Cottages, and it was then closed.

Harry Winnington was Landlord of the old Ring o' Bells and he moved into the new Ring o'Bells when it opened in the 1920s. Under each side of the stone sign on the new Ring o' Bells, there was placed a penny, by two of the bricklayers working on it.

In the little cottage, next door to Billy Walsh's shop, lived George Frith, a tall man but with quite a stoop by virtue of his trade as a cobbler. His cobbler's shop was in Station Road on the left hand side looking towards Acton, a very old half timbered building, now demolished. He was well known throughout the district as a very good cobbler and was always busy.

Billy Walsh was a regular at the Gate Inn, always standing in his favourite corner of the bar smoking his pipe. One of his favourite topics was the hiring of bicycles for which he charged 3d an hour, and very often they were not returned until late evening with punctures in both wheels. He lived in Church Lane at first, but moved into living quarters at the shop when Miss Hoole died. Miss Hoole was the sister of Sam "Saddler" Hoole who repaired harnesses on one side of the shop, while his sister sold ladies' wear in the other. Sam, who repaired all the harness for Nook Farm, used to sit cross-legged on the floor amongst a pile of harness. He was a small bespectacled man, with monkey-like features, who would travel anywhere for a fight and was not bothered by the size of his opponents; the bigger the better.

His sister was always telling him to quieten down and not to fight, but he would take no heed; the excitement was in his blood. Big Irish farmworkers were no match for this little man who would outbox them, ducking and weaving, before putting them down with a mighty blow. He was often called in to help the less fortunate folk threatened by the bullying characters of the day. After he died, his sister carried on alone at the shop, until she too died, and Billy Walsh moved in. Billy was a portly little gentleman, bespectacled and jovial. As well as hiring bicycles, he repaired them and sold them, and built up a thriving business selling items of ironmongery, ice skates, fishing tackle and fireworks, but he would never sell air gun pellets. His wife sold ladies' clothing in the other half of the shop, just as Miss Hoole had done. In the Second World War Billy became Chief of the Auxiliary Fire Service which manned a mobile pump, to assist with fire-fighting.

At one time, Derby Spruce was Landlord of the Wheatsheaf and when his wife died, he took on a barmaid, named Alice. He organised a fund for a special bicycle for Fred Lewis who had lost a leg in the First World War. Fred became friendly with Alice, and the Landlord (who had wanted her for himself) banished him to the Ring o' Bells, where he met Clara, whom he later married.

Alice left the Wheatsheaf and another barmaid was taken on and old Derby began to become very possessive of her too. The local lads plagued him about it and he used to give them money to drink elsewhere.

Tom Gatley went shopping to Warrington with this new barmaid, in Arnie Forster's taxi and on return, Tom took a washing basket of crockery out of the car and helped the lady out, feet first into the crockery basket, breaking all its contents. She must have been prone to disasters; Harry Woolley tickled her legs while she had a pile of empty glasses and they all ended up smashed on the floor.

Derby Spruce brought, in a basket, two pigeons to my father, at Nook Farm. His pigeons were the envy of all the pigeon flyers and before he brought them to Dad many had tried to buy these two, Eric Johnson's dad being the most persistent.

The Volunteer does not seem to have existed long, presumably after 1879 when this house, and the one adjoining it, had diamond-paned windows, and were known as the Old Manor House. This is where William Horner began his creamery business, before moving to Bryn.

Hiram Curwell was the very first man to cart milk to Horners, at these premises, with a donkey and cart. Paul McGregor, who lived in a bungalow at the bottom of Littledales Lane, also carted milk, with a donkey and cart, but Hiram was the first.

The Reverend Charles Spencer Stanhope was the vicar and he received £341 a year plus his residence, the old vicarage, and 30 acres of glebeland. There was also a strong Methodist following in the village and although the early history of Wesleyan Methodism in Weaverham is little known, it is undisputed that on April 8th, 1774, the Rev. John Wesley rode from Little Leigh, by Weaverham Gate and Bryn, to Chester and it is possible that some villagers had heard him preach at Little Leigh and had come under his influence.

Mr Thomas Forster came to the village in 1813, from Burtonwood, Lancashire, to reside at the old Smithy House, near Weaverham Gate, and it is known that Mr Henry Sanderson was connected with Methodism from around that time. Mr Sanderson lived at Mere House Farm and died in 1833. Services were being held in various cottages at that time and it is supposed that Mr. Forster's cottage was the last one to have held such a service. Although it is not known at what date the first chapel was built in Weaverham, it is known that the Hartford old chapel was built in 1833 and that one was built at Weaverham soon afterwards. It was a plain, oblong building, quite comfortable inside, and was heated by a stove and lit by candles. The chapel was situated at the top of a narrow side street, the "Wynt" (now Chapel Street), off High Street. There was no vestry, nor any spare ground outside, but evidently there was a coalhouse somewhere, as records show that in 1874, one shilling was paid for a lock and staple for the same. At each end of the chapel there was a gallery of pews raised by steps up to the walls. The pulpit was against the middle of one of the side walls and around its front and two sides sat the choir. The opposite seats were usually used by men. The Sunday services were in the afternoon and evening. In order to give people the opportunity to attend the Parish Church afterwards, the afternoon service was held at 1.30 pm. The service was subsequently held at 2 pm.

At that time there was no evening service at the Parish Church, the latest service being held in the afternoon, at 3 o'clock. It is not known when bible society classes were first formed at Weaverham, but there are tickets dated 1844, issued to Thomas Forster and his wife Ann. At one period, a small band which included a bass fiddle accompanied the services and later in 1877 a reed organ was introduced to assist with the singing.

A number of local preachers resided in Weaverham. In fact, at one time Weaverham sent out more preachers than any other village in the Northwich Circuit. They usually travelled on foot or horseback. Sometimes, if two or more were travelling in the same direction, they would acquire a horse and trap for the journey at their own expense. Travelling home on dark winter nights, they experienced some strange happenings. I often recall the tale told by my grandmother's uncle, Adam Forster, whilst travelling home from preaching a service at Kelsall. He was returning to Village Farm, Weaverham, and he was accompanied by a friend, both of them travelling on horseback. Grange Lane, from Bryn Smithy to Weaverham, was a dark foreboding way and as they came down past the lodge, Adam was leading the way. They approached the bridge over the stream when, suddenly, the ghostly figure of a woman sprang up behind Adam. The horse's pace quickened and Adam was gripped with fear. The other followed awestruck. Over the railway bridge they went and, suddenly, the ghostly figure alighted and vanished down the old lane past Nook Cottages, which was once the only way to the Grange Hall.

Adam's companion shouted "Did you see that, Adam?"

Adam had seen her and the two lost no time in getting back to the little farm in the village where they related what had happened. The "Grange Lady" had been seen by many on their travels in the vicinity of the old Hall, at Hefferston.

It is not known who were the actual Trustees of the old Chapel, but the veterans at that time were: Thomas Wild, Weaverham Wood; Henry Sanderson, Wallerscote; John Gerrard, Nook Farm; and William Forster, Village Farm.

Village Farm was the home of preachers for many years, being considerably nearer and much more convenient to them than "The Wood", or "Wallerscote", where the houses were also open to them.

The present chapel, in Forest Street, was built in the year 1878 on land kindly given by A.H. Smith Barry, Esq. (Lord Barrymore). My great grandfather, David Forster, was involved in the building of it. When he tendered to build the chapel, he undercut so much, it completely broke him. It cost £1,800 and, with the aid of a grant from the General Chapel Fund, the whole of the debt was cleared by 1894. It was opened on June 18th, 1879, the preacher being the Reverend Henry W. Holland, then Chairman of the Hull District. It was a great occasion for him because he had spent his early days in Weaverham, with his uncle, Mr. Lea, at Lake House Farm, and he was a great friend of Mr. Henry Sanderson, senior.

The first Trustees were Messrs. Henry Sanderson, senior; Thomas B. Moreton; William Forster; Daniel Wrench; John Wild; David Forster; Henry Sanderson, Junior; Ezra Gandy; Charles Hancock; John Gerrard; William H. Moreton; Robert Heywood; John Roberts; Frederick Ellison and Charles Gleave.

A pipe organ was installed in 1895 and for about 30 years, Walter Hickton was the blower. An amusing incident occurred one Christmas when the carol service was in progress. Walter called to the organist, requesting that he played "While Shepherds watch....". The organist, embarrassed by the sudden request, signalled back to Walter that he couldn't change the order of the hymns.

Walter shouted back: "Aye well, tha' can play what tha' wants but I shall blow 'While Shepherds watched'."

When the new chapel opened, it was decided to start a Sunday School, in the old chapel, which was altered to accommodate this new project. The school opened on April 11th, 1880, with 33 scholars attending in the morning, and 39 in the afternoon... a sad reflection on the number attending the chapel services today in the 1990s. The building soon became too small and a new school was built at a cost of £1,350 and opened, on October 5th, 1903, by the Reverend Marshall Hartley. The old chapel was partially taken down and a caretaker's house erected on the same spot.

There was a flourishing Sisterhood and an excellent Men's Bible Class (in the late 1920s).

During these early years of the chapel, one of the most exciting days for the children of the village was the annual Sunday School Outing to Overton Hills.

Local farmers and businessmen supplied horses and carts. These were market carts or wagonettes fitted with seating arrangements and the horses would be decorated as if for a fete. The journey was as much a part of the day out as the time spent at Overton, and the children were dressed in their best Sunday clothes. The day chosen for the outing was the Thursday before Whit Sunday and everyone prayed for a fine day as the procession of horses and their various vehicles proceeded towards Frodsham. It was a most colourful occasion and the children would sing merrily as they jogged along on their journey. Mr Fairclough, from Mere House Farm, sent a horse-drawn wagonette, and Mr Frankenburg, from Hefferston Grange, would send a horse and spring cart, driven usually by Alan Rustage, who, on leaving school, went to work at the hall. He recalled to me that the first time he took a load of children to Overton, he became separated from the procession and did not know the way. He had to rely on the horse which did not fail him and he eventually arrived safe and sound.

On reaching the pleasure grounds, the drivers unloaded their children, and the Sunday School teachers in charge of them, and then the horses were taken to either the little farm adjoining the grounds, or to the Belle

Mont Inn, where stabling and parking was also available. Enough hay was carried for the day and the horses were watered. There was an area of sand for the children who could also buy buckets and spades. Amusement stalls, swingboats and chairoplanes were amongst the fairground amusements. There were hobby-horses and the ever popular Helter Skelter, a prominent landmark that could be seen for miles shining brightly in the sun. It was a fair height with steps up to the top where the spiral shute to the bottom was full of children speeding down it on the little mats provided for the descent. Needless to say, this was in great demand all day. Donkey rides were also available. There was a large tearoom where the children were assembled for afternoon tea and the day was always a huge success. Some of the older children and grownups would have a special treat by visiting the yard of the Belle Mont Inn where, in a large cage, a performing monkey would give a non-stop acrobatic show to all who cared to watch, stopping only to feed on a few titbits thrown to him by the crowd who thoroughly enjoyed every minute of his antics. By late afternoon, the children would climb wearily back onto their various forms of transport ready for the long enjoyable journey home with the horses clip-clopping their way back to the village. By the time Alan Rustage arrived home at the hall, at Hefferston Grange, the peacocks would be beginning to roost on the low branches of the beech and oak trees in the grounds. He would unyoke the horse from the cart, feed and water it in the stables, and then probably turn it out to pasture for the night.

The Helter Skelter, which was sadly taken down some time after World War II, was built in 1908 at a cost of £300. It was an 80-feet high wooden tower and in its heyday attracted crowds of day trippers. On its first day alone, over 3,000 rides were made at a penny a time. It stood for 70 years or more, before being dismantled, and was as familiar a landmark as Blackpool Tower.

These wonderful days out in the magical children's playground continued well into the 1930s; not only with the Sunday Schools, but with other clubs and fellowships such as the Rechabites, as the older villagers will remember, with the horse-drawn vehicles of former years giving way to newly appearing motor lorries provided by local businesses, such as Burgess Bros..

There were lots of other events to look forward to expectantly; the Forester Club held Annual Fetes at both Weaverham, on Gerrards Park, and at Acton Bridge, on Manning's field, opposite the Station Hotel, now the Hazel Pear. Bands used to play for dancing on the field at Weaverham, or in the Club Room, at Acton Bridge. It would usually be Royle's Fair in attendance and the last music for playing by the dance band was always a selection of hymns, ending with "God be with you 'til we meet again." This went on while Mr Royle was entertaining the committee with a few drinks in his caravan. The fair would always arrive on a Thursday, open on Friday night, and would be open on Saturday afternoon and night, Monday night, and leave for its next venue on Tuesday.

Foresters always started the proceedings on a Saturday afternoon with a procession, with marching bands and with the popular so called "Jazz Bands", such as the favourite Whalley Road Band, and during the afternoon there would be all sorts of competitions, tug o' war, egg and spoon races, three-legged races, and other entertainments, as well as the more serious running events.

Local sportsmen such as Eddie Gordon, George Redford, and Fred Allman, used to meet on Pitstead field, on what is now Walnut Avenue and where The Salter stood, to train for the various cycle and running events held at the local fetes.

One such event was the "round the houses" race at Frodsham Carnival. Joe Shallcross was picked and heavily backed to win. He was told to stay behind the local best runner until just before the finishing line and then burst past him. This he did, only to be passed on the line himself to come second, much to the dismay of his friends, some of whom had lost their last shilling. Another contestant, in the cycle race, fell over the line with his feet firmly strapped into the pedals and could not be released in time to be presented to the Judges, and lost his first place. I think the rider was Hugh Scott.

As well as all the fun of the fair, such as the steam-engined driven hobby horses with its accompanying organ music, swing boats and all manner of stalls and coconut shies, there would, invariably, be a boxing booth. The fair would have a night finish at 11.00 p.m. and since the pubs finished at 10.00 p.m., it would give drinkers an hour on the fair before close. So for the last hour the ground was full of revellers, with the last half hour on the hobby horses being free.

Less vigorous was Sandiway Flower Show, which used to be held every year on New Park and at one of these shows, on August 4th, 1914, the festivities were brought to a standstill with the announcement that war had been declared on Germany, and would any Army Volunteers present report immediately for duty. These shows carried on for many years and Albert Holden used to show produce there. He had trained at Delamere House and said old Hughie Wilbraham, who liked to claim he grew every known variety of apple, pear and plum in his orchard, could go to sleep on any of the field gates on his estate, just leaning with his head in his hands, and was often found in this position by his estate workers. At one of these shows, Jack Gleave was riding the chairoplanes and urged his friends to spin him around. They spun him around so many times that on getting out he was so dizzy he could not stand for half an hour, and vowed never to ride them again.

The Oddfellows Friendly Society also held an annual fair on Manning's field, their members parading in their regalia of a blue sash, worn over the left shoulder, and I have been told that the fair was at some time held in the field behind the Gate Inn. Then there was the Annual Rose Fete which used to be held always on the second Saturday in July. The teachers organised the whole affair, with the Queen, from the top class, chosen by vote of all the schoolchildren, and Mrs Turner specialising in the Maypole Dance. The Rose Fete used to be held on Mr. Darlington's field, opposite the Hanging Gate and did not move to Lake House until a few years after the Second World War.

There were few incidents in the village life which aroused more excitement than the local lad who flew his biplane over his girlfriend's house and then, hoping to fly over the old mill at Bryn where his father was the miller, banked too steeply, lost control and altitude and hit the ground at Hefferston Grange, narrowly missing a clump of trees on the Top Park. This caused one of the wheels to break off as it bounced high in the air again, only to come down rather heavily on the top of a large holly bush.

My father, who was ploughing with horses in a nearby field, watched the scene with amazement. He saw the plane, which after all was little more than a large kite with an engine and held together with struts and wire, take its downward dive, momentarily going out of sight behind the trees and buildings before bouncing upwards into full view before once again vanishing as it came down to rest precariously in the lofty holly bush near the far lodge in the corner of the wood. This may have saved him serious injury because it would have been impossible for him to land on one wheel and he could have crashed into the far lodge which could have been fatal in such a flimsy aircraft. Jimmy Johnson,who was peeling potatoes for dinner in the little cottage at the end of Forest Street, heard the plane circling and also watched it go down, and hurried to the scene of the crash.

My father tied up the horses and rushed across the fields to find the young pilot, who had escaped with cuts and bruises after scrambling out of the wreckage, rather dazed and shaken, but thankful to be alive.

His name was Freddie Stubbs and he had flown Sopwith Camels in the Royal Flying Corps at the end of the Great War and was still in the Service, the year being about 1919. Hundreds of people flocked to the scene of the crash.

Aeroplanes were a rare sight in those days. Very soon, the local policeman was there to protect the wreckage from souvenir hunters. Eventually a guard of airmen arrived to keep watch over the plane until it could be recovered and taken away. Fred's mother (they lived in Cuddington Hollows) had come down into Weaverham to tell everyone proudly "Our Freddie's coming over" and this became a catchphrase in the village for some time afterwards. In fact, the story was retold over again for many years, until the Second World War when there seemed to be more aeroplanes in the sky than motor cars on the roads, and crashed aircraft, Allied and enemy, were not an uncommon sight.

Freddie's girlfriend was a Miss Youd, from Station Road, and years later, he admitted he had been showing off a little. They were later married and lived in Station Road, opposite Wilson's Drive. It was a pity that the flight ended so abruptly, but Fred was still in one piece and rejoined the RAF at the beginning of the Second World War. Although no longer allowed to fly (he had caused some damage to his eyes through reluctance to wear goggles whilst flying in open cockpits), he took charge of a barrage balloon unit in the North East.

The mill at Cuddington Hollows was always known as Horner's Mill and the propeller from the crashed aeroplane hung up there for many years, and could, possibly, still be there. My father had a wheel cap, which has since vanished, and I have a strut from the broken undercarriage, a beautifully polished piece of hardwood still smelling of dope and stamped "Whitehead Engineering".

Freddie's father is the first remembered miller at the mill and he was followed by a man appropriately named "Miller". You could get a bag of wheat ground for a shilling and it would be divided into Thirds, Bran, and Flour, enough to do no end of baking. The mill was a wonderful sight when working with the huge waterwheel turning all the machinery, much of it beautifully made out of hardwood.

After the death of Mr. Frankenburg, who had followed Robert Heath into Hefferston Grange, the estate was once again up for sale and at this time there was considerable alarm in the village when it became known that the Corporation of Warrington were considering the area for the building of a Sanatorium, to house and treat the ever growing number of tuberculosis victims. This dangerous infectious disease was spreading at an alarming rate and at that time the only treatment (apart from drastic surgery to remove infected areas of lung) was rest, good food and fresh air, and this had led to the Corporation coming out into the countryside to choose a site on which to build a Sanatorium.

Several sites had been considered and the choice had been narrowed down to the area of land at the top of Withens Lane, or to the Hefferston Grange site, and the latter, with its secluded grounds and walled garden was chosen.

The old hall would provide excellent accommodation for the staff, while the adjacent Park Land would be ideal for the position of the hospital buildings. The prevailing winds from the Mersey Estuary, bringing with them the air from the pine forests of Delamere, would be extremely beneficial. The estate was duly purchased and work began.

Soon the foundations were laid and a miniature railway track was laid out so that bricks and materials could be easily moved about the site to wherever they were needed. The Warrington Borough Surveyor, Mr Howson, designed the buildings. The overall contract was given to Fairdoughs of Warrington, and a bricklayer, by the name of Ike Hewitt, did much of the building. Materials were brought in by horses and carts, some from Acton Station and some from Northwich. Grandfather George, who now had the tenancy of Grange Farm (the Home Farm) as well as having purchased Nook Farm, lent a cart to carry bricks from Thompson's brickworks.

Young local lads had a wonderful time, playing in the hoppers at night along the railway line when the workers had finished for the day. With the exit of the Frankenburg family and no occupiers of the hall itself, there had never been such a free and easy time round the old Grange. Whilst it was being prepared for its new arrivals, Mr Holden was to stay on as head gardener and with his home in the lodge, at the end of the main drive, he soon took over the role also of gatekeeper. He was a man of great character and as a gardener he was second to none, having been apprenticed at Delamere House and later having worked at Oulton Park. Here, at Hefferston, he lived for his work and throughout his working life he was able to grow sufficient fruit and vegetables for the patients and staff. Mrs Waterman became the caretaker and lived alone in the hall for a considerable time.

The adjoining wards were built near to the old hall and two separate wards were built a little further away. Women were to occupy the wards on the north side, and all these were linked by roadways with the hall, which was to become the Nurses' Home. Six wooden huts, each on a revolving base, were built, to be turned in any direction, to suit the sun, or prevailing wind. The wards, able to house up to 80 patients, were so designed that the beds could be pushed out under the verandahs when weather conditions permitted, so providing the patients with the maximum amount of fresh air.

A large wooden recreation hut was sited in a convenient position, between the men's and women's wards, with facilities for darts, billiards and dominoes. There was also a well-stocked library and teaching facilities, for the small number of children who were patients, and a bowling green for the not so ill patients. There was even a small shop where relatives visiting patients could buy refreshments and sweets.

The large ward, set nearest to the old hall and sheltered by rhododendron bushes and a copse of fine old trees, which had grown around the moat area, was to be known as the "Nursing Block". Here, patients in a more advanced state of the disease, could be cared for with the utmost devotion by wonderful staff who worked tirelessly, without regard to the dangers to their own health, whilst dealing with this very infectious disease.

The Sanatorium opened in 1921 when the Matron, Miss Emma Yaxley, arrived with her staff and soon patients from the Warrington district began to arrive. The Medical Officer of Health at that time was Dr Joseph, a dedicated man who became deeply involved with the new Sanatorium. He paid regular visits and was very interested in every aspect of the place and insisted on strict discipline over staff and patients. He was keenly interested in the natural conservation of Hefferston and when some of the patients carved their names on trees, he threatened to discharge them if it happened again.

Some of the first patients to be admitted had contracted tuberculosis through the effects of mustard gas in their lungs during the First World War. It was a truly terrible disease and little hope could be given to anyone who was seriously affected with it, and very few of the early patients survived, although some, George Summerfield and Ernie Unsworth were two, spent several years as patients. During the 1920s and '30s, the death toll was very high with several deaths a week.

Life went on very much the same at the Hall with Matron Yaxley assuming the status of the Lady of the Manor, with servants, just as in the days when it was a country house, but with neither butler nor footman, but she was respected and supported by her staff. Mr Holden, at the main lodge, was head gardener, supported by his assistants, Jack Barker and Walter Newall, and at the West Lodge, first Mr Bloor and then Mr Makin, were engineers, looking after the electrical and machinery side of the Sanatorium.

George Ward was the sole porter, handyman and jack-of-all trades. A truly remarkable man, he devoted his life to the institution and many times worked twelve hours a day or more. For years he had one afternoon off a week when he would walk for miles around the district. He was a pillar of strength to patients and staff alike, and could always find time to give a helping hand on the Grange Farm, with cow calving or harvest time.

The two horses, Punch and Bob, which were kept at the Sanatorium lived there for many years. Sadly, after the outbreak of the Second World War, they were taken away to be destroyed as it was thought to be uneconomical to keep them. This was very sad and later regretted and I do not think such a thing would be allowed to happen today. Of the two horses, Punch did the grass mowing and Bob did the cart work. George Ward used to take Bob to Acton Bridge Station, to pick up Matron Yaxley and nurses, off the last train from Warrington. Old Bob could be heard for miles around the district as he trotted home on the clear, frosty, moonlight nights.

Summer and winter alike, George used to go into the station yard with Bob and the shandry to pick up his passengers off this late train, and villagers, hearing the clatter of hooves on the still night air, would say, "There goes th'owd Sanny Express".

The horses had a shed to feed in during the summer, but in winter times they were kept in the Coachhouse stables where they were fed, watered, bedded down, and mucked out by George who used to take them to Rafe Broad's smithy to be shod. When Rafe retired from the smith, he continued to shoe Punch and Bob, coming up to the Grange to do so. On one such occasion, whilst shoeing one of them under the old horse chestnut tree, he accidentally dropped a nail which found its way into a cow's foot. When the nail was eventually found and pulled out, the cow dropped as though dead, but after a while she got up and made a slow painful recovery.

When Matron Yaxley retired, about 1942 or '43, her place was taken by Mrs Dorothy Lee, who became the new "Lady of the Manor". She first of all came to live at Tilston Hayes, in West Road, which had been taken over, some time after 1941, by the Government, to house nursing staff at the Sanatorium and the new Emergency Hospital. The Limes, in High Street was also taken over. Later, when Mr. Holden retired and vacated the East Lodge, at the main gateway, Matron Lee and her husband moved into this house. Len was a wheelwright on the railway and each evening he would be seen walking along the track from Acton Station to Grange Wood where he would then take the old path across the park to his home.

Matron Lee reigned supreme for many years, seeing the end of the war celebrated at the old hall. Miss Cummings, the Assistant Matron, resided in the Matron's quarters in the hall itself. For many members of staff, this old house was their only home and they worked there for most of their working lives.

One such person was little Sarah "Nellie" Alcock who had been there ever since the Sanatorium opened. She wore heavily-lensed glasses and amongst her many jobs, she was kitchen maid and also tended the small flock of hens and ducks which the Matron and her husband had established in the grounds. Although she never married, she was, in early days, always amongst the lads of the village who came up to the Grange in search of girlfriends. Everyone knew Nellie and the Grange was her home where she lived and worked and eventually died.

George Ward remained porter and boiler attendant; Eddie Machin was now engineer, and Jack Barker had succeeded Albert Holden as head gardener. After Mrs. Dunne retired as cook, a position Mrs Ward had held at one time, a Gwen Rowland took over. She was a heavy-smoking woman, rarely seen without a cigarette in her mouth, and who was later to become Mrs Clarence Holt. By this time, and following his demob from the army, Clarence had become a porter at the hospital, because it was decided there was now too much work for one man, and this would allow the porters to have more time off and enjoy a shorter working week. After all, the war was now over and life could be taken a little less seriously.

It was a happy place, so different from the early years of the Sanatorium when very few villagers would venture past the railway bridge for fear of contracting the deadly disease, and when the Sanatorium and the old hall, with its beautiful gardens and park, remained a very private place. Others came to work from nearby villages, many coming by bicycle from Northwich and district, as did two women nicknamed Abbott and Costello, for one was short and dumpy, the other tall and thin.

Many funny stories were told of those years, such as the time when one woman sold about half a dozen hens in feather to staff friends. These were hard to come by in those years and somewhat of a luxury, but everyone was aghast at the end of the following week when the woman's husband was in court for stealing half a dozen hens from a neighbour.

Then there was little Eileen Hook who used to fall asleep by the hot-plate, only to be caught by the wily old Matron Lee. A potato pie supper with dancing was often held in the old house and young men from the village would be invited to help make a reasonable mixture of boys and girls, and many a good night was had by all. Tom Clarke, a male patient in the Sanatorium, used to help as he got better and, later, he became one of the staff, as a male nurse, and made Hefferston his life, and died there.

Eric Travis, who met and married his wife Stephanie, a Ukrainian girl who was nursing at the Grange, worked at Hefferston for 35 years as a male nurse, carrying on at the geriatric hospital when the Sanatorium closed down.

As the village moved into the 1920s, so it had began to grow. In 1920, Brunner Mond and Company bought, from Lord Barrymore, Owley Wood, on which to build a new estate, to house their increasing workforce, so quickly was the Chemical Works expanding. Workers had been recruited from all over the country, some from as far as Portsmouth, and some especially skilled men from abroad. To house these new workers, 250 houses were built, creating great excitement and much employment. The building materials were brought to Acton Bridge Station and then carted by horses to the site. There was a clubhouse for the men and the estate had its own water supply, each house being fed from the tower built in Owley Wood Road, at the top of the wood.

Weaverham Well had supplied the old village with water since at least Saxon times, and it was still from this same source when cottages began to receive piped water fed from the tower at the top of Brickley. Prior to this, each cottage would either have its own well and hand pump, or would share a well with neighbours like the row of terraced houses which stood in High Street, next to the Wheatsheaf. This terrace had a communal well, round the back, from which each household drew its own water.

Ernie Denning worked the pump to fill the tower. He was a tinsmith by trade, like his father before him, and used to solder milk churns for Horners' Creamery, and would do the pumping at night. He lived with his sister, later to become Mrs Moore, at the shop in High Street which Bill Hornby moved into from the Wharf.

The supply from the well became hardly adequate and so, in about 1912, an additional supply was pumped from Crabtree Green, and the old well water was condemned shortly afterwards, but even so continued to quench the thirst of many a walker on a hot day.

In 1932, the first council houses to be built in Weaverham were completed and named Forster Avenue, after Councillor David Forster. These cut a road across what had been two fields and joined Northwich Road with Wallerscote Road.

So many improvements were talking place rapidly in these years of the Twenties and Thirties. The North Western Road Car Company introduced a bus service, which was cheaper and infinitely more comfortable than the old horse drawn shandries and early motor wagons. I think the single fare to Northwich was threepence.

There was a small motor driven train, called the "Dodger" which travelled back and too all day long, between St.Helens, Warrington, Over and Wharton, and Winsford, stopping at Acton Bridge and Hartford en route. On Saturday nights, the last trip started from Warrington at 11.00 p.m., bringing people back from the Hippodrome and Royal Court Theatres. The return fare was a shilling, and on the dimly-lit station platform, if a ticket had been mislaid, a piece of cigarette packet would be proffered instead to the porter, either Bill Saunders, or Arthur Yoxall. This same Dodger would also pick up the milk at 7.45 in the mornings, for St. Helens Co-op.

Great improvements were made to the drainage and sewerage systems, with proper sewerage beds being made off Well Lane. Prior to this, night soil had, for years, been dumped on a field to the rear of Hefferston Grange.

But there was still no street lighting, and why a Village of Moonbeams, you may ask ?

Well, on November 1st 1928, there appeared a fascinating little story in the Manchester Evening Chronicle, under the heading "Village of Romantic Gloom, Lovers' Retreat."

The story begins in the low-beamed dimly-lit sitting room of "Poplar Cottage", in High Street. This old cottage was said to be three or four hundred years old and was the home of the Bebbington family. It was, and still is, a black and white timbered building with a thatched roof. The windows were deep-silled and the walls covered with a thick mantle of ivy. Charles Bebbington, village sexton and local historian, was being interviewed by a reporter, from the Manchester Chronicle.

"Why is the village called 'Lovers' Retreat' ? " asked the reporter.

The old sexton smiled gently and replied: "You know that our streets are not lighted and the moon has been known to improve romance. Perhaps that answers your question. The moon still provides all our outdoor lighting just as it did when Edwin, the King of Mercia, held the village. Nor were there any lamps when King Edward I visited Weaverham in 1277, on his way to lay the foundation stone of Vale Royal Abbey. There was a time when the village was self-contained and every trade in the country was represented in these few miles of pleasant countryside. There were weavers, coopers, saddlers, tinkers, chandlers, joiners, blacksmiths, wheelwrights and farmers, and for aught I know they all worked and played by the light of the moon. An attempt was made to light the village by oil lamps about fifty years ago (1878) and these were maintained by public voluntary contributions. But all this died out after about thirty years and we are still without light."

Here the old historian paused and then added with a trace of unhappiness: "But it is coming at last. Walk three hundred yards down the road and see the Rural District Council representative, David Forster. He'll tell you all about it."

The reporter passed through the low-beamed door and out onto the street and, leaving the old church way back on the right, headed for what the villagers called the "Great North Road". In a shop was advertised a dance to end at 2 am.. There was no lack of dances in Weaverham at that time. It was a village of moonbeams and late dances and when the moon forgot to shine, stormlamps would light the way home for the revellers in the small hours. A return of the "Polka" and the "Bustle" would have put Weaverham back into the last century.

David Forster, the Rural Council representative, was at his ironmonger's shop, by the old village tree, which has sheltered many pairs of lovers in its time, with its wonderful village seat arranged around the base of it.

He said: "Yes, we have light shortly; we have applied to the Ministry of Health for powers to instal street lighting and we are awaiting a reply."

The old tree at this time of year was shorn of all its foliage, but stood loyally facing a buffeting in the strong wind and was still able to afford a rendezvous. Many times the wicked gleam of car headlights picked out the figures of courting couples, closely huddled together on the seats arranged around the base of the old tree. Many times must a lovesick swain have breathed a solitary oath at a searching flash of light before it disappeared as suddenly as it came, to cast a glare for the moment on the spinney beyond.

Asked whether he thought the lovers of the village might object to the streets being lit up, the Councillor laughed merrily and said: "Ah well, they mightn't want it, but they'll soon get used to it."

But that would remain to be seen !

The Weaverham Electric Company was formed in 1910 and a few of the village houses were wired for electricity and this supply carried on until the company went into liquidation in 1920, when it was taken over by the Northwich Electric Company. However, much of the village still had no electric supply up to the 1930s and I remember well many farms and cottages, particularly those on the outskirts of the village, using oil lamps for their lighting. Supplies of oil could be bought from Forster's Garage, or from travelling salesmen, such as Ernie Sage, who came round the village in his van on Saturday afternoons, stopping at various vantage points from where the villagers could go and purchase domestic utensils, oil and other requirements. One of his stopping places was on a little grass triangle where Grange Lane, Forest Street and West Road converged. There was very little traffic in those days and I clearly remember going to his van for paraffin for the oil lamps and shippon lamps for Nook Farm where electricity was supplied in the early 1930s.

In the days of early village lighting, previously mentioned, there had been about half a dozen lamps erected at the most important places. John Whitley, who was also Sexton of Weaverham Church, was the lamplighter. In fact, he was the last man to hold this position in the village. He held the job for many years, maintaining and lighting the lamps each evening. Very often, he was plagued by young lads who followed him round blowing the lights out and generally annoying him. But the old lamp-lighter was endowed with much patience and carried on doing his duty steadfastly, thus keeping the village reasonably lit at its key points. Through winter snows and blustery nights, and winters were much more severe in those days, "Old Snirt", as he was nicknamed by the village lads, trudged the streets with his lamps and ladder. He kept his lamps and oil in the stables of Holly Hurst, in Church Street. This form of lighting was abandoned as the old lamp-lighter became too frail for the job, soon after the first decade of this century, and who was to know that most of those mischievous lads who had taunted the old lamp-lighter would, before another decade was over, be fighting for their country on the fields of Flanders ? It was on those battlefields that the cream of our village lads died as one old Russet recalled. Tom Gatley, who recalled blowing the lamps out on many occasions, was one of the first in France, with the Royal Artillery. Once more, the village was in darkness, "Old Snirt" and his lamps were just a memory, and the villagers were once more relying on the "Man in the Moon" for his light.

The old tree I have just mentioned, which became known as The Village Tree, was a Lime tree and was planted at the "Gateway" to the village on a grassy triangle, across the road from the Gate Inn, at the junction of High Street with West Road and Sandy Lane.

The planting of the sapling, in the Autumn of 1852, was witnessed by an ancestor of mine, Samuel Moss, who at that time as a boy of 12, lived in Gorstage with his parents. The landlord of the Gate Inn, known now for the last many years as the Hanging Gate, was James Wing, and at the village smithy, close by, lived Thomas Forster, who, with his family, had been blacksmiths since 1813. The smithy stood at the corner of West Road and Station Road.

As the tree grew, a surround of wooden seats was placed around its base and it became a popular rendezvous for young sweethearts. Starting its life when Queen Victoria had been on the throne just fifty years, it lived through the reigns of King Edward VII, George V, George VI, and well into the reign of Queen Elizabeth II. When the planting took place, the road lived up to its name "Sandy Lane" and its surface, consisting mainly of sand, became deeply rutted by the wheels of coaches and other horse-drawn vehicles. This was clearly remembered by Tom McCann, an Irish workman who lived and worked for my grandfather at Nook Farm, and for the previous tenants during the latter part of the 19th Century, and whose story I have already told.

What changes the old tree must have witnessed during its years of life. The main one was the transition from horse-drawn vehicle to the motor car. The old smithy became less in demand, and the Forster family built the first motor repair garage in Weaverham, with Arnold Forster becoming one of the village's first car owners. By this time, the surface of the road had been greatly improved becoming by now macadamed, but for some time to come motorcars and horse drawn vehicles were to share the village roads.

Perhaps the most frightening night of the old tree's life was during the Second World War, when a parachute mine landed at Nook Farm, destroying the farm, and blowing debris to within yards of the Gate Inn and village tree. Incendiary bombs were also dropped and fell within yards of the inn, exploding in the road near to the old tree.

As the years passed, the traffic increased to an almost unbearable degree, making it unsafe to cross the roads to the seats, particularly since the traffic could pass in any direction either side of the tree. It was not until later that a 'keep left' system was introduced, and so the seats were removed, with the island around the tree becoming ever smaller. Very few travellers had time to admire the "Village Tree" as they hurried past in their cars. To many it was just another obstacle.

The tree belonged to another age, when village life was much slower and it was not until the construction of the Weaverham by-pass that a degree of tranquillity was restored around it.

The little green, on which the tree was planted and on which it stood until 1997, when it was sadly felled, but happily now replaced by another sapling, belonged to Greenall Whitley, the brewers, who owned the Gate Inn, and it was only the timely intervention of the licensee of the time, Fred Moseley, which saved the tree from destruction some years ago when some misguided Local Government official decided to have it felled. Let us hope this new tree will grow in stature and survive for many years.

Although the population had risen from 2,714, to about 4,000, Weaverham remained a rural community, a relatively unspoilt village and a very nice place to live.

Residents of the old village and Owley Wood were learning to live happily together; they united in worship at church and chapel, compared babies at the Welfare Clinic held fortnightly at the Church House, and joined in social activities, whist drives, concerts and dances. They shared one football team and one cricket team, and only between the two Scout Troops, 1st Weaverham and 1st Owley Wood, was there any rivalry.

The First Weaverham Boy Scouts were formed in 1926/27 by Colonel Heald, Mr A.C. Gregg, and Nant Chetwynd. The headquarters were in the stables of the old Ring o' Bells, just outside the gates of St. Mary's Church, but soon afterwards a new Scout Hall was built in Church Street, at the expense of Mr A.C. Gregg, who was the great great great-grandson of the founder of Styal (Quarry Bank) Mill, and on land donated by Lord Barrymore. Mr Gregg farmed at Ash House, in Acton Bridge, where he had a large fruit farm, and was a great benefactor to the young people of the village. Bill Elson's Uncle Jim was a Cubmaster, along with Bill Fletcher, and he remembers going to camps which were held in Gregg's Orchard, on a flat piece of ground by the stream. This stream formed the boundary between Crowton and Acton, and having been joined by Crowton brook, which provided the water for Crowton Mill, it was quite wide here and fairly deep and only a few of the older scouts could leap across it, and only after a long run up. They used to tease "Pop" Ryan into chasing them and would escape by jumping across the stream. It was only about half a mile before it flowed into the River Weaver and at that time was a well known trout stream, and fishermen used to come from a distance to fish it. Bill also remembers going to a camp in the Isle of Man, which was held in conjunction with a Territorial Army Camp. Colonel Heald, having served in the Great War, was a Territorial Officer, and idolised by his Scout Troop, and as the Senior Scouts became of age they too joined the Territorials, so that when war was declared they, along with the Colonel, were amongst the first to go.

Bob Roberts was at this camp with the scouts and during a walk in the mountains Bob began to run down a hill and overan himself and to stop he ran into a tree with his arms outstretched. This saved him careering downhill, but he broke both wrists, although it did not stop him becoming a successful and much-admired professional boxer in later years. This camp would have been held in about 1936. Also in the early Thirties there was much excitement in the village when it became known that a scene for the film "Bulldog Drummond" was to be "shot" locally. Crowds gathered by the stone bridge, over the old arm of the river, near to Acton Swing Bridge, but unfortunately the first night's "shoot" was cancelled due to heavy rain. However, the following night was fine and the crowds gathered again to watch the excitement. A large saloon came down the road towards the bridge, with a dummy at the wheel and a stunt man driving from a position on the running board on the side of the car, hidden from the camera. The car sped down the road, careered off the railings leading up to the bridge, shot over the bridge and into the new river, taking most of the railings with it. Then there was the "rescue" when an actor was pulled from the water and carried into the Leigh Arms.

Also in the mid Thirties, Bill was in the garden at The Woodlands, in Station Road, one Saturday morning, when he heard an unusual noise, and rushing to the garden hedge and looking out, he saw an aeroplane, a biplane, circling around. This descended and landed in the field behind the Hanging Gate; there were no power lines or pylons in those days. The pilot was John Cobham, and he flew all that Saturday, trip after trip, until dusk giving flights at 2/6d a time to passengers, most of whom had not seen an aeroplane before. Incidentally, the windmill which stood in Station Road was not demolished until about 1910 when The Woodlands was immediately erected, exactly where it had stood.

I recall sitting in the classroom at Forest Street, on the afternoon of January 15th 1937, when suddenly the peace was disturbed by the sound of low flying aircraft. The weather was appalling and heavy drizzle had ruled out any reasonable visibility. The planes seemed to be circling the village for some time. When I got home from school, I found out that one of the planes had crashed within yards of the spot where nearly 20 years earlier Freddie Stubbs had landed in the holly bush.

This time the plane was an Avro Anson, flying with two others from Woodford to Speke. The bad weather had become even worse than expected, and the aircraft had become completely lost. The pilot of this one, K6286, decided to look for a large flat field in which to land, and getting away from the built-up area came down, from the west, at Hefferston. Suddenly, he saw power lines ahead and managed to lift the nose up to climb over the top of them, missing them by a few feet, but this led to him overshooting his intended touchdown point and his speed took him through the hedge of the next field, and, catching his right wing on an old oak tree, the plane spun around and came to rest in the roadside hedge of Grange Lane, within a few yards of the holly bush which had cushioned Freddie's fall.

The pilot was unhurt but shaken and he was able to find his way to the hall from where he was able to telephone for help. Eventually, the RAF sent a contingent to guard the crashed plane, until it could be dismantled and taken away. Talk was that the Anson was a new type of bomber, but it was, in fact, used mainly as a reconnaissance and training plane during the Second World War. I well remember sitting in the plane with my grandfather and the village policeman, Bobby Savage, at the controls. It was something I will never forget, especially the very strong smell of dope with which the fabric had been heavily treated.

4

A VILLAGE AT WAR

IN this second half of the 1930s, the continued Nazi aggression in Europe made it increasingly likely that War would eventually break out, and it was in early Spring 1938 when the Corporation of Warrington who, as well as owning the Sanatorium, also owned quite a lot of land around the Grange, were approached by the Ministry of Defence to supply a patch of land to accommodate an Emergency Red Cross Hospital. As it was a matter of utmost urgency, it was agreed to use part of a field rented by my grandfather. This was fenced off and very soon work started on building six hutments, to hold a total of 80 patients, who could be either wounded servicemen, or civilian casualties, from air raids.

A London firm from Slough came to build the hospital, with the help of a lot of local labour. Such was the urgency, that medical supplies, such as stretchers, crutches, trolleys and spinal carriages, were among the many accessories delivered before the building was completed. As children, we played on the site, watching the workmen and even taking it in turns to ride in the spinal carriages. Little did I realise that I was to be first casualty to need one in that hospital.

The place opened, provisionally, in early 1939, and volunteer Red Cross nurses came to work in it. Women and girls from all walks of life came to offer their services. The Emergency Hospital was to be run in liaison with the Sanatorium and Big House, under one Matron. As the long hot summer of 1940 came to a close, many of the older Weaverham residents were becoming very apprehensive. They wondered why the Emergency Hospital had been built so quickly on the outskirts of the village. Was the Government expecting so many casualties from air raids ?

The collapse of France, and the evacuation from Dunkirk, had taken place and still the new hospital remained empty. The village was being denuded of men; hundreds had rushed to join the Forces as war was declared.

Leaflets about Home Defence started to land on the nation's doormats in the Summer of 1939. Blackout instructions were sent out in July 1939, and some people began to dig air-raid shelters. A large village shelter was built in Forest Street, about the position of the present-day entrance into Fieldway. The school had its own shelter, where the school car park is now.

There was only one school, Forest Street, and there was another large village shelter at the entrance to the Cricket Field. Roads began to be more dangerous because of dimmed car lights, due to blackout restrictions; on narrow roads a top speed of 15 mph was recommended and on main roads 30 mph. The general public was beginning to get alarmed about the possibility of gas attacks, and gas masks had to be carried everywhere.

On the 14th May, 1940, the Secretary of State for War, Sir Anthony Eden, broadcast a call for volunteers to be known as the Local Defence Volunteers, the LDV, cruelly pilloried by the youngsters as Look, Duck and Vanish. Men between the ages of 17 and 65, of reasonable fitness, were wanted. The response throughout the country was overwhelming and within 24 hours over a quarter of a million men had volunteered, including many First World War veterans. Their main task was to look out for parachutists.

From May 1940, the public was beginning to realise that there was a possibility of invasion. In July 1940, Winston Churchill suggested that the LDV should in future be known as the "Home Guard" and by the beginning of August, the War Office had grouped the new force into battalions and zones. Weaverham became "D" Company, the 13th Battalion, the Cheshire Regiment.

During the winter of 1940, Home Guards were issued with serge Army -issue battle dress and American Springfield .300 rifles. These had been packed in grease for years and had to be soaked in boiling water for hours before they could be made ready for use. The Browning Automatic machine gun was also issued and the instruction book had to be carefully studied for the mechanism to be understood, and the gun stripped down and reassembled over and over again.

The Weaverham Home Guard trained at the Scout Hall, in Church Street, and Harry Hargreaves had the armoury behind his shop, in Esthers Lane, and the rifles were stored there.

Corporal Jack Barker, the head gardener at the Grange, and Lance Corporal Bill Cooper, who worked on George Darlington's farm in the village, were in charge of the Browning Automatic. Training sessions in the Scout Hall and in local woods and fields took place regularly, much to the amusement of schoolchildren who could not take it seriously.

The local Home Guard guarded the Dutton Arches and had a lookout post on top of Weaverham Church Tower. I have to say that the view from the top of the Church Tower at blossom time was breathtaking. You could hardly see a home for fruit trees; it really was a village in an orchard. Sadly, these orchards have all gone.

The swing bridge at Acton was also guarded, with sleeping accommodation in the outbuildings of the Leigh Arms for those off duty.

The Weaverham Platoon Sergeant was Tommy Johnson, and the Platoon Commander First Lt. Percy Hearn, and later Captain Bill Morris. For men not able to serve in the Home Guard, there were other duties which many men undertook, such as Air Raid wardens, and the Auxiliary Fire Service. An emergency First Aid centre had been set up, and equipped, at Dr. Shaw's stables, at Ivy House, and each night it was manned by local volunteers who were trained by St. John Ambulance men and women. Mrs. Armitage, from The Woodlands, Station Road, was in charge, and she paid out of her own pocket to have a large dish of hot pot made at Alf Woodward's Inglenook Cafe. Mrs. Woodward prepared this meal which was collected each night by one of the staff at the centre, but during the summer months, sandwiches and salads were available. Geoff Burgess was in charge for the first period, assisted by Eddie and Jack Nagle, Mary Nagle, Arthur and Jack England and their wives. They had, at their disposal, several private cars and a van, to act as an ambulance should the need arise.

There were some embarrassing moments for the Home Guard, such as when Jack Gleave was cycling to Dutton to see his girlfriend when an air raid started and he was pulled up and arrested by the Home Guard's Syd Woodward, who knew him well enough, and detained until proof of his identify could be established. Perhaps he had been arrested for his own good because, being out on such a night, was foolhardy, to say the least, as the shrapnel from exploding anti-aircraft shells was lethal. He recalled hearing the whistling of the falling bombs aimed at the arches and thinking they had his number on them.

Incidentally, standing by the farm gate at Church Farm one night about midnight, my father and Jack Gleave heard the dull thud of exploding bombs.

Jack said: "Did you hear that, they're bombing Sheffield tonight?" Sure enough, the following day, it was reported in the newspapers that Sheffield had received a number of bombs.

I wonder if this was the same night that Arthur Short told me about when he went rabbiting at Dutton, with Reg Brown. The rabbits were feeding on some turnips in a field there and their warrens were in some gorse bushes at the top of a hill. All the nets were stretched out when Reg said: "Hush, that's Gerry coming," and sure enough the plane was the forerunner of a wave of bombers attacking the Runcorn and Liverpool area. Suddenly, all hell was let loose, the gorse bushes were set alight by incendiaries and a stick of five or six bombs fell across the area. The blast of the nearest, which fell about 100 yards away and blew Arthur and Reg to the ground where they lay for some time; the nets were burned and the rabbits with them.

And that same night, George Preece, going to work in his car to Rocksavage, was surprised, as he was passing through Dutton Hollows, by the sudden appearance of a German aircraft which made three passes over the area dropping bombs each time. George drove his car into a barn and fled into the open countryside for safety. When the raid was over and he turned for his car, he was warned: "Don't go near the barn, there is an unexploded bomb."

However, George ignored the warning and removed his car, but the next morning, as he passed the same spot, he was shocked to find the barn had disappeared, blown to smithereens by the bomb which had a delayed action fuse.

On another night, Arthur Short was on Home Guard duty with Bill Clark, on the Church Tower, at Weaverham. They were working a two on/two off system. However, when it came time to be relieved, there was no sound from below so Arthur said: "Just give a ring on the bell." Pulling a bell rope, the huge bell started to swing and a loud peal sounded out. Of course, church bells were to be the warning of enemy paratroops. The more Arthur hung on to the bell to stop it swinging, the more it rang, bringing out the vicar in his night attire and his houskeeper. Many more people also got out of bed with fears of being surrounded by German troops.

Shortly after this, there was suddenly an influx of evacuees as the target cities were emptied of children, those coming to Weaverham were from the Liverpool area, which was being devastated by bombing. Within a year, as the Blitz lessened, three quarters returned home, but others stayed for years.

Mrs. Tarbuck recalls returning home from holiday with her four-year - old son and recalls travelling on a train packed with soldiers.

"It was very upsetting, each time we stopped at a station on the Lancaster, Preston, Wigan and Warrington line, there were sad scenes of families seeing men off to war. When we got home I was told there was an evacuee to be taken in, and he was Jack Rooney, aged six or seven, from Liverpool."

The little boy stayed for two years and went to Forest Street School and was visited by his mum at weekends, and Mrs Tarbuck was thanked by a certificate signed by the Queen.

The war progressed quietly and peacefully enough for us in the village until my own life was to be devastated. My most horrific memory of the Second World War takes me back over half a century to November 28th, 1940, when I was just 14-years-old and living at Nook Farm with my grandparents, George and Edith Moss.

I had lived at Nook Farm with my grandparents for most of my early life, having gone to live there when my sister Eileen was born, to ease the burden for my mother, and, as happened very often in Cheshire farms, my grandmother was loath to let me return home. Therefore, I remained while my sisters, Eileen and Doris, and my brother, Ken, were brought up first in Nook Cottage and then at Hefferston Grange Farm, and so although I visited my mother and father regularly, I was at Nook Farm with my grandparents that fateful night.

Nook Farm, with its lovely old ivy-clad farmhouse, stood at the junction of West Road with Grange Lane, which came to be known as "Moss's Corner." The farm was thought by many to have the prettiest farmhouse and buildings in the village, with its lovely garden and apple and pear orchard, especially at blossom time in the spring. It was just over a year since the outbreak of the war and already there had been about 40 air raids on Merseyside. Apart from the anti-aircraft guns, there seemed to be no other opposition as, during the long summer evenings just past, it was possible to follow the air raids on Runcorn, by watching the little balls of black smoke with their red centres from the exploding anti-aircraft shells.

This day, Thursday, 28th November, had been dismal, becoming quite foggy by early evening. In the nearby wood, owls were hooting ominously as if they had a premonition of what the night had in store

Before 8 o'clock the fog seemed to be clearing a little, and searchlights began sweeping across the night sky. Soon afterwards we could hear distant gunfire and it was not long before the familiar drone of German aircraft could be heard, although no warning sirens had sounded. It was not until some time afterwards that we learned that due to the widespread fog across the country, the bombers had flown around the coast to attack Liverpool from the Irish Sea, thus taking the early warning system by surprise.

It was soon evident, by the number of aircraft overhead and the intense barrage of anti-aircraft fire, that this raid was going to be heavier than anything we had experienced before. The dull thud of bombs exploding not too far away was becoming alarming and frightening. My grandfather had retired to bed early, to prepare for an early start on the milking the next morning, and we had decided to stay by the warm kitchen fire, rather than go to the cold air-raid shelter, as we had done on most previous occasions. This air-raid shelter we had built in the orchard, well away from the house and farm buildings, but because of the cold, and I also had my homework to do, we stayed in the kitchen with the farm fire burning in the grate.

The noise was increasing, almost beyond endurance, and when an old cat, which had been sharing the hearth with us, went to the door to be let out, I seized the opportunity to have a look outside.

I followed the cat across the cobbled farmyard as she ran through a passageway between the buildings and scampered off across the fields. We never saw her again. Over towards Overton Hills, the orange glow of fires in Liverpool could be clearly seen, and clusters of flares suspended by parachutes hung like huge chandeliers in the sky, lighting up everywhere like day. It was a very frightening sight.

Suddenly, a large 500lbs, bomb exploded a few fields away and the blast shattered the glass in a garden frame leaning against the farmhouse. Then, as if sown by some giant hand, shoals of incendiary bombs exploded with a brilliant blue flash along the fields, at the side of the railway, which must by now have been clearly visible to the bombers above. I was worried about the danger by fire to the two large haystacks standing in the stackyard. I ran back into the house and as I got inside my grandfather was coming downstairs to join us. Once again, we settled down around the hearth. Then, suddenly, there was a blinding flash of light, a mighty rumble, and the old house shook and disintegrated around us.

Only the huge oak beams saved us from being crushed to death as the house fell upon us, filling the air with dust and the acrid fumes of the soot from the chimney; soot which we were to taste for weeks because of the amount we must have swallowed. I remember hearing no clear explosion, just a prolonged deep roar. I was hurled from my chair and ended up under a pile of debris. My grandfather remained calm and took charge of the situation. Although he was deeply shocked, he had no actual injuries. Unfortunately, I had been in a position with only the window between myself and the terrible blast and, consequently, I was dreadfully injured by the flying glass.

There were six of us in the farmhouse at the time, my grandparents, two aunts, an uncle, and myself, and also a little fox terrier Pip who had been so frightened by the noise of the earlier part of the raid that he had been almost hysterical. My uncle, who had been sitting next to me, suffered severe head and face injuries on his right side, while I received serious injuries to my spine, head, face, left eye and left arm.

I could not speak to tell anyone where I was, but after a careful search in the darkness, my grandfather found me, removed the rubble from around me, took me outside, and laid me down in the rubble-strewn garden. It was some time before I found my voice; my left arm would not move, and with my right hand I felt the terrible damage to the left side of my face. I found myself blind in my left eye and with very little vision in my right, and I could feel the blood running down my back.

Not knowing the extent of my injuries, my grandfather had laid me down on some coats he had brought from the wreckage and covered me with others. My grandmother, even though she was in a very bad state of shock, and with cuts to her face and arms and a nasty eye injury, prayed that we might all see daylight.

Still the planes droned overhead. There was no let-up in the gunfire and the shrapnel was falling like hail. Cyril Catley, the village chemist, and Chief Air Raid Warden, happened to be patrolling on foot in West Road, and although he was blown off his feet and through the hedge at Tilston Hayes, the home of Mrs Burton, he managed to get to that house and telephone for help. He had no trouble getting into the house to telephone as the front door had been blown off its hinges. It seemed like ages as we waited in the intense cold, bleeding profusely from our injuries, for help to arrive. Soon more wardens arrived, followed by a couple of cars, converted into makeshift ambulances, to take us to the stables at Ivy House, Dr. Shaw's house, where there was a First Aid Post with some St. John Ambulance men on duty. They were local villagers, among them Walter Glenister, Geoff Burgess, and Jack Nagle, who had manned the

Post since its foundation at the beginning of the war. However, my grandmother and I had serious eye injuries and were taken to Hartford Hill in Darwin Street, where a doctor was in attendance. We ended up, after a nightmare ride through the air raid, back at Hefferston Grange Red Cross Hospital.

I do not remember much of the journeys between the First Aid Posts and then eventually to the newly-built Red Cross Hospital, but I do remember the feeling of relief to be back in a warm building where we could be attended to by the wonderful nursing staff, which included many local Red Cross volunteer nurses.

Meanwhile, back at the farm, villagers were risking their own lives releasing the cattle that had been trapped in the farm buildings. The shippons by now had no roof and Cattle Warden, Arthur Dean, a local farmer, assisted by other villagers, released those cattle which were in distress and made the others as comfortable as possible until morning came. Although all the cattle survived, they were badly affected by the experience. A collie dog and a pet rabbit survived in a building next to the house.

I was told later that a parachute mine had dropped in the gateway to the farmyard, about 20 yards from the house, where it exploded immediately on contact with the ground. These parachute mines, or land mines, as they were also called, were a comparatively new weapon, designed to cause maximum blast damage and to break morale. They consisted of an aluminium container containing 1,000 lbs. of high explosive, suspended from a 27-feet diameter parachute, of artificial silk.

Windows were broken over a wide area of the village and nearby houses damaged. The gate hinges from the farmyard gate were blown nearly half a mile to the Gate Inn, and even today, fragments of the aluminium container can be found in the fields, hundreds of yards from the spot where the explosion took place.

Photographs of the damage were taken the next day by Ernie Lamb, who worked at the farm. I am lucky to have these photographs because at that time it was an offence to take photographs of bomb damaged buildings for fear of giving comfort to the enemy, should they fall into their hands.

Ernie gave me the photographs after the war and told me had also had a very narrow escape during the raid. He had been sitting on the roadside seat, opposite the farm, and as the ferocity of the blitz increased he decided to walk his girlfriend home, to Hefferston Grange, where she lived. It was extremely foolhardy to be out as shrapnel from exploding anti-aircraft shells was falling like hail, and it could kill. He then hurried back past the farm to Mary Brown's chip shop, at the bottom of Forest Street. The shop was a popular eating place and it was business as usual, air raid or not.

As Ernie arrived, an enormous explosion shook the shop and broke windows everywhere. Fear gripped the whole village as people realised something dreadful had happened. The seat on which Ernie and his girlfriend had been sitting was twisted and broken beyond recognition and had been blown over the hedge. The next morning, young Bill Walsh, arriving for work at Nook Farm, was met at the crossroads by the village bobby, Constable Savage, and was told the terrible news. As dawn came, he was shocked to see the devastation caused by the blast. Telephone lines were down, water mains were broken, and there was a crater filled with water. As the War progressed it was not long before Billy Walsh (who sadly has recently died) joined the RAF, and he was to go on many bombing raids over Germany as an air gunner in Wellington Bombers.

After extensive surgery, followed by skilled and dedicated nursing at the Emergency Hospital, I was restored to a reasonable level of fitness, even though I was never ever again to be 100% fit, nor was my eyesight ever to be as good as it should have been.

I was in hospital for weeks and lost a lot of time off school, which I had to make up for by staying on for an extra year. In the weeks of convalescing, I learned to play the accordion and then the piano accordion, all of which was to give me a great deal of pleasure in years to come, as well as a second career as a professional musician.

My first engagements were at the new American Army Camp, at Delamere Park. Just before the war, the Wilbrahams had built for themselves a new house, Delamere Manor, and the old hall, which stood at the far corner of a great park, was demolished. This park was taken over by the Ministry of Defence and a huge American Army Camp built on it, where they held regular dances at which myself and friends used to play. We also played throughout the rest of the war at the regular Saturday night dances at the Church House, and at other venues, arranged by local groups, to provide comfort funds for our troops abroad.

The presence of this camp and others in the district, such as the ones at Marbury Park and Marton Sands (soldiers were also billeted at Oakmere Hall and Weaverham Grange) brought an upheaval in the quiet village while they trained for the invasion of Europe. Children used to run behind the trucks loaded with troops as they passed through the village and would shout, "Any gum, chum?".

But as D-Day drew near, all these troops disappeared overnight and quiet again descended on the village and it continued on its quiet way until the war drew to a close. On the 8th May, 1945, church bells rang out and the village High Street was thronged with people as they danced and laughed in the afternoon sunshine. There was joyous relief on the faces of all who filled the village centre as VE was declared.

On that night, local shopkeeper's daughter, Rosie Hornby, and her husband Ernie Wilkinson, set up a stage outside their home, and with accordion and drums, played all the old songs until well into the night. People were reluctant to go home, so great was their joy and, even when the last strains of music had died away, many still walked about, their happiness overflowing. But, as well as joy, there was grief and sorrow for those whose lives would never be the same after losing loved ones and having seen their hopes and aspirations come to nought.

But, despite my own personal trauma, I look back on those years with nostalgia, and I am glad I lived through them. I count these years amongst the happiest of my life and all my friends of my generation when we recall these years, while passing the time of day, are of the same mind. People were so kind to one another. Those who had gave gladly to those who had not, every man was brother to his neighbour, and there was comfort and happiness in his neighbour's presence. The village was one family, no-one would let harm befall another, and how sad that now we sometimes walk in fear. For schoolchildren those years were especially wonderful. Everywhere there was freedom to roam and play and, with there being so few menfolk at home, there were so many opportunities to earn pocket money, working on the farms, setting potatoes, or at harvest times, or even picking fruit at Mr Gregg's.

Bill also reminds me that the old football field was no longer in use. Those who had graced its turf, like Albert Johnson, who went on to play for Everton, and his mates of the old Weaverham team, had all gone to war, but the goalposts were left standing; this was a luxury as usually two coats placed on the ground had to suffice. Here, all the lads from the village would gather to choose sides and then play all day. The cricket field was also abandoned for the duration and, only occasionally, would they would play football on it and then be chased off by Mr Vaughan.

There were no bailiffs on the Weaver, so you could fish for nothing, and at Pettypool, Lord Delamere's old keeper, Mr Thayers, would let you have a boat for half a crown and you could fish then, all day and night. Nowhere else was there a gamekeeper, and fields and woods, which had been seriously out of bounds, were now an adventure land for exploring and birdnesting, like Cunningham's Wood, at Forest Hill, while Captain Cunningham was away in the Army. After school, you could cycle up to Horners Mill and catch eels, or tickle trout, in the stream below the wheel, or, in the Mill Pool, catch big trout, with a rod and line and a worm. How these idyllic moments from times long ago so endure.

Another wartime story, recalled and written out for me by my old friend Bill Elson, reads as follows:

"During the War most of the men of working age except those on work of National Importance were away in the Armed Forces. Consequently, there was a shortage of labour on local farms, particularly at harvest times.

I was at the Grammar School and on occasions the whole of the Fourth and Fifth forms were sent out in term time to help gather in the potato crop. I remember several times going with the rest of the form to Walker's Farm, at Gorstage, to harvest potatoes, and to Barlow's at Dane Bank. At Christmas time, however, we were not required on the farms, but there was work at the Post Office, either sorting or delivering, to cope with the greatly increased seasonal mail. But this work was only available to those pupils who had reached the Sixth form. At Christmas 1945, I therefore applied for the job at the Post Office and was duly sent for to deliver mail from Weaverham Sub Post Office. The Post Office was in the High Street and Mrs Hughes was the Postmistress. The Sorting Office was in Chapel Street, or more commonly known as Chapel Wynt. This Sorting Office still stands 50 years later, but, of course, is used for other purposes.

The mail for the district was brought out from Northwich Main Office, every morning at 6.00 a.m., and we sorted the mail into appropriate bundles before leaving on our rounds. As well as myself and another schoolfriend, there were two regular postmen, Ezra and Jack Clarke, bachelor brothers who lived in a cottage in High Street. Each of us had a regulation Post Office fixed-wheel bicycle. These were backpedalling, with no brakes and no freewheel, and to stop, one had to stand up and press hard on the back of the pedal to lock the back wheel. Incidentally, there was an extra payment per week for cleaning and maintaining the bicycle, but I cannot remember how much this was.

My deliveries began with Forest Street and then down West Road, following on into Station Road. The route continued on the left over the station bridge into Milton Rough, Sandfield Terrace, and the old water mill at Milton. From the mill there was a footpath over the mill stream and across the fields to Onston. At this time, the path was wide and firm and was never ploughed over and was suitable for cycling and pushing a pram, and there was a gate at either end, not a stile. From Onston, the road continued to Gandy's Mill and on to Bent Lane, Crowton, and thence into Marsh Lane, where the last delivery was at Sandhole Farm, an old sandstone built farm on the hillside. The Marsh had been the stage for the Cheshire Hunt Point to Point races, and was to have been its permanent home, but because of the War it was abandoned and never reinstated, but at this time the jumps were clearly visible in the hedgerows and were well maintained.

After Sandhole Farm, one cycled back into Crowton Village, delivering the road through the village as far as its junction with Norley Lane, and then I returned through the village and turned into Ainsworth Lane, carrying on along this road as far as Peck's Brow, a group of cottages on the brow of the hill overlooking Pickerings o' the Boat, and then down into Pickerings. Pickerings o' the Boat was in fact named after the family who had lived there, Colonel Pickering being one of Cromwell's most able soldiers. At Pickerings, one crossed over a stream by means of a substantial wooden bridge, to the side of the river. At this point, there was a post on top of which was an iron cradle in which was suspended a large brass bell which was rung by pulling a rope attached to it, causing it to swing freely in its cradle. On the far side of the river were some cottages, occupied by Waterways employees.

They were originally lock-keepers' cottages, built there at the time a lock stood on the river at this point. If I had mail for the far side of the river, I would ring the bell and a man would emerge from one of the cottages and, by means of a windlass, would wind a bridge across and walk over to take the mail from me.

From Pickerings, the road continued to and through Oakhill Farm, to the last deliveries on the route, which were Railway Cottages, two cottages near the foot of the Viaduct. From here one cycled through Acton Cliffe and back to Weaverham Post Office with mail which had been collected en route. The Postman had to carry with him stamps and small change, since there were no Post Offices on this route and the Postman was obliged to sell stamps to, and accept letters for posting from anyone who asked, and, of course, there were a number of post boxes to be opened en route. The last time I did this round was in November 1945. The regular Postman, Harry Collier, was now reestablished on the round now that the War was over and I was back at school. However, Mr Collier was standard bearer for the British Legion and had been chosen to attend the ceremony at the Cenotaph and unless he could get someone to do his round for the few days he would need to be away he would not be able to go. Since he knew that I knew the route and would be acceptable to the Post Office, he asked me if I would cover for him and I was happy to do so. Everything was as I had previously described it. The bell was still on its post and the bridge was duly wound across the river when I rang it. Unfortunately, the bridge was washed away in the great flood of 1946 and never replaced, but for some time afterwards while the cottages still housed Waterways employees, a rowing boat was provided for the same purpose. When I recently cycled along the river to Pickerings some fifty years later, the post is still in position with the cradle on top, but sadly there is no bell."

The weeks following the end of the war were in some ways unsettling. I suppose we were all unwinding. There was such relief that it was all over and we had survived, but there was sadness too at the thought of the changes which were overcoming the old village, changes with which I would have to come to terms and which I might not like. My thoughts were turning not only to what the future may hold in store for me, and the direction my own life might take, but I constantly reflected on the appearance of the old village and the way of life of its people, as if to get it forever etched in my mind. I reflected on the stories told to me by my grandfather and it was a shock to realise that through his eyes, and his stories, and the stories of others, I could look back over 150 years into the lives of all these people, men and women, honest workers at their toil, who had graced this ancient village and trod its quiet ways and whose stories here are told.

It was only by consulting the Censuses of former years (extracts of which follow) could I convince myself of the long years encompassed by Grandfather's memory.

On 3rd November, 1846, John Moss, a widower and labourer, married Mary Rowe, a spinster and servant. Both were resident in Cuddington at the time of the marriage. The father of John Moss was Josiah Moss, from Handforth Brook Farm, and the father of Mary Rowe was James Rowe, of Cuddington. Both James and Josiah were farmers.

Weaverham Census Records

Census 1841	Gorstage	Born
Josiah Moss (Farmer)	60 years Head	
Sarah Moss	60 years Wife	
John Moss	20 years Son	
Sarah Moss	15 years Daughter	
Maria Moss	15 Years Daughter	
Thomas Clark	15 years Male servant	
William Green	10 years Male servant	
Samuel Hornby (Farmer)	55 years Head Widower	
Mary Hornby	20 years Daughter	
Thomas Hornby	15 years Son	
John Hornby	10 years Son	
Elizabeth Harrison	35 years Female Servant	
Peter Hodkinson	20 years Male Servant	
* Thomas Forster (Blacksmith)	50 years Head	Burtonwood
Ann Forster	45 years Wife	Lowton, Lancs
John Forster}	20 years Son	Weaverham
William Forster} twins	20 years Son	Weaverham
Abraham Forster	15 years Son	Weaverham
Henry Forster	12 years Son	Weaverham
George Pope (Blacksmith)	25 years Boarder	Weaverham
Martha Mainwaring (Female Servant)	15 years	Weaverham

* Thomas would be 22 years old when he came to Weaverham). Ann would have been 17 years.

Census 1851		
Thomas Forster (Blacksmith)	60 years Head	Burtonwood
Ann Forster	55 years Wife	Lowton, Lancs
Henry Forster (Blacksmith)	21 years Son	Weaverham
Harriet Forster (Scholar)	8 years Grand-daughter	Weaverham
John Forster (Blacksmith)	30 years Head	Burtonwood
Sarah Forster	40 years Wife	Moulton
Adam Forster (Scholar)	5 years Son	Weaverham
William Forster (Carter)	33 years Head	Weaverham
Sarah Forster	28 years Wife	Ashton
Thomas Forster (Scholar)	10 years Son	Weaverham
Mary Forster (Scholar)	8 years Daughter	Weaverham
David Forster (Scholar)	6 years Son	Weaverham
Betsy	Baby Daughter	Weaverham

Census 1861	Grange Hall	
Robert Heath (Landowner and Farmer)	46 years Head Unmarried	Middlesex
Mary Lilley Heath	19 years Niece Unmarried	Liverpool
Fanny Emma Heath	15 years Niece Unmarried	Liverpool
Mary Tunnifcliffe	59 years Housekeeper	Eccleshall

Census 1871	Nook Farm	
John Gerrard (Farmer)	63 years Head	Kingsley
Fanny Gerrard	61 years Wife	Preston Brook
William Gerrard	20 years Son	Weaverham
Elizabeth Gerrard	29 years Daughter	Weaverham

Census 1881	Gorstage	
John Gleave (Farmer)	46 years Head	Weaverham
Eliza Gleave	46 years Wife	Crowton

Elizabeth	21 years Daughter	Crowton
Emma	20 years Daughter	Crowton
Alice	18 years Daughter	Crowton
Tom (Scholar)	11 years Son	Crowton
Henry (Scholar)	8 years Son	Crowton
Joseph	3 years Son	Crowton
Annie	1 year Daughter	Crowton
Daniel Woodward (Bricklayer)	29 years Head	Weaverham
Elizabeth	25 years Wife	Warrington
Thomas	Son	Crowton
Samuel	7 months Son	Weaverham
George Woodward (Bricklayer's labourer)	33 years Boarder	Weaverham

Census 1881	Sandiway Bank	
John Bolton Littledale (Retired Broker)	58 years Head	Liverpool
Mary Bolton Littledale	35 years Wife	Liverpool
Minitte M. Bolton Littledale (Scholar)	14 years Daughter	Weaverham
Edith M.Bolton Littledale (Scholar)	10 years Daughter	Weaverham
May Bolton Littledale (Scholar)	5 years Daughter	Weaverham
Rosa Woodyat	14 years Visitor	
Mary Hobson (Governess)	38 years Unmarried	Birmingham Heath
Mary Ann Wilson (Lady's Maid)	26 years Unmarried	Crook, Westmoreland
Ann Binzley	31 years Unmarried (Cook)	York
Alice Hignett (Kitchen maid/servant)	22 years Unmarried	Weaverham
Mary Chatterton (Housemaid)	22 years Unmarried	Lower Bebington
Frances Taptey (Housemaid)	30 years Unmarried	Prestall, Lancs

Census 1891	Littledales Lane	
Samuel Hindley (Gamekeeper)	47 years Head	Antrobus
Susanna	37 years Wife	Wigan
Jane (Scholar)	11 years Daughter	Weaverham
George (Scholar)	8 years Son	Weaverham
Sarah (Scholar)	6 years Daughter	Weaverham
James	4 years Son	Weaverham

Census 1891	Keepers Cottage, Beach Lane	
David Hindley (Gamekeeper)	40 years Head	Antrobus
Beatrice	38 years Wife	Gt.Budworth
John (Gardener's asst)	19 years Son	Weaverham
Margaret (At home)	17 years Daughter	Weaverham
Joseph (Scholar)	13 years Son	Weaverham
Lois (Scholar)	12 years Daughter	Weaverham
Rose (Scholar)	10 years Daughter	Weaverham
Oswald	3 years Son	Weaverham
Florence	2 years Daughter	Weaverham
Fred	3 months Son	Weaverham
Mary Dennison (Seamstress)	67 years Mother-in-law	Weaverham

Census 1891	Church Street	
Joseph Johnson	58 years Head Married	

(Gen. Labourer)		Weaverham
Alice	59 years Wife	Kingsley
Joseph	22 years Son Unmarried	
(Coachman)		Kingsley
James Clark	14 years Boarder	
(Gen. Labourer)		Kingsley
Thomas Gleave	38 years Head Married	
(Grocer & Farmer)		
Mary Gleave (Grocer)	38 years Wife	
Emily Gleave (Scholar)	12 years Daughter	
Mary Eleanor Gleave	8 years Daughter	
(Scholar)		
Sarah Adern	37 years Sister-in-law	
	Unmarried	
Sarah Platt (Farmer)	42 years	Weaverham
Maggie Platt	8 years Daughter	Weaverham
Thomas Platt	12 years Boarder	Weaverham
Census 1891	**Forest Street**	
Joseph Burgess	50 years Head Married	
(Gen Labourer)		Over
Hannah Burgess	58 years Wife	Shurlach
William Burgess	22 years Son	
(Gen Labourer)		Sandiway
Joseph Burgess	19 years Son	
(Gen Labourer)		Sandiway
Alice Burgess	13 years Daughter	
(Scholar)		Weaverham
John Forester	76 years Head Married	
(Blacksmith)		Weaverham
Frances Forester	60 years Wife Married	
		Weaverham
Lucy E.Woodward	19 years Stepdaughter	
(Gen.Servant)		Weaverham
Emily S.Ennis	5 years Boarder	
(Scholar)		Weaverham

Census 1891	**Nook Farm**	
David Forster	46 years Head	Weaverham
(Joiner & Blacksmith)		
Sarah Forster	44 years Wife	Weaverham
Edith Forster	21 years Daughter	
		Weaverham
Thomas Forster	20 years Son	Weaverham
(Joiner)		
Louisa Forster	18 years Daughter	
		Weaverham
William Forster	16 years Son	
(Blacksmith's apprentice)		Weaverham
Arthur Forster	14 years Son	Weaverham
(Joiner)		
David Forster	11 years Son	Weaverham
(Scholar)		
Elizabeth Forster	9 years Daughter	
(Scholar)		Weaverham
Clara Forster	7 years Daughter	
(Scholar)		Weaverham
Fred Forster	6 years Son	
(Scholar)		Weaverham
Arnold Forster	3 years Son	
(Scholar)		Weaverham
Arthur Tomkinson	40 years Head	
(Gen Labourer)		Withington
Elizabeth Tomkinson	39 years Wife	Linden
Alfred Tomkinson	19 years Son	Swettenham
Albert Tomkinson	16 years Son	Sharston
Eleanor Tomkinson	14 years Daughter	
		Cranage
Alice Tomkinson	10 years Daughter	
(Scholar)		Sandiway
Ada Tomkinson	6 years Daughter	Gorstage
(Scholar)		
Arthur Tomkinson	3 years Son	Kermincham
Charles Tomkinson	1 year Son	Hale

John Moss was born to John and Mary on 25th July, 1847 at Cuddington, and the birth was registered by Mary, on 9th August, 1847, and on 26th September, 1872 this baby, John Moss, now 25-years-old, a labourer and a bachelor, married Mary Gleave, a spinster, and daughter of Farmer George Gleave of Church Farm, at Weaverham Parish Church.

One of the sons of this marriage was George Moss, born 30th July, 1873, and on 1st June, 1899 this same George, now aged 25 years and a bachelor farmer, married Edith Forster, a spinster aged 29 years and the daughter of David Forster, builder and blacksmith. George lived at Beach Farm and Edith at the smithy in Station Road. The marriage took place at Weaverham Wesleyan Methodist Church in the presence of David and Clara Forster, and the newlyweds went to live in Salisbury Terrace. Stanley Moss, my father, was born to George and Edith on 1st April, 1900, at Salisbury Terrace, before they moved to Nook Farm, where I was to spend my childhood. One of my earliest recollections as a very small boy, long before I went to school, was hearing my grandfather talking about "the Hall" and I longed to see what the old building looked like.

The opportunity came when I was taken by one of my aunt's across the fields, under the railway bridge and up to the Hall Farm, to watch the threshing machines at work in the stack yard, at the Home Farm. I can still recall the scene with the men working frantically to keep the hungry machine going. The whole thing seemed alive as it shuddered and creaked as the sheaves of corn were fed into it. The air was full of dust and chaff from the grain and of smoke from the steam engine which I can clearly recall with its name emblazoned on the front of the boiler: "King Edward VII".

As we left the bustle and noise of what was to a small boy a wondrously fascinating scene with its loud hum of machinery and its smell of burning coke, steam, smoke and oil, my aunt took me up through the farmyard, past the stableyard, with its large stable buildings and old coachhouse surmounted by the clock tower, and there at the end of an avenue of rhododendrons, stood, in all its glory, the old hall.

It was a large red-brick building and as a small boy I was filled with wonderment and was fascinated by the number of windows in its frontage. I had no idea of the profound influence the old hall had already had on my life and would continue to have in the future. As we walked home across the park and through the wood, my head was full of wonder and even at that young age, I was aware of an aura of brooding mystery about the place, a mystery that was to intrigue me more and more over the years and would nurture in me a resolve to delve into the lives of those who had over the centuries made the Grange their home and the estate their playground, and whose lives had been inexorably bound up with the lives of those living in the village over which the hall held dominance. And where could I start, other than going back to the earliest records of the village's existence?

The ancient village of Weaverham was easily accessible from the sea by way of the Mersey and the River Weaver which, until it was canalised in the 18th Century, was tidal as far as Saltersford. It was known to the Vikings, as there is a Norse map in existence showing its site on the Weaver. Earlier still, it was known to the Romans, as Roman coins, dating back to the 1st Century AD, can be found in every field in and about the village and there is also the age-old tradition that at least two Roman roads converged on the hamlet, to join at one point near the church before descending down into the Weaver Valley for a river crossing, either by ford, or bridge, somewhere near to Saltersford.

In fact, according to the one-time sexton and local historian, Charlie Bebbington, the church is built on a section of it. There is also evidence in the form of field names, such as Pavement Ends, which was the name of the field at the bottom of Withens Lane where the Youth Club and the Community Centre now stand. W. Thompson Watkin, in his "Roman Cheshire", published in 1886, was in no doubt that Withens Lane, which existed in its entirety until 1947, and which many local people will remember with nostalgia as being one of their favourite quiet ways, was one such road, being a continuation of Littledales Lane and Bradford Mill Lane, in Whitegate, all sections of the same Roman road.

The other road he projected was one leaving Watling Street at Crabtree

Green and descending through Cuddington into Weaverham, by way of Gorstage and, possibly, falling into another road coming from the direction of Eaton, where there is a known Roman Villa, all converging on Weaverham for a river crossing. None of this can be proved because before Watkins' time no-one was seriously interested, and neither has any scholar since, and over the last decade any evidence which could have remained has fast disappeared. However, in the park, near the hall, coins have been found bearing the stylised horse legend of the Gallo Belgic tribes of the 1st and 2nd Centuries BC, and until recent years, near the hall, were grouped together three large stones which could have been Ice Age relics, or the remains of a cromlech.

In the 7th Century, it is known that Theodore, Archbishop of Canterbury, established the Parochial System and so the parish of Weaverham was formed and apart from this one reference, we have to arrive at the Conquest and the Domesday Book for the first undisputed written commentary on the Township and Manor.

This commentary, under the heading "Roelau Hundred", is too well known to require further mention here, other than to say that before the Conquest it was held by the Saxon, Edwin, Earl of Mercia, brother-in-law to King Harold who, for a time after the Conquest, was allowed to keep his lands, possibly due to the fact that he was supposed to be uncle to Hugh Lupus. However, in 1068, Edwin joined in an uprising against the Normans and Hugh Lupus was sent to quash the rebellion which he did with such zeal that the whole Manor was laid waste. There were insufficient men left to cultivate the land and "burgesses" had to be brought in from Chester for this purpose. Its value fell from X pounds to 50 shillings.

Hugh Lupus seized the Manor and it remained the property of the Earls of Chester until King Edward I bestowed it upon Roger, Lord Clifford, who settled it as a dowry on his wife, the Countess of Lauretania, of Beaufort in France, whom he had married on his way home from Palestine. At Clifford's death, however, in 1286, the whole Manor, comprising the townships of Weaverham, with its hamlets of Milton, Gorstage and Sandiway, Acton, Crowton, Cuddington cum Bryn, Onston and Wallerscote, and all Clifford's goods and chattels, except his wife's jewels, were seized for debts due to the King. Edward then bestowed the Manor, with its "Church, mills, homages and services", on to the Abbey of Vale Royal, and this was confirmed by Royal Charter in 1299. It was valued at £25.3s.10d a year and remained in the possession of the Abbey until the Dissolution, by Henry VIII, in the year 1536.

Hefferston Grange became then one of the granges of Vale Royal Abbey and after the monks took up residence they became a familiar and conspicuous sight in their white cassocks and black cloaks as they walked the lanes around the old hall on their way to the church to carry out their religious duties. The monks of Vale Royal belonged to the Cistercian Order who were devoted to manual labour and were excellent farmers and horticulturists and they would be seen tilling the fields around the hall growing corn which they would take to the mill at Onston. This mill, at that time, would have had a horizontal wheel, as was the custom in those years. They also bred large numbers of cattle. They dispensed charity and food and were skilled in the use of herbs for medicine. They copied the scriptures and classical writings, thus preserving them.

So for over 250 years, the successive Abbots of Vale Royal ruled over the Manor and village of Weaverham. The Abbot had a Court, which he held fortnightly, the old sandstone Grammar School, in Forest Street, being reputed to be the Courthouse and a prison, and this Court claimed an exclusive criminal jurisdiction, in capital and other causes, over all within the boundaries of the Manor and "over all natives whatever offence committed".

Justice was administered by the Abbot's bailiff, selected from the younger sons of the County land owning families. Lands were attached to the office, and duties of summoning the tenants of the Fee of Weaverham in wartime, and of claiming the bodies of the Abbot's tenants from other Courts. The villagers were required to attend the Abbot's Courts at short notice. If they had pigs eating acorns in the nearby forest, then the Abbot demanded payment at the Abbey Mill and the daughters of tenants were not allowed to marry outside the Manor without the permission of the Abbot. When any "native" died, his pigs, capons, horses at grass, his domestic horse, his bees, pork, linen and woollens, and his money in gold and silver became the property of the Abbot. The standing corn and any that had been harvested had to be divided between the widow and the Abbot, and the Abbot was allowed to purchase a hen or duck for 2d, and a duckling in Lent for 11/2d and was to have the first offer of any corn or hay which was for sale.

In time of war, the "natives" were liable to be taken to keep watch at Chester Castle. The local inhabitants intensely disliked these harsh and oppressive customs and transgressions against Monastic tyranny were constant and the Bailiff was a busy man as the Vale Royal Ledger Book which records Court proceedings will confirm. So, despite the good works done by the monks, there was enmity between them and the "natives" which sometimes flared up into bitter violence. In 1321, John Boddleworth, a monk, was caught and murdered by sons of the family of Oldyntons who then played football with the severed head, so it is said. But, perhaps, the only proof of this event was the discovery of a headless skeleton in one of the many coffins uncovered within the confines of the abbey during the last full scale excavation of the site, carried out by F.H. Thompson, who was, at the time, Curator of the Grosvenor Museum, in Chester. It was said that after this episode, some monks would travel between the various Granges and the Abbey only at night without carrying torches and that beech trees with their smooth bark were planted along the routes so the monks could feel their way.

The Cistercians were a foreign Order, from Cisteaux, in Burgundy, and this Order is noteworthy as being the first to refuse to be subject to the Bishops of the Established Church, owing, instead, direct allegiance to the Pope. So, in this way, they were a foreign garrison within the country, owing no allegiance to its laws and contributing nothing to the revenues of the English Church. This may have contributed to its downfall and the confiscation of all its properties and possessions at the Dissolution when the Abbey and its lands, together with the Granges of Conersly, Bradford, Ernsley, Merton, Petty Pool Mill and dam, and Bradford Mill, were granted to Thomas Holcroft, an Esquire of the King's body, from Holcroft Hall, near Leigh, in Lancashire, for the sum of £450.10s.6d. And four years later, the Manors of Weaverham and Over, together with Hefferston Grange and Onston Mill, were granted to him, he now being the newly knighted Sir Thomas Holcroft, subject to an annual rent of £10.0s.4d and the Manor of Cartmel, in Lancashire, given in exchange, in the consideration of £464.10s.10d. Thus was brought to an end the rule of the Abbots and the Grange was left awaiting a new occupant. In 1542, Sir Thomas Holcroft sold Hefferston Grange and its land, together with Onston Mill, to Peter Warburton, third son of Sir Piers Warburton of Arley Hall.

The remainder of the Abbey lands in Weaverham and the detached part of Whitegate within Weaverham, were sold by a grandson of Sir Thomas to the Marbury family, of Marbury Hall. Thomas Marbury had three daughters, but no male heir and on his death, the estate passed, in 1708, pursuant to a decree in Chancery to Richard, Earl Rivers, upon whose death, again subject to decree in Chancery, it was purchased by his son-in-law James, Earl Barrymore. The estate remained in the possession of this family until 1930, when on the death of the last Earl, the manorial rights came to an end and the estate was dispersed, much of it being purchased by ICI, and parts by sitting tenants and others.

The Holcrofts remained at the Abbey for two generations, during which time the building was much altered. Some parts were razed even to the foundations and the stonework scattered and sold by the cartload, leaving the present manor house but a fragment of the original magnificent structure which had been the largest monastic building in England, larger even than Fountains Abbey. Until recent years, many of the stones could still be seen about the village, forming garden walls and property boundaries and some are said to have been used in building the stone bridge over the Weaver, near to Acton swing bridge.

In 1616, the manor house was sold by the Holcrofts to Mary, Lady Cholmondeley, daughter of Christopher Holford of Holford near Plumley and widow of Sir Hugh Cholmondeley. A son in direct descent was, in 1821, created Lord Delamere, of Vale Royal, and the house remained in the possession of the family until the end of the Second World War, when for a time it became the headquarters of ICI Salt Division.

5

HEFFERSTON GRANGE

THE WARBURTONS

THE first of the Warburtons to take up residence at Hefferston was Peter, third son of Sir Piers Warburton, of Arley Hall, and his wife, Elizabeth, daughter and heiress of Richard Winnington, of Winnington. He came with his wife Alice, daughter and heiress of John Coupe, of Abbots Bromley, in Staffordshire. He would have found an austere building, some parts of timber, but mostly a great deal of heavy stone masonry and retaining many of the features of the fortified moated manor house of the Norman Earls and the Saxon Earl Edwin. Some of these features included the remains of the moat and an enormous stone trough, to hold water sufficient to stay a long siege, and, in the cellar, a beautifully moulded sandstone doorway, as well as the great sandstone blocks which supported the mediaeval buildings. As one of the Granges of Vale Royal Abbey, under the occupancy of its monks, its main purpose had been to provide, store, and supply grain for the use of the Abbey.

Peter and Alice had six children. First was Anne, who married Thomas Fitton of Siddington, in the County of Chester. Second was Eleanor, who married into the Hurst family, of Oscote Green, Co. Derby. The third child was Peter, son and heir, who married Magdalin, daughter of Richard Moulton, of St. Albans, who was auditor to the Exchequer of Queen Elizabeth I. The fourth child was William, who later resided in Skelton, County of Nottinghamshire, and married one of the Brooke family, of Norton. Then their third son was Richard, who became Sir Richard, Pensioner to Queen Elizabeth I. He married Anne Vasor, who was Maid of Honour to Queen Elizabeth. Lastly, there was Thomas, who died unmarried.

Peter and Magdalin inherited Hefferston Grange and had eight children. First was Sarah, then Theodosia, then Francis, followed by Mary Anne. The fifth was Peter, son and heir at last, who later became Chief Justice of Chester and married Alice, daughter and co-heir of John Gardener of Kimbleton, Co. Worcester, Esq.. The sixth child was William, who married Anne, daughter of Richard Warburton of London, Esq.. Seventh child was Thomas, who married the daughter of a London merchant, and eighth child was George Warburton.

From 1620 to 1735, the Warburtons were patrons of the vicarage of Weaverham, under the Bishop of Chester. Peter Warburton, the Justice mentioned above, who was living at the hall in 1641, was described as, "That learned and religious gentleman" and his motto was "Christ is the Christians' all." This was put up in every room and ordered to be engraved on rings given at his funeral. He was also known as "This religious Judge Warburton of Helperstone - a gentleman that greatly affected retirement and privacy and spent the greater part of his time in reading and prayer."

His house at Hefferston was "a little sanctuary to the silenced ministers and those that cohered to them." The cause of Non-Conformity he approved to his dying day. An escape tunnel, albeit a narrow one, is known to exist to this day. It is interesting to note that Judge Warburton's father, Peter, died on the 7th August, 1617, and besides owning the estate at Hefferston Grange, he held the advowson of the village of Warburton, from 1597, and charged the profits of the advowson with the maintenance and education of his fourth son, George, reserving the living for him at the next vacancy.

The Will of Peter Warburton, of Hefferston Grange, Esq. 20th June, 1617. Probate granted 18th September, 1617 to son and heir and one of the executors:- "The Hefferston and Onston Mill to my wife as parcel of her "jointure" and after to my son Peter for life To my wife: My whole interest in the tithe corn of Cuddington and Onston for life. To my son Peter, his heirs and his assigns: The present profits of the advowson and the next presentation of the moiety of the parsonage of Lymm and Warburton on condition that he present my son George parson of the said moiety of the said parsonage upon voidance of the present minister, Mr Shelmerydne.

My son Peter to maintain his brother George in learning out of the profits of the tithe until presented and then my son George shall serve during life.

To my son, George: All those grounds I hold in Warburton of my cousin Warburton of Arley, paying up the rents due for the same.

Whereas my son, Peter, has covenanted to pay £1000 for the expense of my younger children, £300 to my daughter, Theodosia, at marriage to the content of their mother and £20 apiece until marriage - £200 apiece to my sons William and Thomas when they shall come to their Prentice ships or at 24 years. If one die, the survivor to have £400.

All my utensils, household staff and husbandry ware to my wife and son Peter, he to be dutiful to her, and be an aid to his brothers and sisters.

To my daughter, Garrett (sic) Garnett, £10, and to her daughter, Mary, £10.

Unto my wife: My coach, furniture and coach-horses and ye gray nag she used to ride on; the rest and residue to the younger children - Francis, Theodosia, William and George.

To my daughter-in-law one of the cotts which she shall choose.

To my serving men, Bebington and Henskall 20/- apiece. Unto my hired servants and maidservants....

To my sister Wolls - one gold ring with a......

To my brother William a loop gold ring now in my chest.

To my niece Wil... and my niece Hyde a piece of fine gold of 11s. apiece in my chest.

To my cousin Warburton of Arley - one of my best colts.

To my daughter Bere - a speer royal, in my chest.

My executors to cause to be made a "work pryee" and given to my cousin Mary
Wilbraham.

My wife, son Peter, and brother William to be executors.

My cousin, Warburton of Arley to be Overseer.

Signed: Peter Warburton

Sealed subscribed and delivered to his Beloved wife as his last Will and Testament
in the presence of John Grymosdiche, James Gerrard, Thomas Bebington, Richard
Woodyer, Hugh Hammett, James Gerrard and others."

Inventory of goods at Hefferston
* (Interesting to compare prices, then and now)

7th August 1617, includes at Hefferston Grange the following:

In Cawley Meadow - 5 fat Kine	15. 0s. 0d.
Four ronk oxen	£10. 6s. 8d.
In Black Keepe - 10 Kine and 1 Bull	£27. 0s. 0d.
In Ley moor - 10 calves	£5.10s. 0d.
Four score and seven sheep	£20. 0s. 0d.
Eight oxen	£37. 0s. 0d.
Three horses	£30. 0s. 0d.
19 old swine and 6 pigs	£10. 0s. 0d.
Geese	15s. 0d.
15 acres of Barley	£50. 0s. 0d.
Rye, Barley and Oats	£4. 0s. 0d.
Saddles, Bridles and all furniture for the stable	£ 1. 8s. 0d.
Forty cheeses	£1. 0s. 0d.
All the coopery and two spinning wheels	£10. 0s. 0d.
Brass	£20. 0s. 0d.
Pewter	£14. 0s. 0d.
Leases of Cuddington, Warburton Ground and mill, money and plate	£30. 0s. 0d.
Linens	£40. 0s. 0d.
Tables, stools, forms, cupboards and cheese presses	£20. 0s. 0d.
Wearing apparel	£20. 0s. 0d

Praysers (Valuers) - John Parker,
Lawrence Woodson, Richard Williamson, Richard Pearson, Robert Allot.

At Warburton

Half of three acres of barley	£5. 0s. 0d.
Half of 4 acres of oats with four butts of barley lying on the Town Field	£3. 6s. 8d.
One bull	£2.10s. 0d.
Cupboard, Table, Bedcast and two forms	£1.10s. 4d.
Swine trough	2s. 0d.

Praysers or valuers - Richard Rowlandson,
Drinkwater (junior) John Rowlandson, Richard Drinkwater.

From the contents of this will, it can be seen that the Hefferston farm
was being farmed in a typical Cheshire style of that period, growing bar-
ley, rye and oats and rearing cattle, sheep and pigs. Also some geese were
kept and, in the dairy, cheese was being made. Oxen were being used for
draught purposes and, no doubt, would be kept inside during the winter
months, as we learn from Daniel King's "Vale Royal", while the cattle win-
tered outside.

The children of Judge Peter and Alice Warburton were: Peter, Thomas, Henry and Geoffrey, who sadly all died in infancy; the fifth child was Robert, son and heir, who married Elizabeth, daughter of Alderman Berkeley, of London. Robert was buried at Weaverham, on April 7th, 1696. The sixth child was Peter, who married Theodise Somers, daughter of a London merchant, and they settled at Abbots Bromley, in Staffordshire. The seventh child was Elizabeth and then there were Anne, Sarah, Abigail, Hester and Theodise, 12 children in all.

Robert and Elizabeth had six children. They were Thomas, who died unmarried in 1694; secondly Peter, son and heir, who died unmarried at the Grange on 27th May, 1717 and was buried on 1st June, 1717; the third son was John who married the aforesaid Hester, daughter of Peter Warburton, but John died in 1718.

Then there was Mary Warburton, heiress to her brother Peter and she married the Reverend Matthew Henry of Broadoak, Flintshire, on 8th July, 1690. Mary died 12th August, 1731 and was buried at the Trinity Church, Chester, 14th August, 1731. Matthew had already died on 22nd June, 1714 and he too was buried at Trinity Church. The fifth child was Alice who died unmarried in 1709 and was buried at Weaverham, on 6th October, 1709. The sixth child, Esther Warburton, died unmarried, in 1710, and was also buried at Weaverham.

The children of the Reverend Matthew Henry and Mary Warburton were: first of all, Esther Henry, born 27th September, 1694, who married a Londoner named Buckley; then there was Elizabeth Henry, who was born in 1701 and died 14th November, 1752, and was buried at St. John's, Chester. She had been married to John Philpot, Esq. of Chester (a descendant of Sir John Philpot who was Lord Mayor of London 1378-1379) who died 9th December, 1764, and was also buried at St. John's, and they had a daughter Mary; the third child was Sarah Henry, born in 1703 who married Bailey Brett of West Bromwich; the fourth child was Theodosia, born in 1708 and who married Randle Kay, of Whitchurch, in 1717, and they had a son born 27th March, 1735; the fifth child was Philip Henry, the only son and heir, who changed his name to Warburton and made his mark by becoming M.P. for Chester, in 1747. He was born in 1700 and died unmarried in, August 1760, and was buried at Weaverham.

Matthew Henry was the son of Phillip Henry born 24th August, 1631, and the grandson of John Henry, a Welshman whose father was Henry Williams. In this case, the son took his father's Christian name, which was often the custom in Welsh families at that time.

Although John Henry was poor when the family lived at Britton's Ferry, near Swansea, he left home early in life to seek his fortune in London. One account says that he had only fourpence in his pocket when he reached London, but he must have had a reasonable education and been well brought up because he soon became well known in the city and, while still quite young, entered the service of the Earl of Pembroke as the

"Earl's Gentleman." Soon he became "Keeper of the Orchard", at Whitehall, and shortly afterwards, "Page of the Backstairs", to the Duke of York. Matthew Henry once said of his grandfather: "He lived and died a Courtier, a hearty mourner for his Royal master, King Charles I."

There is no doubt that John Henry's connection with the Court had been both intimate and friendly. His son Philip, who was near to the two princes in age, being one year younger than Charles and two years older than James, was on friendly terms with both of them. The two princes were often at the Henrys' house in those early years and there is no doubt that Philip as a child visited the Royal household. Philip's mother was said to be a "virtuous, pious gentlewoman who did not seek the Vanities and Pleasures of the Court".

So it was that Philip grew up in important surroundings and at the age of 13, he became a pupil of Headmaster, Dr Busby, at Westminster School. Dr Busby was, reputedly a strong disciplinarian, who ruled "with a rod of iron", or rather a "birch". Philip Henry only once suffered at his hands, but admitted he deserved his punishment. Dr Busby was a distinguished and remarkable man of "piety and justice" who said that at one time he had educated 16 of the Bishops of the Church and, surprisingly, although he was so stern, he gained the affection and love of his pupils.

After four years under Dr. Busby, Philip Henry was chosen with four other pupils from Westminster School to attend Christ's Church, Oxford. Philip's Godfather, the Earl of Pembroke, was one of the Electors and gave him £10. On account of the Civil War and his loyalty to the Royalist cause, John Henry must have been very impoverished at the time. No doubt, Philip's close association with the Royal family would have bearing on the type of friends he made.

At Christmas 1648, Philip obtained leave of absence from his college and went to London to spend Christmas with his father, John, at Whitehall. By this time John was a widower, still living in his old house as Keeper of the Orchard.

Many of his old companions and fellow servitors had long gone. It was nearly seven years since Charles had left his palace and at last, on 20th January, 1649, he was brought back there under arrest on his way to Westminster to face his judges. Here is Matthew Henry's account of that occasion so memorable in the lives of his grandfather John and father Philip, at that time a youth of 18 years.

"The King passing by his door under guard, when he was going to Westminster, that which was called his "Tryal" enquired for his old servant Mr. John Henry, who was ready to pay his respects, prayed God to bless his Majesty and to deliver him out of the hands of his Enemies, for which the Guard had like to have been rough with him."

Ten days later, Philip formed one of the packed crowd that saw Charles

Page 106

I go bravely to his death. Then two companies of troopers immediately scattered the crowds and the great event was over, to the bitter personal grief of the loyal and affectionate little household of Henrys.

Philip Henry took his BA degree in 1652 and preached his first sermon at South Hinskey, in January 1653. He was not yet ordained, but Cromwell was Lord Protector of the Realm in those days and such a young man as Philip Henry, full of religious zeal, would certainly be considered competent to preach the Word.

Soon after this Philip was engaged by Judge Puleston, of Worthenbury, in Flintshire, to be a Tutor to his sons and to act as Preacher at Worthenbury Church "on the Lord's days." He came to "Emeral", the Pulestons' house, in 1653, and he was so much appreciated that Judge Puleston built him a very handsome house and soon Philip Henry married the daughter of a local man, a Mr. Matthews, who was at first by no means in favour of the match. However the couple married in 1660, but two years earlier, in 1658, Lady Puleston had died and her death was a great blow to Philip as she had shown him great kindness when he had joined their household. Then in 1661, when Judge Puleston died and there was no more kindness shown to him by the Emeral household as the Judge's heirs had no regard for him. His annuity was withheld and on 31st January 1661, Philip entered in his diary, "Things are low with me in the world, but threepence left".

The Act of Uniformity was passed on 24th August, 1661, Philip's birthday, and on that day 2,000 faithful Ministers of Christ were ejected from their livings. Philip now belonged to the company known as the "silenced ministers".

Judge Warburton, of Hefferston Grange, was sympathetic to the cause of the "silenced ministers" during his lifetime at the hall and there is still a tunnel leading from the grounds to the cellars at the Grange. This tunnel, well made of brick, is quite narrow, but would have been big enough for a servant to take food to anyone hiding in the area around the cavity walls which had a secret door to the cellar.

Although the penalties for preaching at unofficial assemblies could mean seven years transportation, which meant working as a slave in some West Indian colony, Philip Henry sometimes spoke at such meetings, and strange as it may seem, he became friendly with Dr. William Lloyd, Bishop of St. Asaph, a friendship which grew, as was demonstrated by the many calls of the Episcopal carriage at Broad Oak.

At least in these troubled times Philip Henry, by the generosity of his father-in-law, had a comfortable home in the old farmhouse at Broad Oak. It was here that his family were born, but, sadly, his eldest son died of measles. However, his second son Matthew, after being very ill with the same complaint, survived. It is not surprising that Matthew became a serious-minded boy and very studious and who could read a chapter from the Bible when he was only three-years-old. Although other children came along, they were all girls, and eventually Matthew had four sisters.

It was Spring 1685, when Matthew Henry went to study at Gray's Inn, London, and it was a little over two years later that he married Katherine Hardware, at Tarvin Church, on July 19th 1687. Matthew had by now started to preach the Word among the Godly families of Cheshire. Katherine had heard him preach many times, at her father's house, Mouldsworth Hall, near Tarvin, and it was Matthew's sisters who had led to their friendship and eventual marriage, after which they went to live in Chester. Matthew was ordained in 1687, in London, by no less than six prominent Non-Conformist Ministers and now he was an accepted Pastor of the congregation who worshipped at the Old Meeting Place, in White Friars, Chester, where, eventually, a new chapel had to be built, in 1700, when the congregation outgrew the old place.

Sadly in 1689, after 18 months of marriage and happiness, Katherine, his wife, died. During the winter of 1688/89, smallpox, the scourge of that period, claimed Katherine and left Matthew with a newly-born daughter. Philip Henry, devastated at the death of his dear daughter-in-law, the only daughter of Samuel Hardware, baptised his little grand-daughter in Matthew Henry's chapel and it was said, "There were no dry eyes in the congregation".

In Trinity Church, Chester, there is a memorial brass put up in Katherine's memory which reads: "ad Patrian migravit 14 die Febri 1689 anno aetatis 25".

Matthew buried his head with sorrow into his books and in his work as an Evangelist, but Mrs Hardware, his mother-in-law, decided that Mary, the youngest daughter of Robert Warburton, of Hefferston Grange, was ideally placed to become Matthew's new wife. No doubt she steered Matthew towards the old house, said to be a "little sanctuary to the silenced ministers and those that adhered to them."

Matthew married Mary Warburton on the 8th July, 1690, a marriage destined to bring happiness, and it pleased Mrs Hardware, whose own family were kin to the Warburtons.

James II visited Chester in 1687 and had discussions with many people and listened to their views on the repeal of the Penal Laws and Test Act. Matthew Henry was one of the persons to meet the King, and Matthew – as the son of James' old playmate Philip – expected him to be tolerant of his views.

By his Declaration of Indulgence, 4th April, 1687, the King suspended all penal laws against all classes of Non Conformists, and authorised both Roman Catholic and Protestant Dissenters to perform their worship publicly. From then on, Matthew Henry did much to bring some "spiritual cheer" to the local Cheshire villages as he went about his work with a lightened heart. He gave monthly lectures at Mouldsworth, Bromborough Court, Beeston, Middledale and Burton, Whitchurch, Wem, Prescot and Boreattan, where he was a constant visitor in the house, as his father had been before him, and, on one occasion, he was called to an important congregation at Hackney, London. On many of these occasions, when he was travelling far from home, he would take his wife Mary back to the Grange, to stay with her brother, Peter Warburton, until his return. Matthew loved the Grange because of its quiet tranquillity. However, he was now suffering from failing health, one of his troubles being diabetes, and on a journey to preach at Nantwich he was thrown from his horse near Tarporley. Determined not to let his congregation down at Nantwich, he continued his journey and preached the service, "but not with his old fervour and liveliness".

After the sermon, he was about to journey to Doddington, at the invitation of Sir John Delves, but he found he was unfit for the journey and was taken to a Minister's house in Nantwich where he died the next day, 22nd June, 1714, at the age of 51 years.

Matthew's wife inherited Hefferston Grange when her brother Peter died unmarried on 27th May, 1727, and when Mary died in 1731, the old Grange and its estates were inherited by her son, Philip Henry, who then assumed the name of Warburton.

Philip lived as Squire of Hefferston Grange until 1760, when he died unmarried after making his mark by becoming Member of Parliament for Chester in 1741. He made a lot of changes to the old hall, almost completely rebuilding it, changing its appearance from the mediaeval structure which had stood so long to the red brick-faced building which stands today. He had the building re-roofed and at the same time had the new downspouts decorated with the Warburton crest, the Saracen's Head, which are there to this day.

Philip kept a pack of hounds at the hall and hunted the area frequently, living the life of a true country gentleman. The stabling accommodation at the Grange, together with the large area of ideal hunting country made the place perfect for such pursuits. With the passing of Philip Henry Warburton, and no male issue of the Warburton family to carry on, the old Grange became the property of Mary Philpot, as a dowry upon her marriage, to Nicholas Ashton, the wealthy squire of Woolton Hall near Liverpool. Mary was the daughter of Philip's sister Elizabeth, who had died in November 1752, and she married Nicholas Ashton in December 1763.

THE ASHTONS

Nicholas Ashton, J.P., D.L,, although coming into possession of Hefferston Grange on his marriage to Mary Philpot in December 1863, had no intentions of living there. He was far too fond of Woolton Hall which he had purchased from the Molyneuxs, of Sefton, and to which he had made many large additions, both to the building and to the grounds. The hall is described as being a noble stone mansion, with extremely beautiful gardens and grounds, with rich and extensive plantations. The hall was also convenient for his work in Liverpool where he had offices in Paradise Street. Also he had been appointed a Magistrate and, in 1770, he was made Sheriff of Lancashire, all the more reason for him to remain at Woolton Hall, which he did for the rest of his life, dying there in 1833.

Nicholas was descended paternally from the Ashtons, of Ashton-in-Makerfield, a collateral line of the family of Ashtons, of Chadderton. He was born 19th October, 1742, and had been presented to the Pretender, in Derby, in 1745.

His father, John, projected the Sankey Canal of which he, Charles Gare, James Crosbie, John Blackburn the younger, and Richard Trafford, were styled "undertakers." There is no doubt that John was deeply involved in the slave trade, as were very many of the Liverpool Merchants.

The first slave ship was said to have left Liverpool in 1708. It was a barque of only thirty tons and carried fifteen slaves from the West Coast of Africa to the West Indies. By 1747, there were as many as thirty ships engaged in the trade and, by 1760, the number had risen to sixty nine-ships, or over seven thousand tons of shipping.

It was the Treaty of Utrecht that had opened up new possibilities of trade with the Western World. In this Treaty there was a clause by which Spain granted to Britain the contract to supply negroes to her American Colonies where labour was scarce and plantations of sugar cane, sugars, and tobacco were fast growing. Not only was the trade legal, it was encouraged by a commission, sometimes offered by the Government, for every healthy black landed in the plantations.

The people of Liverpool looked upon this traffic as merely a branch of the ordinary sea-borne trade and few saw anything of which to be ashamed. By 1790, the city possessed 5/8ths of the English slave trade and by now almost all the Liverpool Merchants had a hand in it. By 1800, enormous profits became possible when a good slave would fetch £100, although the average price was between £50 and £60. The slaves were rarely landed here, but a ship would load up with Manchester and Yorkshire cloth as well as hardware, firearms, hatchets and knives, and exchange these goods on the West African Coast for slaves who would be sold on the slave markets of the West Indies and America, where the vessels would then thoroughly wash out their holds and load up with sugar, rum, coffee, tobacco, cotton, and other produce to be sold at a good profit on the Liverpool Market.

In 1772, it was decided that since slavery was unknown to English Law, any black slave who touched English soil became free immediately. However, before the legislation became enforced, there were a few little black boys who were dressed up in Oriental trousers and a turban to accompany ladies of fashion, carrying a cup of chocolate or bearing a prayer book to Church. Figures show that between 1783 and 1793, including both years, 305,737 slaves were carried, at a total cash value of £15,186,850. Although few slaves were actually brought to Liverpool, the following advertisements would be seen in Liverpool newspapers:

(1) "Wanted immediately, a negro boy, must be of full black complexion ... not above 15 or 16 years of age."
(2) "To be sold at the Exchange Coffee House in Water Street this day. Eleven Negroes to be sold per the Angola."
(3) "To be sold by auction at George's Coffee House betwixt the hours of 6 and 8 o'clock a very fine negro girl, about 8 years of age."
(4) While one Auctioneers advertisement groups the following items together:
"2 boxes bottled cider. 12 pints raisin wine. 6 sacks of flour. 3 Negro men, 2 Negro women, 8 Negro boys, 1 Negro girl".

Sales occasionally took place in the coffee house, but also in shops, warehouses, and on the steps of the Customs House, beside the old dock. A common method of auction was by "candle" when bidding went up to the last flicker of a short length of candle, or when a pin stuck in a candle fell out. When sold, a slave would be branded with his master's mark "O.O" or "31DD", DD being the common Liverpool brand.

However, opposition to the slave trade, by Abolitionists, Quakers, Methodists, and others, was the beginning of the end of the trade and of slavery itself. The last ship to leave Liverpool was the "Mary", with Captain Hugh Crow in charge. She carried 400 negroes to their destiny in the year 1807, over one hundred years since the trade began. There is no doubt that Nicholas Ashton, who played a great part in developing the salt trade between Cheshire and the Americas, was also engaged in the slave trade, as were his friends. His daughter, Elizabeth, took as her second husband, George Williams, of Little Woolton, who was heavily engaged in the business and who became a target of the Abolitionists and had his house ransacked.

Nicholas, however, turned his attention to the even more lucrative trade of Privateering which had also become big business in the Port of Liverpool, and he had a very narrow escape one afternoon in March, 1793, when his newly-launched Privateer, "Pelican", was cruising in the Mersey. She was manned by 94 chosen seamen and a Ball had been arranged by their host. Many of the invited guests were dressed for the occasion and the Ball was in progress when suddenly a gust of wind heeled the "Pelican" over and she instantly filled with water and sank with a terrible loss of life. Nicholas was not on board because he was waiting with a friend at Woolton Hall for a coach to arrive from London carrying a merchant friend who had been invited to the celebration. Fortunately for them, the coach had broken down and they had been delayed for the repair, so when the coach eventually reached Liverpool it was all over. Only about 32 people survived.

Mary Philpot died in 1777 at the age of 37; her mother had been 39 at Mary's birth. The children she bore to Nicholas Ashton were:

1. John, born at Liverpool August 9th 1765. He died at Hefferston in 1814, one year before his son died at Waterloo, and is buried at Weaverham Church.

2. William, born 28th September 1773, who died in Martinique in the year 1796 in Service. He was Colonel of the 79th Regiment.

3. Thomas, born 1775, died 1816 unmarried.

4. Henry, died in infancy.

5. Sarah, died in infancy.

6. Mary, died in infancy.

7. Elizabeth, born 1766 and died 1820. Elizabeth married twice; first to William James and on his death she married George Williams of Little Woolton, who had his house ransacked.

8. Mary, born 1777, and who died 1852 at Carlisle.

Nicholas Ashton married for the second time on 23rd January, 1781, to Catherine Hodgson, daughter of Thomas Hodgson, of Liverpool, who died 19th May 1806, but not before bearing three children who were:

1. Joseph, born 15th May 1783, and who was buried 15th March 1836,Childwell.

2. Ellis, born 15th April, 1789, and who died in 1869. He was MA of Brazenose, Oxford, took Holy Orders and was Rector of Huyton.

3. Henry, born 4th October 1795 and died 22nd December, 1870.

The children of John Ashton, Nicholas's eldest son, and the only Ashton to take up residence at Hefferston, and that was for only a short time, and his wife, the daughter of John Jarrett, were:

1. John, born at Woolton 10th March 1796 and died a Captain in the Guards at Waterloo on the 18th June, 1815.

2. Herbert, born Woolton 10th November 1797, died Nice on 21st March 1876 and is buried there.

Herbert Ashton had entered the Royal Navy on 14th April, 1809, when he was eleven years of age, and he served in HMS "Implacable", of 74 guns, under Captain Byam Martin. Many years later, when "Implacable" put in at La Corunna, in Northern Spain, Herbert met his brother, John Ashton, who was serving in Wellington's Peninsular Expedition. The two brothers were never to meet again.

When Wellington's Army crossed the Pyrenees, marching through Bayonne, Toulouse, and on to Brussels, John Ashton was a Captain in the 3rd Foot Guards. He was killed on 18th June, 1815, defending the Farm of Hougoumont, Waterloo, and lies buried in the orchard there. He was 18 years of age. There is a tablet in St. Joseph's Chapel in the Village of

```
TO THE MEMORY
OF THE UNDERMENTIONED GALLANT OFFICERS
OF THE SECOND BATTALION
OF HIS BRITANNIC MAJESTIES
THIRD REGIMENT OF FOOT GUARDS
WHO BRAVELY FELL
IN THE BATTLE OF WATERLOO
ON THE 18TH JUNE 1815
THIS TABLET IS INSCRIBED BY
HON COLONEL
HIS ROYAL HIGHNESS
PRINCE WILLIAM FREDERIC
DUKE OF GLOUCESTER AND EDINBURGH
FIELD MARSHALL OF HIS MAJESTY'S FORCES
LIEUT COLONEL THE HON. SIR ALEX GORDON KcB
CHARLES FOX CANNING
CAPTAINS: WILLIAM STOTHERT
THE HON. HASTINGS FORBES
THOMAS CRAWFORD
JOHN ASHTON
ENSIGN SIMPSON
```

Waterloo, which I reproduce above.

There is another plaque to Crawford on the wall of that orchard at Hougoumont indicating his resting place, leading us to suppose John Ashton is also there.

"Implacable" survived at Portsmouth as a Sea Cadet training-ship, until December 1949 when she was sunk as the Government of the day would not afford to restore her.

Herbert Ashton's second wife was Marie Peronn Usannaz, who died in Paris 1900, but his first wife was Heloise Clement, who died in 1849, and was buried at Kensal Green.

The following in memoriam verses were written soon after Waterloo:

"Hail, youthful Ashton in thy field of blood;
Thou bloom of honour gathered in the bud;
Thy prime career of martial life began
With spirit fit to shine in glory's van;
Comrades who groaned to see thee yield thy breath,
Yet almost envied thy heroic death.
Accept the country's Praise! thy mother's tears!
Whose heavenly sorry Heaven itself reveres!
Kissing in agony affliction's rod
She yields her pride murm'ring to her God."

In the second half of the 18th Century, there was published a novel ("Mervyn Clitheroe" by William Harrison Ainsworth) which caused a sensation in Weaverham.

William Harrison Ainsworth was the son of Thomas Ainsworth, a Solicitor, and was born at Manchester on 4th February, 1805. He was educated at Manchester Grammar School and articled to the firm of which his father was a member, proceeding to London in 1824, to complete his legal training, at the Inner Temple.

At the age of 21, he married a daughter of John Ebers, the Publisher, and started in his father-in-law's business, but this proved unprofitable and he decided to attempt literary work. Some of his early work had attracted praise from Sir Walter Scott and this encouragement decided him to take up fiction as a career. In 1834, he published "Rookwood" which was an immediate success, and, thenceforth, he was always occupied with "historical" novels. He wrote some 40 such stories, of which the best known are "Jack Shepherd", 1839, "The Tower of London", 1840, "Guy Fawkes", 1841, "Old St. Pauls", 1841 "Windsor Castle", 1843, and he also wrote "Lancashire Witches".

The story of "Mervyn Clitheroe" is centred around an old hall, which, for the sake of the story, he calls "Owlarton Grange", but which is readily recognised as Hefferston Grange.

Weaverham, its streets and familiar landmarks, and named places in the near neighbourhood are so accurately described as to make one wonder how the author could write of it with such familiarity.

The Grange itself is depicted, with astonishing insight, as it would have been in earlier times. But then, on learning that the author died in 1882, and was buried at Kensal Green, where Herbert Ashton's first wife was buried, makes me believe that Ainsworth and Herbert Ashton had become closely acquainted in that part of London, and that Herbert Ashton had provided a great deal of the local knowledge and folklore that Ainsworth had woven into his story. Three roads in Owley Wood – Clitheroe Road, Mervyn Road, and Ainsworth Road – are named after the author and book, and because of its reference to witchcraft and hauntings at the Grange, the Reverend Francis Long banned his family from reading it, but this made them more eager to find out more.

The third child of John Ashton, of Hefferston, was Richard, who died at Gorstage Hall in 1869. He married Louisa, daughter of Sir John Lister Kaye, Bn., in 1850, and she died at Gorstage Hall, in 1870.

The township of Acton had been part of the ancient inheritance of the Duttons, from whom it passed by marriage to the Gerrards and the Fleetwoods. It was sold by the latter to a Mr Scrase, of Brighthelmstone, from whom it was purchased by Nicholas Ashton who was always looking to buy more land. However, after Nicholas Ashton's death, in 1833, followed by the death of John Ashton's widow, the Acton lands were disposed of, and from his share of the proceeds, Richard Ashton built Gorstage Hall. The fourth child was William Ashton, H.E.I.C.S., born 1798 and who died 1882. He was Collector of Cuddlore and Cuddapah in the Madras Presidency, India.

Fifth was Mary Ashton who died 24th September 1866.

Sixth was Harriet Ashton, who married the Dean of Carlisle.

Seventh was Frederica Ashton, who died 2nd January 1884.

Eighth was Julia Ashton, who died 14th April 1892.

Since Nicholas Ashton had never had any desire to live at Hefferston, it had been necessary to lease out the hall. Fortunately, the Tarporley Hunt Club had been formed on the 4th November, 1762. The Grange was ideally suited as a hunting lodge, being situated close to the Hunt head-quarters, having good stabling facilities, with room for a number of hunters, and a coach house. The house was spacious; there was plenty of horse pasture and space for a gallop; it was ideal, and consequently there was no shortage of people wishing to take up the lease.

Among these was Thomas Tarleton, later of Bolesworth Castle, who was a member of the Hunt and one time President.

In 1805, Bishop Dr. Henry Majeudie translated from the See of Chester to Bangor stayed at Hefferston, courtesy of Nicholas Ashton, while his new residence was being made ready, and soon afterwards John Ashton moved into the Grange, joined the Hunt, and became its President. John's stay, however, was not a long one. He died in 1814, one year before the death of his son at Waterloo, and is buried at Weaverham.

Another prominent Hunt member to take up the lease was Thomas Brooke who moved in shortly after John Ashton's death. He was brother to Sir Richard Brooke, of Norton Priory, and was M.P. for Newton, as well as having, in 1810, been made Sheriff of Cheshire. He died in 1820 and his brother's widow, Lady Mary Brooke, then acquired the lease and moved into the house with her daughter, Charlotte Frances, and her nephew Henry, who later moved to Ashbrook Hall and Church Minshull.

Lady Mary was the daughter of Sir Robert Cunliffe, Bt., of Saighton, who had also been involved in the slave trade and privateering out of the Port of Liverpool and was a business associate and friend of Nicholas Ashton. It was no surprise then that Nicholas granted the lease of Hefferston to Lady Mary for her lifetime and she remained in residence until her death, in October 1852 in her 92nd year. Herbert Ashton, who was now heir to Hefferston, had been obliged to honour his grandfather's agreement, but now, on Lady Mary's death, he was free to dispose of the hall and its land and complete a sale which had been held somewhat in abeyance during her occupancy.

Woolton Hall had come into the possession of Ellis Ashton, Herbert's uncle, who sold the hall and its grounds, in 1865, to James Redcliffe Jeffrey, Esq., of Compton House, Liverpool. Woolton Wood, another part of the Woolton Estate, was sold about the same time by Henry Ashton (another of Herbert's uncles by Nicholas's second marriage) to Francis Shand, Esq.. It would appear then that all Nicholas Ashton's estates in Lancashire and Cheshire were being disposed of, and the deal which Herbert Ashton was waiting to complete was the sale of Hefferston Grange, with its land, to one Robert Heath.

THE HEATHS

HEATH OF KEPIER
ARMS: Party per chev. or and sa,, in chief two mullets, in base a heath cock wattled gu.,counter-charged.

CREST: On a wreath, a heath-cock's head erased sa.,wattled gu.

This branch of the Heath family had their roots in the County of Middlesex and the first 'Heth', of whom there is any documentary evidence, is recorded by the Heralds as being "a gentleman", and thus it may be inferred that the family occupied a good position and had an estate in Middlesex, probably land which they held or occupied by the recognised system of tenure, or military service, under the Sovereign. The earliest records show a John Heath, who was probably born not later than 1470. His son lived at Twickenham and his grandson, also John Heath, purchased, in 1568, the estates of the dissolved hospital of Kepyer, in Co. Durham. The fourth surviving son of Nicholas, then acquired lands in Little Eden, Co. Durham, which, later, at the age of just eighteen, was inherited by a grandson, George Heath. By his second marriage, George Heath had six children, his heir being Henry Heath, a 'Master Mariner and Ship Owner' whose son, Henry Fearon Heath lived at Westoe, Co. Durham and married Mary Carlen. Their fifth son, Robert Heath, was born 25th July, 1815, and baptised London, Pentonville, 16th August, 1815.

Robert was educated at Witton Wear Public School, near Durham, as were his brothers, who were Henry, baptised 28th September, 1802; Edward baptised 2nd October, 1804; John Carlen Heath, 1810; Sherman, 1812; and George Yeoman Heath, born 1819, and baptised at South Shields, 20th October, 1819, and described as being of Westoe.

It would appear that John, Robert and Sherman were named after John Robert Sherman, a friend of Henry Fearon Heath and a fellow Insurance Broker, of Highbury Park, Co. Middlesex. There were also two girls, Fanny, born in 1807, and Ellen, born in 1817.

On leaving school, Robert came to Liverpool, to complete his business studies, where he was later joined by his brother, Edward. Edward, the second son, entered the mercantile marine and at a very early age commanded his own ships, making South Shields his headquarters. He later became associated in business with the firm of Gwyer Brothers, of Bristol, Russian Merchants, which led to his marriage with Anne, eldest daughter of William Orchard Gwyer, who was a prominent person in Bristol commercial circles. The family were of Welsh descent; its name being originally spelt "Gwydr". This lady's brother, Samuel Gwyer, was the representative of a firm in St.Petersburg where he attained a high social standing, amassed a considerable fortune, and became a "persona grata" in Imperial circles.

In the meantime, Edward had moved his business to Liverpool where he too had earned for himself a reputation for absolute integrity and the esteem of his fellow citizens and a substantial position in the commercial circles of that city.

Robert Heath then formed a company with Edward, but, shortly afterwards, went out to join his brother Sherman in America. Robert was the complete opposite to Sherman, who was a flamboyant character, being clever, artistic, a good musician, a singer with a lovely voice and a good dancer. He could also sketch and was good at wood carving, but he also had the ability to organise business and by the time Robert arrived from England, Sherman had built up a thriving commercial enterprise in New Orleans.

The three brothers thus had a wonderful opportunity, each contributing his own skills, to develop a successful mercantile business covering the Southern States of America, with a base in New Orleans and a home base in Liverpool.

All went well until tragedy struck when Sherman, on a business trip to Florida, contracted yellow fever and died in Pensecola in September, 1839, aged only 27. Robert, however, continued with the business and even expanded by purchasing a cotton plantation in Louisiana, to export good quality cotton to Lancashire in his brother Edward's ships.

He did manage to make a trip home in 1841 when, with his brothers, he travelled up to Durham to visit the Heath families' several ancestral homes in that county. On his return to Louisiana, he took with him his sister Ellen and, as well as taking her to see Sherman's grave in Pensecola, he took her on a tour of the Southern States. These were hazardous journeys covering great distances, mostly on horseback, through some unsettled country, including some Indian Territories.

Robert continued to look after his interests in Louisiana but, as the years went by, there was growing opposition to the use of slave labour in the cotton plantations, and growing unrest between the North and the South which was to eventually erupt into the Civil War. So Robert, concerned about the possible conflict, decided the time had come to wind up his business interests in New Orleans and return, to settle down in England. And so, in 1849, having sold his enterprises in America, he arrived home in England, a handsome young bachelor of 34 years, and a very wealthy man, looking for an estate he could farm and on which he could breed horses, a passion in which he had successfully indulged in Louisiana where he had become a skilled horseman, as well as a gifted handler and breaker.

Robert lived for a while at Liscard, on the Wirral, where his friend Bolton Littledale's family lived at Liscard Hall. Here they had a wonderful dairy farm, years ahead of its time, and sold milk and dairy products over a very wide area.

Captain Bolton Littledale was also looking for an estate and eventually bought 400 acres at Sandiway Bank and, more than likely, made Robert

Heath aware of the impending sale, by Herbert Ashton, of the Hefferston Estate. Robert had already inspected several properties in the County of Durham where his brother John had always wanted the family to become landowners again, but he held the opinion that the soil of Durham was heavy, cold and unfertile, and not suited to the breeding of horses. He settled then on the Grange Estate which he purchased from Herbert Ashton for £30,000, a great deal of money it would seem to me for these times. However, he was not able to take possession right away as Lady Brooke had the tenancy for her lifetime and it was not until about Christmas 1852 that he was able to move into the property and begin to create the sort of farm he wanted.

The house was described as "large and handsome, standing on the site of an old Monastic appendage, hence its name, "The Grange". The estate comprised about 500 acres divided at the time into four farms: Grange Lane Farm, Nook Farm, Milton Farm, the Home farm (sometimes called Grange Farm) and a watermill.

Robert Heath lost no time in joining the Cheshire Hunt, along with his friend Bolton Littledale, and the pair soon became popular members. They also took on a gamekeeper, Sam Hindley, who looked after both estates and whose expenses they shared. Robert was at first greeted with fear and suspicion. He was a tall man, well over 6 feet and heavily built, who, according to Grandfather George, developed a stoop in later life. He spoke with a strange Colonial accent.

Rumour soon spread among the villagers that he had been a slave dealer, but this was hardly possible, since the slave trade was over before he was even born, but no doubt he would have used slaves on his plantation. He was an aloof man, class-conscious, who would warm to and socialise only with his peers and preferred at first to communicate with his workers only through his farm bailiff, who was a wonderfully knowledgeable man by the name of Samuel Hodkinson, a local man from Gorstage, where he lived with his wife and three children. Until his death, at the age of 62, on 28th July, 1881, Mr Hodkinson was to remain a good and faithful servant to the "Squire", as Mr Heath had become known. There is a wonderful memorial stone to his memory in Weaverham churchyard.

Mr Heath had obviously learned a lot about farming during his stay at Liscard and also kept himself abreast of improvements in husbandry. Neither was he too proud to learn from Samuel Hodkinson and together they built up a herd of shorthorn cattle of which the Squire became very proud and which kept the Home Farm dairy busy making cheese and butter.

There was also a large flock of sheep and the usual farmyard poultry, with geese and ducks revelling in the large duck pond which was situated in the stackyard by a large hawthorn hedge with several fir trees on its Eastern side. On the northern side of the stackyard, Robert Heath built a wonderful Cheshire barn, which he commemorated by inserting a decorative stone into one of the pillars with the inscription "R.H." and the date "1864". On the western side of the stackyard, was the large two-storey barn into which had been installed a horse-gin, or as Cheshire folk would say, "a ginny ring." This was a shaft fitted to a type of capstan which, in turn, was connected to a geared system, so that when the two horses, which were required to turn it, were walked round in a circle, it drove a mechanism which was suitable for grinding corn, or pulping turnips. It also had a number of other uses. Only the larger farms in the village were equipped with these and it was said that some horses were ruined for other work, as they were unable afterwards to walk in a straight line.

Next to the barn was a stable to hold two pairs of shire horses, with a loft above for hay and, just before entering the stackyard, stood a beautiful round dovecote made of brick, an impressive building in the traditional 17th Century style, about eight yards in diameter and with a domed roof, topped with a cupola through which the birds entered. The birds laid their eggs in nests recessed into the inner walls from top to bottom of the dovecote and easy collection of eggs, or young birds, was made possible by means of a "potent"; this is a central revolving pole to which a ladder is attached by means of two stays. The pigeons were of the "Blue Rook" variety and each pair produced two chicks eight times annually, which were culled at four weeks when the "squabs", as the young birds were called, were still covered in down and the flesh was salty and fat and were used to make pigeon pie. The pigeons were well cared for and managed and were an important part of the domestic economy.

Next to the stable, and opening out into the front yard, were two shanties, one of which accommodated a permanent Irish worker and the other an itinerant, that is a seasonal worker who came for such work as harvest or potato picking. The shippon, which held about 18 cows, joined on to the main barn and another large barn stood next to the shippon, with the dairy and cheese room close by.

Mr Heath's private stables for the coach horses and hunters stood between the Hall and the farm buildings at the end of the main drive which wound its way past the Georgian icehouse on the left, hidden in a clump of rhododendron bushes and covered by a large mound of soil with a monkey puzzle tree growing out of it. The drive then continued past the Hall and round to the stable with its clock. The clock, with its white cupola and weather vane, could be seen for miles on a clear day; its position on top of the steeply sloping roof added great character to this notable old building. Between these stables and the farm buildings, was the cobbled yard with its horse boxes, coach house and tack room surrounding it.

At the Grange, Robert Heath became a very successful breeder of carriage horses and hunters, winning awards at shows across the county and despite permanent damage to his arm sustained in a horse riding accident in America, he was able to master the most awkward of animals. If any of the heavy horses became difficult to handle, he would be able to go up to it, quieten it and harness it without difficulty.

Robert remained in partnership with his brother, Edward, in Liverpool, but sadly Edward began to suffer from increasing ill-health and in the census of 1861, two of Edward's children were shown as staying at Hefferston, as follows:

Robert Heath, Head, Landowner & Farmer, 45, Unmarried. b. Middlesex.

Mary Lilley Heath, Niece, 19, b. Liverpool.

Fanny Emma Heath, Niece, 15, b. Liverpool.

Mary Tunnicliffe, Housekeeper, 59, Eccleshall, Staffs.

Mary Jane Matthews, Servant, Unknown, Unknown.

Edward, who died in 1862, had another daughter, Jessie Anne, but there were no sons.

For the first 18 years of his life at the Grange, Robert Heath remained a bachelor, working hard to expand the farm. One of his innovations was a boiler house, where he could boil up swill and potatoes for his pigs which were housed in brick-built sties at the rear of the farm and by 1870, he had a large flock of sheep looked after by a shepherd who in 1891 was Thomas Chaplain, a Somerset man who lived with his wife, Dinah, in the South Lodge.

One local man, Harry Mercer, crippled with arthritis, had the job, at a very low wage, of mending all the sheep hurdles, pulling them up and tarring the feet and taking for repair, by horse and cart to Bryn Smithy, any which required new feet. By the time he had finished his round from the Dingle to the Wood and to the Back Drive, it would be time to start again. Robert Heath was well respected by his workmen who knew he disliked smoking and when they saw him approaching as they worked in the fields, they would hastily put out their clay pipes, only to light them again as he turned on his heel to return to the hall. They all knew from experience he would not look back once he had left them. He employed quite a few old men from the village for a few hours each week, doing odd jobs and one of the first of these daily odd jobs was to pump water from a well near to the stable door, to fill a storage tank in the attic above the stable. This took two men turning a two-handled pump and, by the same method, they also pumped water from a well near the hall, to a large water tank in the top storey and this supplied the domestic water. There was also an underground storage tank which collected rain water from the roof. The principal farm well was in what is now the garden and this sometimes ran dry.

The Squire acquired an experienced head gardener, George Ferrit, who with his assistants, cared for the walled garden, the pleasure grounds and also the conservatory which the Squire had had built on to the south corner of the hall where he grew many of the exotic fruits that he had been accustomed to in Louisiana, and to remind him of those days he also planted a magnolia tree and azaleas around a rose ring close by.

Mr Ferrit, who lived in the main lodge with his three sons and one daughter, looked after by his housekeeper, Ada Gilbert, was a very fine gardener and kept several greenhouses and hothouses in full use and grew vines and nectarines. He had a fine array of fruit trees, with a large vegetable patch and herb garden within a walled garden where he grew peaches against a wall and he had several orchards growing apples, pears, plums and damsons. The lawns were immaculate with peacocks strutting about and an abundance of shrubs added colour and shelter around the beautiful grounds. One of the garden walks led down to where a secluded pathway passed along the edge of the moat where a lovely summerhouse beside a tall fir tree stood on a bank overlooking the water. Here was complete tranquility, with only the sound of the birds to break the silence, just as it must have been 300 years earlier when the Cistercian Monks were living here. The pathway led through a small wooded area, with wild flowers growing in profusion, snowdrops first, then celandines, cowslips, red campions and then for a while, a carpet of bluebells, followed by foxgloves, all in their time.

At the tops of the tallest trees, rooks built their precarious nests and where the cover was thickest, pheasants were reared by the old gamekeeper, Sam Hindley, who would eventually turn them out into the area known as Heath's Willows, a wild fringe of willows with plenty of cover alongside the Cuddington and Handforth brooks, where he would be seen, with his gun under his arm and his knapsack on his shoulder, scattering a little corn here and there to entice the birds to stay in the vicinity.

Just before the two streams ran into each other, near to the old Onston Mill, an ancient mill from Saxon times, the willows opened out into a lovely old wood containing many oaks, elms, willows, alders, sycamores and many other varieties of trees, which became carpeted with bluebells every year and was always known as "Bluebell Wood." It was a haven for wildlife; badgers, foxes and otters which came upstream from the mill pool at the old mill, but sadly, by 1990, it had been felled and ploughed up. Tenant farmers were under strict orders not to let their dogs wander freely in the fields and any which did so were in danger of their lives, as the gamekeeper was ruthless and would shoot any strays on sight, as well as foxes and cats. It was a well known fact that if a dog put its nose near a pheasant's nest, the eggs would be abandoned and the chicks lost. The foxes, however, presented the keeper with a problem as this was fox hunting country and, as his two employers, Robert Heath and Captain Littledale, were keen Hunt members, he had to balance the needs of the Hunt with those of the shooting parties. The shooting parties, of which Dr. Smith was always a member, would leave Mr Heath a brace of pheasants or a couple of hares, a few rabbits, or a partridge or two, and now and then, the tenant farmers would be invited to shoot. The whole structure of the countryside was designed to provide cover for game and the pleasures of hunting with hounds.

When Sam Hindley retired, he was followed by his son, George, who was just as ruthless with stray dogs and vermin and held the job until, for economic reasons, John Bolton Littledale had to give up the shoot, but was able to place George, who was a fresh-faced man like Grandfather George, in a gamekeeper's position in Wales.

As well as being allowed to grow wild along the brook, the willows were also grown commercially and beds of these were cultivated to provide withes for basket and hurdle making. Nook Farm was probably the last farm in the district where willow beds were kept for this purpose. The willows grew in butts, or large drills, and today the butts can still be seen alongside the brook, going down towards Milton, 150 years after they were first put down. Billy Gorst bought two-year-old willows for use as cornerposts in basket making and Ned Burrows used to cut and bind these into bundles to the length of a wagon, to be carted to Northwich, near Dane Bridge, where Billy Gorst had a business making baskets and hurdles. Ned Burrows used to work for Bailey Bebbington, old Charlie's father, and sometimes for Arthur Moss, and would often sleep out rough, bedding down in straw next to the pig cote. "Shoot" Harry Groves was the last willow cutter. He had his own horse and cart and carried on until the end of the industry in this part of the world. The willows, or osiers, required boggy ground and it was ideal down by the brook, the sets or small sticks of willow were planted in the butts about 3 feet apart, the butts were about 4 feet apart. The wet ground would encourage quick growth and apart from those which were required to grow two years, they were mostly cut every year and the more they were cut the more they would grow, sometimes 20 sticks or more on a stump. They would be cut after the leaves had fallen, usually the end of January or February, so that the old stumps would have a good start for the next year's growth. Then they would be tied in bundles and stood upright in a specially dug ditch, a wet ditch, until about the end of May, by which time they would have begun to shoot again and develop fine root hairs. At this stage, they were easily peeled and it was then they were taken to Billy Gorst where they were skinned through a "cleaver." This was a split piece of wood with a piece of iron each side the split, the osier would be wedged in, pulled through and the skin would come off easily. There were different types of osier, some had nearly black skins, some were of a golden colour and some nearly red. It was reckoned the black skinned ones were the strongest, but when they were peeled, they were almost all white and the true white osiers were used for the most expensive shopping baskets. Some were boiled with their skins left on to make them a buff colour, but for potato hampers and skips, the skins were left on and these were called "browns".

The Squire became a familiar figure driving his large yellow-wheeled trap through the village and on Sundays, he went twice to church in his coach pulled by four horses. He was a zealous member of the church of St. Mary, at Weaverham, and as Squire of Hefferston, he had certain duties which he discharged fully. In 1868, he presented a memorial window to the Grange Chapel; he provided the church with a new organ and helped to pay for the new font. He was Church Warden for many years, but never became a prominent figure in public life, preferring to remain in the background. However, life was to change dramatically for everyone at the Grange when, on a business trip to London, in 1869, Robert met and married, on 9th February, 1869, the young and beautiful Anna Elizabeth Gooday, at the Parish Church of St. Martins in the Field, in the presence of Charles Addison and John Francis Gooday, the bride's father, who was a Solicitor from Sudbury in Suffolk.

It was a shock to his servants at the Grange and the villagers of Weaverham when he returned with his young bride, who was 20 years of age; Robert was 54.

Anna Elizabeth settled in as the new "Lady of the Manor". She was an accomplished horsewoman and joined the Cheshire Hunt, becoming a regular attendant at Meets. She had her own hunters which villagers walking down Grange Lane would see her exercising in the Park every day and her own horse and trap which she preferred to drive herself, unaccompanied. Robert was now persuaded to entertain more frequently and held regular lavish dinner parties, where his wife became the perfect hostess and was very popular with her husband's friends and greatly admired. It was not until 1876 that the first child was born, a baby girl christened Nina Haidee and, to commemorate the occasion, Robert had a new door put on the mansion and a new entrance built. The second child, born in 1882, was another girl, Beatrice, and finally in 1890, Robina Sherman was born.

By now, as the farm was expanding, more local men were working for Mr Heath, including Bill Robinson, who was cowman and Arthur Tomkinson, who was ploughman and teamster. These two lived next door to each other in the cottages by the Wheatsheaf, in High Street. Joe Johnson, from Church Street, was coachman and Jim Hindley and Hughie Nield, who was years later to become bailiff at Grange Farm for Grandfather, were two lads helping with the stock.

Mr Ferrit was still head gardener and late one evening, his son Monty, who was always in mischief, finding the conservatory door unlocked, slipped inside to sample some of the luscious fruit. However, Mrs Heath, who had been walking out in the grounds, came back and realising someone had entered, locked the door and went to tell her husband that she had caught a thief. When she returned with Robert, there was no-one there. In his desperation, Monty had broken out through one of the glass windows and they never did find out who the thief was.

One day, Jim Hindley decided to help himself to a few feathers from the tail of one of a peacock roaming the grounds. After chasing it for a while, he came close enough to catch it, slipped and fell on its tail, stripping it of all the big feathers when it ran off. Unfortunately, just at this moment, Mr Ferrit arrived on the scene to catch young Jim as he gathered a handful of feathers. This resulted in a pair of boxed ears for Jim and a big fright, for Mr Ferrit was greatly feared.

The three girls grew up under the watchful eye of the old Squire who must have been very disappointed that none of them had the same affinity for horses as their parents, although they had all been taught to ride at an early age. Of the Squire's daughters, Miss Beatrice was the most popular and would regularly be seen shopping and chatting to villagers in old Weaverham. Naturally, the Squire and Mrs Heath were hoping their daughters would marry into one of the rich Cheshire families whose sons attended the Hunt Meets, but this was not to be.

Nina grew up quiet and reserved like her father, but much to his disgust, she converted to the Catholic Faith and entered a Convent. Robina, as she grew up, became an excellent shot with rifle and revolver and took part in all the rook shoots organised on the estate. Rook shoots were common among the gentry in Victorian and Edwardian Cheshire. Most estates could boast a rookery or two and shooting parties would arrive in May when it was close season for other game to shoot as many "branchers" or young rooks as they could. They were shot with small guns, or rifles, to avoid damage to the flesh and were plucked by hand, by the cook and her staff, and the tender leg and breast baked into a pie.

I talked some time ago to Lord Delamere's cook, a Miss Wing, who remembers preparing this popular dish for house parties at Vale Royal. Miss Wing came to Vale Royal from Hampshire, where she had been in service, to be nearer to her home at Burton-on-Trent. She also remembers that the train would stop at the bridge for his Lordship so he could jump off and run home across the park and whenever he came home from Africa, he would bring two black servants with him.

It was on one of these trips home, that he called at Weaverham School to ask if there were four boys who would like to go back to Africa with him. Four boys agreed, including a Buckley, from the "Maypole", and a Shallcross, from Acton, and they all prospered.

Jim Walley told me of the story of his Aunt Edna, whose maiden name was Sadler, who would have to wait at "Monkey Lodge" in order to close the gates after Lord Delamere had returned home on horseback. It could sometimes be gone 2 o'clock in the morning and then she would have to walk home to Whitegate in the pitch black night.

As to Miss Robina, she became a rebel and turned away from the way of life she was expected to lead and was constantly in trouble with the old Squire for encouraging lads from the village to go within close proximity to the hall. Her many boyfriends were lads from the village who would meet her at the old iron kissing-gate which swung between two sandstone pillars near the moat, the gateway to a walk behind the walled garden. Another meeting place was the Dovecote, where Robina used to spend hours sitting on the arm of the rotating ladder. One young man she was becoming particularly fond of, was a young stable lad, Arthur Tomkinson, who came from the row of cottages in High Street, near the Wheatsheaf. Arthur's father, also called Arthur, also worked for Mr Heath as wagoner and teamster and living with the Tomkinsons was Raymond Plumridge's mother. Next door lived Alf Wright and next to him the Dillons, but later on Janet Tomkinson, who no-one could ever forget, moved to Dillons' house.

As old Robert Heath crept on in years, naturally there were a few younger men of the hunting fraternity paying attention to his much younger wife.

On one occasion, Joe Johnson, who had taken over the job as coachman at the Grange, in succession to his father, old Joe Johnson, went into the hayloft to throw down some hay for the horses and found Mrs Heath with a local young businessman. Taken aback, the young man offered Joe a sovereign to keep his mouth shut, but Joe refused and for his pains was given a hiding and Mrs Heath, who had no regard for Joe anyway, because of his previous gossiping, sacked him on the spot. Naturally, Joe could not contain himself and soon the whole village knew of the incident. Even at his great age, villagers feared old Robert and it was no surprise when news drifted back that Robert had challenged his wife's lover to a fist fight under the stable clock. A witness to the fight said if it had not been for Robert's great age and his permanent arm injury, he would have given the young man a hiding.

George Hill took over the coachman's job and became well-liked by the Squire, while Joe went into partnership with Eliza Richardson, of 13 West Road, and bought a market cart which he used to take shoppers to Northwich Market and back, eight at a time. He courted this lady for many years, but never married and later branched out into fruit and vegetables, buying fruit, apples and pears to sell in Liverpool. In 1914, to avoid Army service, he got a job with Grandfather George at Nook Farm and stayed until the end of the War, when he returned to his fruit and vegetables and to horse-taxi work. Once, he bought a good load of fruit from Grandfather and stored it in the barn near the road, but Sam Jones and his mates pilfered it and after much haggling, he had to be reimbursed. As an old man, in his declining years, Joe would stand for hours on the corner of Church Street just watching the world go by.

Sadly, on August 7th, 1907, at Hefferston, Robert Heath's long life came to an end at the age of 92 years and he was buried in Weaverham Churchyard. The Heath family crest: "On a wreath a Heath-cock's head, erased Sable: Wattled Gules", which had been granted 4th August, 1558, to his direct male ancestor, had been proudly displayed over the mantelpiece of his study and in his dining room at Hefferston, and remained in position until at least 1940, but then disappeared. There were no male heirs and he was the last of the Heaths, the last male member of a family which had had great wealth, had held great estates and wielded influence it had never abused, a family of such distinction that, to become aware of the extent of its achievements, one would have to read the "Pedigree of the Heath Family of London and Kepyer, Co.Durham", by Cyril Ravenhill Everet, and Cleveland Masterman, a copy of which I have, but which is too lengthy to include in this book.

The friendship between her daughter Robina and Arthur Tomkinson was causing Elizabeth Heath a great deal of distress. She would certainly not accept the young stable lad as a suitable suitor for her daughter's hand and so they decided to elope. One night, Arthur left his parents' cottage in the village and made his way across the park to the Grange where Robina was waiting at her bedroom window. When he was certain the coast was clear, Arthur got the ladder, which was always in place on two hooks under the eaves of the potting shed roof, and with some difficulty placed it against the wall of the house up to Robina's window, enabling her to climb out and down the ladder clutching a few of her treasured belongings. They made their way to Arthur's parents in the little cottage in High Street and from there to Manchester, where Robina took lodgings with Arthur's Uncle Albert, in Myrtle Street. Robina and Arthur were married by Licence on 18th April, 1908, in the Parish Church of St. Clement, Longsight, Manchester, by the Rector, George Hayden, in the presence of Bill Robinson and Katherine Tomkinson. Arthur was described as a teamsman and his father as a farm bailiff.

They then returned to the cottage in Weaverham and it was here that Robina shocked the villagers with her prowess with her revolver. She was a wonderful shot and continued to practise in the back garden and surroundings of the old cottage. Woe betide any stray cats which crossed her path and yet in later years she became a cat lover and kept many pets at her home.

The distress caused to Mrs Heath by the scandal of Robina's elopement, following so closely on her husband's death, decided Mrs Heath to sell the horses and cattle and put the Estate up for sale, which she did in July

1908. The hall and the Home Farm, comprising some 90 acres, were bought by Mr Isidor Frankenburg, but the rest of the estate was not sold and Mrs Heath continued to collect rents on the rest of the properties until about 1920. She advised Grandfather to buy Nook Farm, which he eventually did for £6,000. Cunninghams bought Grange Lane Farm.

On the sale of the Grange, Mrs Heath went to live in a nice house at "Bryn Issa", at Gresford, where she died in 1925, at the age of 77. She was buried at Gresford.

It was assumed, naturally, but wrongly, that Robina must have been pregnant to cause her to elope with Arthur and a long poem about the affair was composed by some wit, which some people could recite for years afterwards. One verse went:

"Robina, Robina, I say have you seen her,
My darling she seems very shy.
If it's a daughter we'll wet it with porter -
If a boy we'll wet it with beer."

However, her son Raymond was born 2nd February, 1909 and celebrated his 87th birthday, in 1996, at Northway, Winnington. He was born in Weaverham, so Arthur and Robina must have been living at the cottage in High Street. Whether or not they had a happy life together, no-one can say, but a second child, Daisy Ellen, was born 20th November, 1911 at Norley. At the time of the writing of Robina's Will in 1950, Daisy Ellen was an inmate of the Royal Albert Hospital, Lancaster. At this time, Robina was living at Holly Cottage, Norley, and died there in 1955, a widow aged 66. Since there is no mention of Arthur in her Will of 1950, I assume she was a widow by then. Raymond was said to have been brought up by his grandparents in High Street, but was sent away to school in London where he stayed for a while, but was not happy and returned to Weaverham. He was well-spoken and never had a local accent.

I cannot say whether or not Robina was completely disowned by her mother, or whether her mother ever forgave her, but in Robert Heath's will, of which I have a copy, she was bequeathed the sum of £2,000, which she was to receive, plus accrued interest, on her 25th birthday. It was said that this was all she ever received from the estate. It is doubtful if Robina and Arthur were ever received at Hefferston Grange, as the Estate was put up for sale almost immediately after the elopement and Mrs Heath then moved to her new home at Gresford.

The last Will and Testament of Mrs Anna Elizabeth Heath

This is the last Will and Testament of me Anna Elizabeth Heath of Bryn Issa Gresford north wales widow.

1. I revoke all wills and testamentary dispositions heretofore made by me.

2. I hereby confirm the Deed dated the twenty sixth day of February One thousand nine hundred and eighteen whereby I have appointed certain Funds under the will of my late Husband Robert Heath in favour of all my three daughters.

3. Executors — I appoint Edward Heath Everett of the Bank of England Liverpool and Lionel Everett the Deputy Chief Constable of Liverpool Executors and Trustees of this my will and I bequeath to each of them who shall prove my will the sum of Twenty five pounds free of legacy duty for his trouble.

4. I bequeath the sum of Three hundred pounds to my daughter Beatrice Rosamund Mary Heath and direct that the same shall be paid to her as soon as conveniently may be after my death and shall be in addition to all other benefits which she may be entitled to under this my will and the said Deed of appointment.

5. I bequeath my Ring with a Diamond in the centre and a pearl on each side to my Sister Bertha free of legacy duty.

6. I devise and bequeath all the residue and remainder of my real and personal property to my Executors upon trust that they or the survivor of them or the executors or administrators of such survivor or other the trustees or trustee for the time being of this my will shall hold the same after

1

payment of my funeral and testamentary expenses and debts and the legacies bequeathed by this my Will and the legacy duty on such of the legacies as are bequeathed free of duty Upon trust for my said daughter Beatrice Rosamund Mary Heath absolutely.

In Witness whereof I have hereunto set my hand this 7th day of Sept One thousand nine hundred and eighteen.

A. E. Heath.

Signed by the said Anna Elizabeth Heath the Testatrix as and for her last Will and Testament in the presence of us both present at the same who at her request in her presence and in the presence of each other have hereunto subscribed our names as witnesses.

Florence Janet Hoskins, Woodlands, Gresford, N. Wales, spinster.
Florence Eleanor Bury, Woodlands, Gresford, N. Wales, spinster.

On the 25th day of May 1925 probate of this will was granted at St Asaph Edward Heath Everett-Heath and Lionel Everett the Executors

This is a true Copy.

2

The last Will and Testament of Robina Tomkinson

M/7
/1

EXECUTORS

COMMISSIONERS FOR OATHS

THIS IS THE LAST WILL AND TESTAMENT of me ROBINA SHERMAN
TOMKINSON of Holly Cottage, Norley, near Warrington in the County of
Lancaster, Widow.

1. I REVOKE all Wills and Codicils by me at any time
heretofore made.

2. I APPOINT WILLIAM GARENCIERES PEARSON of Barrow-in-Furness
in the County of Lancaster, Solicitor; PHILIP LESLIE EARDLEY of
Sunny Bank Farm, Norley near Warrington aforesaid, Farmer and BARCLAYS
BANK LIMITED to be my Executors and Trustees.

3. I DECLARE that the Bank shall be entitled to remuneration for
its services as such Executor and Trustee by fees or otherwise in
accordance with the terms of remuneration charged by it at the date
of my death for its services in acting as Executor and Trustee of a
Will free from duties and deductions and to be paid or retained out
of any part of the capital or income of my estate in priority to all
other payments, and also to any customary share of brokerage
receivable by the Bank and the Bank may in its absolute discretion
determine how any fees or other remuneration payable to the Bank shall
be borne as between different parts of my estate and as between persons
beneficially interested in capital and income respectively of any part
of my estate and every such determination shall be binding on all
persons beneficially interested under my Will and any Codicil hereto.

4. I BEQUEATH to my Son Raymond all my articles of personal use.

5. I DEVISE AND BEQUEATH all the rest of my real and personal
estate whatsoever to my Trustees UPON TRUST after payment of my just
debts and testamentary expenses AS TO my house Holly Cottage to
convey or transfer the same to the Royal Society for the Prevention
of Cruelty to Animals for a home for an Inspector or for an animals'
home.

6. AND as to the residue of my estate and effects UPON TRUST to
sell the same as and when they shall think fit and stand possessed
of the proceeds of sale as a first charge to purchase for my
daughter Daisy Ellen Tomkinson an annuity of Thirty Pounds per annum
for her personal use and for the purpose of providing two holidays

1

per annum away from the Royal Albert Home, Lancaster, her maintenance being already provided for at the Institution.

7. To pay the said William Garencieres Pearson a legacy of Twenty Pounds.

8. To pay the said Philip Leslie Eardley a sum of Twenty Pounds for acting as my Executor provided he shall carry out my wishes as regards my pet animals, which I desire shall be painlessly destroyed by a Veterinary Surgeon (preferably Mr. Greenway of Main Street, Frodsham) by chloroform, and that they shall remain unburied for 24 hours at,least plunged overhead in water to make sure of actual death before burial.

9. To pay to my son Raymond all the income from the residue for life and then to his wife should she survive him, and after the death of both, to pay the said income from the residue to my sister Beatrice Comber for her life.

10. And after their respective deaths to pay the whole of the residue to the Royal Society for the Prevention of Cruelty to Animals and I declare that the receipt of the Treasurer for the time being of the said Society shall be a good and sufficient receipt for the same.

11. I Desire that my Cottage shall not be sold but be used as a home for an Inspector of the said Society or as an Animals' Home.

12. I Declare that any Executor or Trustee who shall be a Solicitor shall be entitled to charge and be paid for all professional or other work done by him or his Firm in connection with my estate notwithstanding that he may be a Solicitor and Executor or Trustee.

13. I Desire that a Medical Practitioner shall open an Artery in my arm after my death to prevent premature burial, and that no mourning shall be worn for me at my funeral,and that there be no flowers or wreaths, and that no tombstone be erected over my grave. And I wish to be buried in Norley Churchyard.

IN WITNESS whereof I have hereunto set my hand this

Robina S. Tomkinson.

2

George Heath of Durham, = Margaret, d. of Thomas
bap 1 July, 1708. bur. Fearton, of Whitley, and
St. Nicholas, Durham, 14 Margaret Foster, his wife,
Aug.,1745. Admin.dated b Cullercoats, Northumberland,
31 Oct., 1747 20 Apr, 1702. m....... d.1747
(Six children) bur. St.Oswalds, Durham.

Henry Heath = Mary, d. of Wm.Hunter, of
Master Mariner Chollerton, Northumberland,
& Ship Owner, bap there 26 July, 1741, m
bap. 1 May, 1738, St.Michael's, Cornhill, London,
St. Nicholas, Durham 16 April, 1768. died 12 July,
d 18 Nov.,1803. bur. 1800, bur. St.Hilda, South Shields.
St.Hilda, South Shields.
(Ten children)

Henry Fearon Heath, = Mary, d. of John Carlen, South
Ship Owner, b. 5 Nov., Shields, afterwards of Westoe,
1768, Mile End, Co.Middlesex, and his wife Mary (d.of Thomas
bap. St.Dunstans, Stepney, Masterman, of South Shields),
Co.Middlesex, 18 Nov. 1768, b. 21 April, 1779, South Shields,
died Westoe, Co.Durham, 17 Nov.,1801,died Westoe, 30 Jan.
7 July, bur. St.Hilda, 1870, aged 90, bur. St.Hilda, South
South Shields, Shields, 4 Feb., 1870.
9 idem, 1825.
(Eleven children)

Robert Heath, of Hefferston = Anna, d. of J.F.S Gooday, of
Grange, Weaverham, Co. Sudbury, Suffolk, b.12 Dec., 18...
Cheshire, b.25 July, Pentonville, m. 9 Feb., 1869, St.Martins -in-
bap. 16 Aug., 1815, St.James, the-Fields, London.
Pentonville, Co.Middlesex, died
12 Aug., 1907, at The Grange.
Will dated 22 Sept., 1902, with
codicil dated 14 Jan., 1905,
proved at Chester, Sept., 1907.
(Three children)

Robina Sherman, b.13 April, = Arthur Tomkinson,(son of Arthur
1889, Hefferston Grange, bap. Tomkinson, of Weaverham,
4 June, 1889, Weaverham Cheshire), of Norley, Cheshire,
Parish Church,m. Manchester, born Weaverham, 20 Sept., 1887.
17 April, 1908.

Raymond Tomkinson, Daisy Ellen,born
b.Weaverham 20 Nov., 1911,
2 Feb., 1909. Norley.

From the Pedigree of George Heath of
Little Eden, Co.Durham

THE FRANKENBURGS

Isidor Frankenburg, the new owner of Hefferston Grange, was born on 18th July, 1845, in Russian Poland and, in 1857, at the age of 12 years, he came to London with his mother Bertha, who had been born in 1810. In 1866, Isidor moved to Manchester and rented a room on the second floor of a building in Hanging Ditch where he began to make outdoor clothing. Despite the terrible setback of having all his stock stolen by his foreman, he was able to firmly establish the business.

In 1867, a French Army representative was in Manchester looking for a company which could supply up to 1,000 waterproof knapsacks per day, which was a huge commitment. Isidor tendered for the order and with the help of his Jewish tailor friends, combined with his own capacity, he proved to the satisfaction of the French Army authorities that he could supply the quantity and quality required, an achievement no-one else in Manchester could match. His initiative won him the contract and with success now guaranteed, he moved to Salford, buying up old unsanitary buildings, demolishing them and building a new factory with new homes close by for his many workers, Jews and Gentiles alike.

In April 1873, he married Frances Ann Slazenger Moss, daughter of the recently deceased Joseph Slazenger Moss, a high class tailor, who traded as J.C. Moss and Sons, in Market Street, Manchester. Frances's brother, Ralph, succeeded his father, but later moved to London to form a rubber and waterproofing company similar to Frankenburgs, which grew to become the Slazenger Sports Equipment empire. The 1881 census found Isidor and Frances living at Clifton House, 398 Lower Broughton Road, Salford, with their five children, along with Isidor's mother, Bertha, now 71-years-old and Isidor's 17-years-old nephew, Alfred, born in Poland. Isidor is described in the census as a manufacturer of leather and rubber goods, employing 78 people.

In 1887, he was elected to Salford Borough Council, becoming Alderman in 1901, and the first Jewish Mayor of Salford, an office he held from 1905 to 1908. He was a Tory, a Magistrate for 20 years and Chairman of the Jewish Board of Guardians. He was also credited with bringing peace to the cotton industry following the strike of 1908. In 1892, he owned two factories: The Greengate Rubber and Leather Company in Salford, manufacturing waterproof clothing, ladies' and gents' waterproof garments, gaiters, Imperial mantles, tennis shoes and leggings, all under the trade mark "The Distingue", and the Irwell Rubber works in Ordsall Lane, making rubber for industrial purposes, for hoses and rubber balls, but ironically, it was Slazengers who were to come to prominence with tennis equipment.

Isidor always showed a great deal of interest in his workers, caring for their health and welfare and for his Silver Wedding Anniversary in April, 1898, he and Frances gave a celebration for 1,100 workers and their families at St. James Hall, Manchester, combining it with their son, Merton's 21st birthday celebrations. His term as Mayor was coming to an end just as Mrs Heath was putting up the Grange and the estate for sale. It immediately appealed to Isidor as an ideal semi-retirement base in the tranquil Cheshire countryside, with plenty of space in which to entertain his workers and friends, and yet within easy reach, by rail from either Greenbank or Cuddington Stations, of his business interests in Salford.

He lost no time in purchasing the hall with its Home Farm and 90 or so acres of land and looked forward to a new life as a "Country Squire" in his mansion house, to which he gave it the name "Hefferston Grange". Previously, for centuries, it had been simply "the Grange" or "Grange Hall" or "the Grange at Hefferston".

However, he did not move into the house until 1909. Although Philip Henry Warburton, in 1741, had greatly extended the house and further alterations had been made by Robert Heath, in 1876, Isidor employed a firm of builders by the name of Woods, of Manchester, to refurbish the house as to his exact wishes and they took over a year to complete the work.

Fred Allman recalled that when he was helping the builders fill in some cavity walls, he came across a tunnel leading away from the house underneath the front lawn. Fred was only a lad at the time and although the tunnel was not very high, he had managed to crawl along it for a short distance when the foreman of the builders ordered him back and the tunnel was sealed.

Isidor was proud of his purchase and had great hopes that his family would continue to live at the hall for many years. He particularly liked the old stable block topped with the clock and cupola which was a prominent landmark. He spent a great deal of money on enlarging the pleasure grounds and gardens; he improved the tennis courts and even created a bowling green where he would organise tournaments when he invited his workers from his Manchester factories to visit and enjoy the amusement grounds at the hall and to breathe the fresh county air.

He would also invite schoolchildren from Weaverham for picnics and afternoon teas, where there would be fresh cream and butter from the dairy where Ella Davies officiated as Dairy Maid, as she had done for Squire Heath. The visitors would paddle in the brook which Isidor had straightened and lined with sandstones and planted along it forget-me-nots and other flowers and ferns. He had made two bays with a view to sailing a boat, but this failed due to lack of depth and insufficient water, except in time of flood. He also cleaned out the moat and stocked it with goldfish, which kingfishers used to take.

The Grange now had its own electricity, as one of Mr Frankenburg's first requirements had been the installation of a Wheatley Oil engine, to provide the power to run the generator for the electric system, which ran throughout the house and outbuildings. The engine house was outside, opening out onto the kitchen yard and the throb of the engine, which was started on petrol switching over to paraffin for its work, and hum of the generator, could be heard from some distance around. It was very reliable, producing a current of 120 volts and was quite safe to work with and even after the electricity had to be taken over by the Northwich Electric Company, it was still 120 volts until well after World War II.

Two old-fashioned lights stood at the top of the drive, between the rhododendron bushes and the little clap hatch, where the footpath came out of the park. This generator was used for many years afterwards by the Sanatorium and was looked after by Mr Bloor, the engineer, who died in 1934 or 35. Some fault in the cable going underground across the gateway to the boiler yard used to cause a shock transmitted to horses' hooves and it was not until Littlers Timber men were using a metal winch, to load wood there, and the winch became live, giving the men a shock, that they realised why George Ward's horse would jump forwards every time he crossed the gateway whenever he turned out with a cart to fetch fish, or other provisions, from the station. The 120 volt power supply was still in use until the 1950s when, by this time, Eddie Makin was the engineer and lived in the West Lodge.

In about 1914, a similar, but less deluxe, Wheatley engine was purchased and installed on a concrete bed in the barn at Nook Farm. A large water tank provided the water for the cooling system. Water had to be carried from the milk house for that first filling and there was great excitement as Tom McCann and his brother carried bucket after bucket of water in preparation for the trial of this new engine. It had to be heated with a blow lamp to vaporise the fuel to start it. It ran for many years pulping roots, straw cutting, etc.. (These engines, I think, were supplied by Birtwisles, of Hartford).

Home Farm was a working farm at the time of Robert Heath's death and although Mrs Heath had sold the cattle and horses, Mr Frankenburg decided to reinstate the farm and took on a Farm Bailiff, Mr Cooper, who classed himself as gamekeeper as well as bailiff and always carried a shotgun about the estate.

Herbert Cooper had an extraordinarily keen eye and could pick out a pigeon amongst the leaves of the tallest trees and shoot it with no trouble. With Mr Cooper's help, Isidor developed a herd of pedigree Jersey cows, each one of which had a bell attached to its neck, and on warm summer nights the tinkling bells could be heard as the cattle grazed in the meadows. There was never any shortage of fresh cream, home-made cheese and churned butter at the old hall.

Alan Rustage worked there as a lad under Mr Cooper and he recalls the donkey which pulled a light mowing machine to cut the lawns and the sides of the drive and was fitted with leather shoes to protect the lawns from its hooves. Alan remembers getting into trouble when Mr Frankenburg caught him riding the donkey which Bill Johnson also used to drive. Alan also had to look after a pair of mongooses which were regularly turned loose in the hall, to rid it of vermin, rats in particular. The chief concern was for the cellars and attics, but these two also gave the house a thorough search. They were far more ferocious and agile killers than cats and they returned to their cage to be rewarded with some fresh raw meat.

Alan also had to look after two Great Danes, one a bitch, the other Prince, who was clever enough to open any gate on the estate with either his teeth or massive paws. Strangely enough, many years later, long after Prince had departed this life, when I was returning home across the park late one dark night, I saw in front of me a huge light-coloured dog which I chased and chased and never got quite near and then it disappeared. When I told dad about it, he said: "Oh, that would be old Prince".

Alan used to walk to work across the park for a 6 o'clock start, with John Burgess, nephew of Joe Johnson, the former coachman to Mr Heath, who was wagoner and did all the cartwork and ploughing. Other locals working on the estate were Henry Oram, who had worked at Buckingham Palace as a footman, and was in charge of the outdoor staff. One of his jobs being to look after the stable clock.

Jim Hindley and Hughie Nield had worked as lads for Mr Heath and stayed on to work for Mr Frankenburg. Jimmy worked for Henry Oram as odd job lad, whilst Hughie Nield helped Mr Cooper with the livestock and many years later, worked as bailiff for Grandfather when he took over Home Farm.

Jack Waterman was chauffeur to Mr Frankenburg, driving him to Greenbank Station each morning, in his new "Sunbeam" car, to catch the business trains. This Sunbeam car was by far the most splendid vehicle in the district and was nicknamed the "Bobby Dazzler" by the villagers. He would come up behind young Arnie Forster, driving his old Ford Tin Lizzie taxi to Northwich with a load of shoppers, the Sunbeam being a much faster car and Arnie being a slow and careful driver anyway. Mr Frankenburg was always on the last minute and the road being very narrow in those days, little more than a lane and no room to overtake, he would get very impatient and say: "Pass him, Vaterman, knock him out of the vay, does he not know I have a train to catch?"

Another car on the road would be Herbert Percival's, who was branching out with an old Ford to complement his horse-drawn taxi service. It was said that Mrs Atherton, Frank's mother and a woman named Laura Harvey, had bought the wheels for Herbert's car due to their fondness for a tipple at the "Style."

Mr Frankenburg was not an easy man to get on with; he would send for Grandfather to discuss farm business and, having completely forgotten what he wished to discuss, he would greet him with:

"Vot brings you here, Mr. Moss ?"

He said to his bailiff: "Cooper, if you stop smoking I will buy you all your clothes; if you don't I vill buy you nothing," but Mr Cooper, a small sharp-eyed man, liked his pipe far too much to give it up.

Mrs Frankenburg did not share her husband's enthusiasm for Hefferston Grange. She was very happy with her friends in Manchester and spent a great deal of time away and in her periods of absence, would stay at her favourite Manchester hotels. Apart from Miss Mary, none of the family seemed particularly happy at the Grange, except perhaps Isidor's youngest son, David, who suffered from a complaint which affected his balance, causing him to fall down and Grandfather remembers him tumbling off the gate at the back drive on the day of the Pageant.

David seemed happy enough looking after a number of hens with the help of young Rookie Woodward. These hens had been established in brick-built hen houses for his benefit, in the expectancy that the outdoor life could only improve his health. Each of these hen houses was named after one of Mrs Frankenburg's favourite hotels.

Mr Frankenburg and his family had been living at the Grange only about five years when, in 1914, the Great War broke out and even though he was employing many local people and in spite of the fact his middle son, Sydney, was an Officer in the Army, having reached the rank of Captain in the Manchester Regiment, there was deep suspicion in the village about the old foreigner on the doorstep. There was even talk of having him interned, such was the hysteria generated by the conflict. As if to show which side he was on, he entered into a great deal of war work, holding charity evenings at Hefferston, concerts at the Church House and other fund-raising events to provide soldiers at the Front with food parcels, warm clothing, socks and gloves. The Frankenburgs' eldest child, Jessie Mary Frankenburg, was always referred to as "Miss Mary", even though she had become a widow, having married, in 1895, Captain Henry Dreschfield, of the 13th Manchester Regiment, who was killed in action 19th February, 1915 aged 47. She spent nearly all her time on charity work.

Isidor bought a Red Cross ambulance which was initially based at Hefferston, and garaged under the arched passageway, in the old stables. It can still be seen how the arch was modified to accommodate the vehicle. Jack Waterman, as well as being chauffeur to Mr Frankenburg, also drove the ambulance, but when Jack was called up for the Army, a Mr Schofield, who was also head gardener, did some driving and lived in the South Lodge. He eventually left after a disagreement with his employer and, since there was now a great shortage of manpower, a Miss Hatton became head gardener and lived in the lodge. Miss Hatton was a very capable gardener and the grounds remained as lovely as ever with the peacocks roaming round freely as they had in Squire Heath's day, presenting a wonderful display as they strutted about the lawns. Miss Hatton used to say that Mr Frankenburg liked to be the smartest man on the train and called to see her every morning to select a red carnation.

Sadly, early in 1917, Mr Frankenburg became ill and on 6th May, that year, aged 71, he died at Hefferston after a long illness. He was buried at the Jewish cemetery at Whitefield, Manchester. Among the mourners were his brother Julius and his wife's brother, Isaac Slazenger Moss. The floral tributes included those from Mrs J. Slazenger Moss, his wife's mother, and those from his wife's brothers, Horatio and Albert Slazenger Moss.

Mrs Frankenburg then gave, to the War Department, the ambulance and the use of the chauffeur to pick up wounded soldiers at ports and take them to hospital. The chauffeur did not return to Hefferston after the war.

The main lodge, at the drive gate, had been a simple ground floor building, but Mr Frankenburg had had this made into a house, in the hope that one of his sons, either Captain Sydney, or David, would eventually like to stay there. Throughout the war, Captain Sydney's wife lived in the lodge with her children, but the Captain, being mostly away on active service, was an infrequent visitor.

Meanwhile, although still living mostly in Manchester hotels, Mrs Frankenburg kept a watchful eye on the Grange and, wanting to improve the gardens and pleasure grounds, should any of the family in the future wish to take up residence, she appointed the highly recommended Albert Holden as head gardener, in place of Miss Hatton, who was in any case about to become Mrs Tom Gleave.

Dad had memories of Tom and Miss Hatton sitting under the porch of South Lodge on one of Tom's frequent courting visits. Unfortunately, in the last few days of the war, Captain Sydney was very seriously wounded, in France, and was moved to a London hospital. To be near her husband, Captain Sydney's wife moved with her children to London and the lodge and the Grange were empty again, apart from Mrs Moore, who, for long periods in Mrs Frankenburg's absences, was alone, acting as caretaker as the house was full of silver and valuables. Mrs Moore, who also was the cook, was a widow and she and Henry Oram were the last of the old servants.

As I have mentioned before, Henry had worked at Buckingham Palace as a footman and as well as being in charge of the servants and doing odd jobs, he also had to look after the stable clock which throughout the war had its bell muffled. At 8 o'clock of the morning following the Armistice, it was allowed to sound again over the park, much to Henry's delight.

Jim Waterman came home from the war and married Mrs Moore and they went to live in our cottage at the Nook where his first wife had died. Sadly, Jim died of the severe 'flu epidemic, which killed so many people shortly after the war, and his widow stayed on in the cottage until Dad moved in when she went to live at Lymm, only for Jim's two boys, Jack and Reg, to tragically drown in the Dam.

In the latter part of the war, the land belonging to the Home Farm had been taken out of the care of the Frankenburgs, except the top and bottom parks which they were allowed to retain, and had been ploughed up to produce more food, some of the ploughing being done very roughly with a Government tractor. At first, we had the use of only two fields which were let to us by Mrs Frankenburg and the rest was rented out to a Sam Lewis, who came to live in the South Lodge after Miss Hatton. However, he only stayed for about three months, before he surrendered the lease to move to Willow Green Farm. Grandfather only learned of this by chance when Dad, ploughing in the first field by the park, received the information in a casual chat with Henry Oram.

As a result, Grandfather persuaded Ross, the chauffeur, to take him to see Mrs Frankenburg, at the Midland Hotel, in Manchester, and he took along with him a wedding present for Miss Mary who was getting married again. To his dismay, Grandfather found that Mrs Frankenburg had already let the farm to a man named Darwell, a part-time Veterinary Surgeon. Fortunately, Mr Darwell's name had been spelt wrongly on the lease and because of the error, Frankenburgs' lawyers were able to quash the arrangement and instead gave the lease to Grandfather, who, therefore, had the tenancy of both Home Farm, from the Frankenburgs, and Nook Farm, from Mrs Heath. Mr Darwell eventually moved into Cuddington Hall Farm.

When Mrs Frankenburg was absolutely certain that no members of her family wished to make Hefferston Grange their home, she put the property and land up for sale and within less than two years of us getting the lease, the Estate was purchased by Warrington Borough Corporation and conveyed to them on the 11th July, 1919.

A man named Jimmy Smith was the Chairman of Warrington Corporation and a friend of Sam Lewis and when the Estate passed to the corporation, he tried, without success, to have Mr Lewis reinstated in the lease. Eventually, Sam moved to Milton Farm, where Jim Smith was a regular visitor.

After her husband's death, Mrs Frankenburg spent some time at Lyme Park and then at Llandudno, where she died on 31st January, 1930, aged 80 years. She was buried alongside her husband at Whitefield, where the tombstones still survives. Isidor and Frances had six children:

Jessie Mary, born 1875, married in 1895 Captain Henry Theodore Dreschfield, later of the 13th Manchester Regiment, who was killed in action February 19th, 1915.

Merton F. , born 1877, who was living at Park Lane, Kersall at his father's death, and died in 1953.

Joseph R., born 1878, Leonard Henry gained a B.A. (Cantab) and was working at Guy's Hospital in London when he died on the 27th December, 1904 at the age of 26, and is buried Whitefield.

Sydney S., also achieved the rank of Captain and survived his war wounds to die aged 54 in 1935.

David, the youngest, married Joyce Bradley at Harrogate in 1923.

Hefferston Grange and Hefferston Grange Farm with the buildings, gardens, pleasure grounds, park, plantations, willow beds, closed pieces or parcels of land and hereditaments there to belonging and containing in the whole 4 acres 1 rood and 14 perches or thereabouts, were conveyed on 11h July, 1919, in consideration of the sum of £13,200 by Frances Anne Frankenburg, Merton Francis Frankenburg and the executors and trustees of Isidor Frankenburg, to the Mayor, Aldermen and Burgesses of the County Borough of Warrington.

For a reason I have been unable to discover, some parts of the Estate were subject to an annual ground rent of £6.8s., payable to Lord Barrymore, against which the Frankenburgs were indemnified, at the time of the conveyance, by the Warrington Borough Council. This annual ground rent was, however, redeemed in the sum of £128 by an Indenture made 4th March, 1920, between Arthur Hugh Baron Barrymore and the County Borough of Warrington.

As a result of this sale, and as we already know, Hefferston Grange became Hefferston Grange Sanatorium. Later, following 1944 and the discovery, by Selman Waksam, a Russian born scientist working in the USA, of the drug Streptomycin, the first effective cure for Tuberculosis, its function as a TB Hospital soon ceased and it became the Grange Hospital. It finally ended its life as a Geriatric Hospital in 1986 when it fell silent and derelict.

It was at this old hall that my father had met my mother soon after the First World War, when she came to work at the Sanatorium and it was here that I was to meet the girl who was to become my own wife. Born in Lithuania, she had been forced to flee with her family from their small farm as the advancing Russians drove out the occupying German armies. They fled westward, carrying whatever possessions they could, sometimes on foot, sometimes managing to get a ride on whatever type of railway wagon was available, finally reaching the Dutch border, where they settled for a while until the war ended. Erna Plewe and her sister, Hertha, then came to England, to work at Hefferston Grange. Neither of the sisters spoke a word of English, only German, which they had been forced to learn in place of their native tongue when the Germans took over the Baltic States of Lithuania, Latvia and Estonia.

I met Erna at the hall, where I helped her overcome the language difficulties, and we became great friends and married in October 1953. We then spent 39 happy years together.

I fall sad when I look upon the old Grange now, silent and empty, its heart removed and its soul destroyed, staring with sightless eyes across an empty silent park where no-one walks and all those gentle people whose lives have touched on mine, pass a silent host before me, pale figures in the moonlight.

And who will yet remember ... and who remains to mourn?

As for lovely old Nook Farm itself, my home for so many years, with its outbuildings, shippons, stables and ancient barns, it was in such a dangerous and precarious state after the bombing that it had to be taken down, to its very foundations, so that no part of it remained above ground. Because of the lack of resources, manpower and the building restrictions, which were in force during the remainder of the war, and for some time afterwards, it was not possible to rebuild the farm and, as the years went by, to do so became a more and more daunting prospect and, some years later, the cellars were filled in and the site grassed over by the Department of the Environment. After having served for some years as a council yard, the whole site, apart from a few orchard trees, now lies beneath the new by-pass, buried for ever, only in faltering memory recalled.

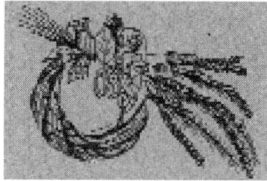

I pray this book may be a fitting memorial to a good man who was proud of his forebears and lived his life that they would be proud of him, and who nurtured these tales in the hope that we who read them might be inspired and enlightened as we share these wistful memories of earlier times.

BILL ELSON

Great Grandfather John Moss
(Josiah's grandson)
at Beach Farm.

Grandfather, George Moss.

Grandfather George's brother,
Harry Moss, of the
Royal Artillery, 1914-18.

Great Grandfather and Great
Grandmother, David Forster
(snr) and Sarah Forster.

Pepper in the milk shandry.

Grandfather George's brother,
Percy Moss, of the Cheshire
Regiment, 1914-18.

Nook Farm at the turn of the century.

An artist's impression... the Moss family at Nook Farm in 1906.

Maypole Inn, Acton Bridge about 1916, showing Ada Buckley as licensee. She married her sister's widower and so, overnight, her nephews became her stepsons, one of whom went to Kenya with Lord Delamere.

Rafe Broad's Smithy, Acton Bridge, now the car park to the Hazel Pear. Ted Rowe's Smithy is next door, on the right, and is still a forge.

West Road. The patrolman is standing with his back to Rose Cottage.

Jack Gleave, of Church Farm.

The Grammar School at the turn of the century, with the headmaster, Mr Trickett.

Above: Sgt. Allen and his first wife, about 1914.
Left: Licensee of The Star, William Wood, with his daughter, Beatrice.

Hornby's... across the road in larger premises.

Hornby's first shop in High Street after moving from Wharf (Nook) Cottages. Rosie is the child on the right.

The Ring O'Bells pub, now demolished.

Tom Gleave and his wife, the former Miss Hatton.

Dr. J.W.Smith.

George Allen on Snowball.

Tom Gleave on his regular Saturday morning walk round the farm.

Forster's Ironmonger's shop, at the corner of West Road and Station Road,
with the Hanging Gate and the Village Tree with the seats.

Great Grandfather David Forster's boys. Arnie is in the driving seat,
with David Jnr. behind him.

High Street, Weaverham, 1923.

High Street, about 1920. Burgess Brothers Drapers,
and Agricultural Engineers is on the right.

Hospital Saturday at Weaverham, about 1925.

Charlie Bebbington's daughter, Nancy, in the doorway of Poplar
Cottage. Nancy eventually went to Australia with Max Fairclough.

Steam engine 'King Edward', at Grange Farm, in the late 1920s.

High Street, Weaverham, 1920. Arthur Tomkinson, who married Robina Heath, lived in the cottages on the right.

Wesleyan Church shortly after completion of the new Sunday School.

Thatched cottage in Forest Street, demolished to make way for the Village Institute. At one time the Whitleys lived here.

The Village Institute which replaced the cottage above.

A chapel trip from Acton. Roy Minshull is fourth from the right, front row.

Sgt.Allen in the stubble.

The author, George Moss, with Jack, the
champion rat-catching fox terrier.
Left: Gipsy caravans at Nook Farm
in the early 1920s.

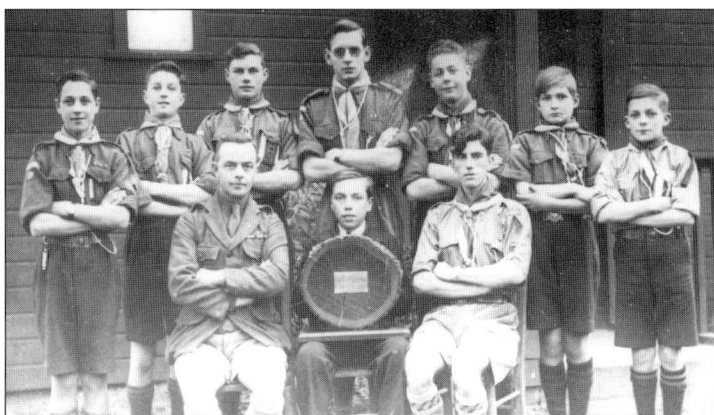
Colonel Heald MBE, TD, with 1st Weaverham Scouts, mid-1930s.

Mainwaring's thatched cottage, in Sandy Lane. Later this was to become Woodward's Cafe.

Woodward's Cafe, now demolished.

Forster's Shop, 1920, showing Little Arnie and David in the doorway.

Hefferston Grange.

Albert Holden with Miss Hatton in the
Conservatory at The Grange.

The old iron "kissing gate" by the
moat, where Robina and
Arthur used to meet.

Hefferston
Grange, 1916.
Miss Hatton
attending the Rose
Garden. The
Conservatory is to
the rear.

Hefferston Grange Sanatorium.

Matron Yaxley with nursing staff in the early years of the Sanatorium
at Hefferston Grange.

Early days at the Sanatorium.

Matron Lee.

Weaverham Army Cadets, 1943.

The Avro Anson which force landed in the Top Park.

The sadness of change... Hefferston Grange eventually
became a derelict ruin.

Nook Farm before the air-raid.

The ruins of Nook Farm after that fateful night. Left is the old house and on the right, the remains of the cart house in which, remarkably, a collie dog survived.

Aerial Photograph dating from the Second World War.

1. The Woodlands
2. Acton Bridge Station
3. Road to milk loading platform
4. Railway Hotel, now Hazel Pear
5. Milton Farm
6. Milton Bank Farm
7. Sandfield Terrace
8. Blue Bell Wood
9. Grange Brook - Willow Beds
10. Site of Onston Mill
11. Cuddington Brook
12. Gandy's Acton Mill
13. Onston Hall

Aerial Photograph dating from the Second World War.

1. Weaverham Wood Farm
2. St Mary's Church
3. Old Football Field
4. Forster Avenue
5. Church Farm
6. Withens Lane
7. Hanging Gate
8. Well Bank Farm
9. Woodwards in the Field
10. Inglenook Cafe
11. Water Tower
12. Air Raid Shelters
13. Lake House Farm